I0764398

THE OLD WORLD

For Mary, Pam, and Karyn
Thank you!

Wilder Publications, Inc.

THE OLD WORLD is a work of fiction. Names, characters, businesses, organizations, places, events and incidents are either the products of the author's imagination or are used fictitiously. Any resemblance to actual persons, living or dead, events, locales or institutions is entirely coincidental.

Hardcover ISBN 13: 978-1-5154-5784-8
E-book ISBN 13: 978-1-5154-5785-5

THE OLD WORLD

by Wilson Roberts

CHAPTER ONE

Canaan, Massachusetts \ Thursday, May 2

HANDS RESTING ON the Porsche's carved mahogany steering wheel, Buckman breathed in the scent of maple blossoms mixed with the aroma of wood smoke rising from the valley below the pullover where he had parked to look at the view and collect his feelings. Trees, thick along the hillsides, cast shadows over the countryside, maple, birch, oak, beech, and ash, with dark stands of hemlock and pine moving into neglected fields and growing around weed-filled cellar holes of burned houses and fallen barns.

In the years away from the Old World section of Canaan, Massachusetts, he'd forgotten how gloomy the place seemed, its forests and high steep hillsides shortening the brightest and warmest of the long summer days, a land where most people still heated their homes with wood, and many still cooked on wood stoves passed on from parents and grandparents, curls of smoke rising from chimneys and lying heavily on the air, even during the hottest days of summer.

Spring, a late comer to New England, compared to the early springs he'd grown used to in Pennsylvania, came even later to the Old World. Fields, long ago plowed and planted in Bucks County, had already yielded spinach, lettuce, and early peas. Here the ground was still unplowed, the most prudent farmers waiting until Memorial Day to do their planting.

It had been a long drive. Hard. Not because the trip from Philadelphia was difficult. That was a simple matter. All he had to do was take the Jersey Turnpike to the Garden State Parkway. Then the Interstates, 287, 95 and 91. Negotiating the traffic of the Cross Westchester Expressway had been effortless considering the problems he had left behind. Cars darting across lanes, trucks bearing down and tailgating him, drivers shooting each other the bird, honking horns and jolting stops to avoid crashing into another car were nothing compared to the tension and fear riding with him, knowing somebody was trying to kill him, might even have followed him.

He would already be dead if he hadn't been nervous, unable to sleep the previous night and heard a car pull into the drive as he lay tossing under the covers; heard the driver get out and walk across the driveway to his front door, each footstep crunching on the gravel. He sat up. There was a loud thud as the book he had been reading earlier slipped from his chest to the floor. Leaning over, he picked up Vonnegut's novel, *Galapagos*, and set it on the bedside table next to the digital clock. It was 2:37.

He had been watching the numbers blink by since he lay down at 11:12. Reading had not helped. There was no comfort in watching TV. Cable news broadcasting, always upsetting, was more disturbing at night. Vacuous people displaying their vacuity on shows about house renovations, real estate flipping, or home shopping held no interest for him. He was not going to lie in bed, wide awake watching reruns of shows like *The Golden Girls, Gunsmoke, Frasier,* and *MacGyver.*

He thought of the recent patient deaths at the Worthington-American, the hospital where Buckman worked. Each of the dead had been suffering from results of the strange uncurable malady they were calling the Tuscan Syndrome, despite it having been sickening people around the globe, but these patients had died from heart attacks, not the neurological damages from TTS.

It seemed to Buckman that the earth had wearied of us, that it was trying to rid itself of the pestilence of human infestation. The Great War of 1914-1918 had produced industrialized brutality and destruction on a scale the earth had never seen before. The deaths of multitudes of creatures, including twenty-one million human beings, the movements of troops, the movements of refugees, people displaced by the disruptions of war, the blasting of forests, fields left contaminated by poisons and weaponry, the emergence of modern warfare with its horrors, all would surely have led into raging despair any spirits of the earth that might exist, any the great soul of the planet there might be. Perhaps the flu epidemic of 1918 was a first experiment in cautioning humanity, earth's attempt to give notice that humanity's actions were placing the species in mortal peril.

We could have paid attention to the warning, Buckman thought. Should have. We did not. Nor did we heed later cautions. International disorder continued as empires collapsed, invented states were created, and false borders established with no concern for cultural values, ethnicities, religions, political leanings of people living within those jerry-rigged boundaries. In the Great War's aftermath, Hitler rose to power promising to make Germany great again, creating a regime so abhorrent that its hateful symbols still raise passions 82 years later.

Buckman half-believed the earth was close to perfecting a human extermination plan. Since AIDS appeared in 1981, scientists had success in understanding and containing, if not curing, the epidemic and pandemic diseases threatening humankind. In 2002 and 2003, there was the coronavirus responsible for SARS. MERS appeared in 2012, and from 2014 into 2016 there was a major outbreak of Ebola. Malformed fetuses resulted from the spread of zika in 2014-2016, and Ebola appeared again in the Congo in 2018. The worst, most intractable pandemic up to the present was the coronavirus behind the ongoing COVID-19 infections. The illness first appeared in 2017 and changed the world as it mutated and spread with relentless pitilessness.

Many had died, more had sickened from COVID. There were people who suffered from the aftereffects of the virus years following their initial infection and long COVID was ever being redefined as its effects kept lasting. Now there was the Tuscan Syndrome, a sickness that appeared in the city of Rada in 2022. Medical researchers had long ago determined that TTS had nothing more than a passing relation to Tuscany, or to Italy, to any country, party, ideology, theology, or specific human activity. It was as if the syndrome arose from the earth and targeted only its current dominant species. Initially the symptoms included pain, ringing in the ears, confusion. Later studies with neuroimaging show major differences in patients' brains when compared to healthy people.

Now, throughout the world people were dying slow, lingering deaths, many on life support in hospitals, as their brains atrophied. In its attempts to deal with the fallout from the Tuscan Syndrome, the American healthcare system, the most backward in the so-called developed world, was in crisis. Medical centers affiliated with large, well-endowed universities were surviving. Public hospitals, funded by tax monies, fees, and insurance payments, were managing to keep open, although many smaller ones had closed, and even some of the larger ones had reduced nursing staff to a few overseers, adopting the old Soviet method of requiring family members to tend to the hospitalized sick and dying.

Despite years of experience in treating TTS patients, medical researchers still had no clue as to the syndrome's cause. Years ago, in 2020 the National Academies of Sciences, Engineering, and Medicine put together a committee that suggested the cause to be pulsed RF microwave energy· Other potential causes or contributing factors of the symptoms that have been proposed and abandoned have included ultrasound, pesticides, or hysteria. All these years later, no one has determined of the cause of the Tuscan syndrome.

Hearing the car, the footsteps on the drive, he moved quickly.

He'd been expecting a move. Lying in bed, staring at the starlight shadows of his window blinds, he'd heard the noises from the drive and managed to slip out the bedroom window, crawl along the back porch roof, slide down a pole and run into the night, hiding in the woods until whoever had come for him went away. It had worked as smoothly as if he'd planned it. Scrunched down behind the rhododendrons, shivering, he'd realized how wired he'd been for this, ready to move without conscious planning.

It made sense for them to come after him. They had to. There was no other choice. He should have thought the whole thing through more carefully before confronting them.

Watching his house through the oak branches with their winter curled leaves, he had tried seeing who was there. Although he'd known why they were after him, he hadn't known who they would send to do the job. It wouldn't have been Castile and Blanchard. They'd send someone more experienced at the removal of people they considered dangerous. He'd squinted, trying to see who was there, but it was too far and too dark to make out anything but the shadowy outline of the house.

He'd shivered and waited. As soon as he'd heard the car door slam, the engine start, and the crackle of the tires head down the lane, away from the house, he'd gone back inside, packed the necessary things, and driven away from his home.

He hadn't had any choice either.

All the way north, his eyes had been on the rearview mirror as much as on the road ahead, driving fast enough to make good time, slow enough to avoid the speed traps. The last thing he needed was a cop pulling him over for a ticket. There was no telling what kind of trouble it would lead to. Castile's connections could easily extend into police networks. Worthington-America's influence was wide and powerful.

Checking the rearview mirror for what seemed like the five hundredth time, he noticed his eyes. They were red, fearful, staring back at him. Rubbing them with his thumb and forefinger, he took a deep breath and arched his back against the seat, trying to ease the stiffness. He'd never seen his eyes look so drawn, tired, runny, not even after pulling thirty-six hour shifts in the ER during his internship and residency.

He looked at them again, then craned and swiveled his neck to see the rest of his face. His hair was mussed and matted, his lips dry, cracked, and sore looking. It didn't look at all like the face he was used to seeing in mirrors. Moving his head, catching segments of his reflection, he felt as though he were looking at a stranger, a haggard, troubled stranger, haunted by what he knew and the burdens of the knowledge. He'd seen similar expressions in patients just coming to full realization of their terminal conditions.

Now he was facing death and running from it. In that respect, he was luckier than most of the patients he'd pronounced death upon. His threat came from the outside, not from renegade cells in his own body. There was a chance for him. More than a chance, now he was back in the Old World.

THE OLD WORLD

He had gotten off Interstate 91 at Graham and taken Route 2 west, going several miles past Canaan Falls to Bethel Road and the ancient narrow steel truss bridge spanning the Canaan Gorge of the Deerfield River. Two miles farther on, he turned right on the Windybush Road, twisting through the Berkshire foothills until he came to the steep turn where it headed down into the deep and remote valley of the Old World section of Canaan.

Looking down he could see the Black Horse Pike curving through the valley, appearing and disappearing around the hills and behind the thick stands of timber. Rusted metal roofs gleamed dully in the already fading sun, chimneys trailing wisps of wood smoke, their fires damped heavily in the warmth of the spring afternoon.

The view seemed unchanged from how it had looked the day he left so many years before. The roads winding along streams and fields, roofs of farmhouses and barns catching the late afternoon sun. He imagined the sweet distant smell of wood smoke filling the air and clinging to peoples' clothes, just as he remembered from childhood. No matter where he might be, the scent of wood smoke brought his memory rushing back to the Old World, almost as though the odor contained and defined the lives carried out there.

He could see the Shippee place, Everett Gould's farm, the decaying silos rising next to Isaiah Heston's barn, still standing. He smiled at the site of buildings that had looked as though they wouldn't last another week when he left twenty-five years before. Wesley Johnson's store, its clapboard sides gleaming with fresh white paint, stood by the side of the Black Horse Pike, several cars and pickup trucks pulled around it.

Scanning the valley, he looked for signs of change, of progress and development. Everything looked unchanged. Unpaved roads and marginal farms, a few fields covered with manure, their owners readying them for plowing. Others with patches of snow around their shaded edges, stubbles of corn and unharvested cabbages, the soil looking as though it would never be ready for spring planting. The Old World seemed as it had been when he left. He looked farther down, past Wesley Johnson's. Another white building caught his eye. Half hidden in a grove of dark trees, its steeple rising above them, was a church.

That was new. There hadn't been any churches in the valley when he was a boy. Folks said the last minister who came in to save souls left cursing the Old World and its people, saying every one of them could go to Hell for all he cared, he was going back to Boston where religion was civilized, and people knew how to respect it. Few people of the Old World had any use for preachers with their Bibles and their rules for living sinless lives and their promises of eventual glory if one could avoid the condemnation of their God and eternal damnation in his Hell.

Looking at the shadowed patches of snow and the early greens of spring, he smiled at the vagaries of the New England seasons, the spring days warm, sometimes hot, the nights cool, people keeping fires in their stoves tamped down, always prepared to toss in a load of wood that would burn quickly, throwing out heat in moments.

Buckman sighed and forced himself to relax. As much as he hated returning, he would be safe here. They'd never trace him back to Canaan. Except for Irene Shoemaker, he'd never said anything about his origins to anyone back in Philly, determined to keep the past behind him. Even if the people after him did find out about Canaan and came looking for him, suspecting he might try running back, no one would help them find him. Not here. Not in the Old World where strangers looking for a person would be ignored, lied to. If they were too persistent, representing too great a threat to a sister, a brother, a cousin, a friend, they would be taken care of in the Old World fashion.

When he left Canaan, he said he'd never return. The climate was terrible, life in the narrow social confines The Old World even worse. Now he was back. Running home to hide. In retrospect it seemed inevitable. Perhaps here he could begin to understand the disintegration he was fleeing by leaving Philadelphia. Perhaps, in some way, it was the same thing he had run from when he left the Old World.

Except for Irene. He ached thinking about her. She had been the best thing to happen in his life since his divorce ten years earlier. Things had begun to happen for them. Words had been said, feelings spoken by both, the tentative, early probings of two people looking for the possibility of commitment. Then he had been forced to run. He knew she would be hurt. But it was better to run, hurt her briefly, than drag her into this deadly mess.

Putting the Porsche in drive, he started down into the valley, toward the Black Horse Pike. It had been years since he'd driven the Windybush. Everything looked the same. If anything, the road was smoother than he remembered. Obviously, the town crew had scraped it recently and there hadn't had been enough traffic to develop its characteristic washboard roughness.

He passed Auntie Martha and Uncle Amos LaTran's house, their rusted Corvair Monza still sitting next to the barn, poles jammed into the front seat and resting under the eaves, holding the side of the building up. He wondered if his aunt and uncle were still living, still there, or if his brother Wilfred and his wife, Charlotte, Martha and Amos' oldest daughter, had taken the place over, as they had been promised they would at their wedding.

As he looked, several chickens darted under a hedge. A dog barked behind the house. Everything looked the same, the house sitting in the shadow of huge maples, a third of its windowpanes replaced with cardboard, the yard in front of it littered with empty oil drums, tin cans and bottles, the ground picked bare by chickens and geese. He expected and needed that sense of things unchanged. He'd been the first Buckman to go to college. The first to leave the Valley. Everyone had thought he was crazy to go. Or uppity. The Old World wasn't good enough for him, they said. Even his parents had tried to talk him out of it.

"Stay on the farm, Billy Buck," his father had said. "Buckmans been working this land, living in this valley since before the Revolutionary War. By god, there ain't no use in leaving it now. Nothing good can come from it."

But he went. From the time he was in the fifth grade and Miss Erdman, his teacher, had told him how exciting the world beyond Wessex County was, he knew he would never be happy living like the rest of his family, staying in the Old World, farming with his father, marrying one of his cousins, doing the same things day after day, year after year, and ending up buried in the cemetery on Christian Hill. Life in the Old World was hard and unpleasant. Buckman had enough of it by the time he was eight and had heard the sounds his father made at night with his mother and sisters.

It made him cry as much as the whippings he and his brothers and sisters received once a week, whether or not they had done anything wrong. Every Saturday night Calvin Buckman would line his children up. Judgment Day, he called Saturdays. He would beat each of them with his belt three times. If they had done something he considered wrong, he would give them an extra three lashes with the buckle end of the belt.

Despite his father's opposition, and several severe beatings to reinforce that opposition, Buckman finished high school and went to the community college in Graham where he found teachers who helped cultivate his mind and convinced him to go on to the University of Massachusetts. After getting his bachelor's degree there, he'd received a fellowship and went to graduate school at Princeton, taking a master's in microbiology and finally to medical school at Jefferson in Philadelphia.

He'd stayed in the city, practicing medicine, splitting his time between an apartment in the city and an eighteenth century stone farmhouse he bought out in Bucks County, near Upper Black Eddy on the Delaware River. He had bought it when he and Hannah were married. It had seemed like the perfect place for them to raise a family, but they divorced less than two years later. He kept the farm, maintaining his hopes for a family, but, after two failed long range live in affairs, he had not felt comfortable enough, safe enough, to marry again.

For a while it seemed as though Irene might change that. Until last night, when he ran back to the Old World. He hadn't even stopped to call her; tell her he was leaving. Had there been time he might have been able to tell her something which could have eased any pain his flight caused, but he'd been afraid. Afraid to hear the sadness in her voice. Afraid of telling her too much. Jesus, he was losing a lot.

He liked being a doctor. Liked the deference people paid him. Liked the power of having life and death information and knowing how to use it to help his patients. Liked the feeling of doing something for people, making them feel better, often really making them better. Liked hearing his name over the hospital paging system. Doctor William Buckman. Doctor William Buckman. It sounded good. Like nothing in the Old World.

Now it was gone. He was running, with no idea when he would be able to stop; the patients, his name over the paging system; the possibilities with Irene, all like they had never been. Everything was as though it had never been. Except for the Porsche. Smiling bitterly, he ran the flat of his hand across the leather upholstery of the passenger seat. At least he had the Porsche.

The Old World would absorb him for a while. He'd hide the car in a barn and fade into the community. They'd never find him here. Who'd ever expect to find Dr. William Buckman in a place like this? Buckman had never expected to find himself here again. He'd believed the Old World was out of his life forever the day he left.

They'd be checking the airports, expecting him to head for the Caribbean, or Europe. He'd cleaned out his bank accounts, cashed in a bunch of securities and left. With Castile's contacts, he'd soon discover Buckman was traveling with a great deal of cash. The last place they'd look for him was a rural community in Massachusetts where people still married their first cousins, where fathers and brothers considered daughters and sisters theirs by right of birth. The kind of money Buckman was carrying would take him anywhere in the world and keep him there in comfort for a long time. The boonies of a Massachusetts hill town would never enter their minds as a refuge.

It wasn't a good place, the Old World, but he knew its ways. He could hide here. All he had to do was tell anyone who asked that he was in trouble on the outside and they would cover for him, with no further questions. And few would even bother to say anything. They'd see him and forget they had. The Old World would be reliable thanks its indifference.

A mile above the Black Horse Pike, the Windybush twisted through a sharp horseshoe bend. Three quarters of the way through the bend, he saw Clay Presnell's old grey farmhouse. Standing behind a thick hedge of budding lilacs, it was a rambling cape with three awkward ells jutting off in different directions, heavy chips of paint peeling off the clapboards.

When he was a boy, he'd ride his bicycle up here and help Clay milk his cows, hay his fields. Clay, in return, taught him to hunt and fish. He showed him the hollows deep in the woods where there were still wild turkey and taught him how to cook squirrel so you could almost make yourself believe it was fried chicken, if you kept your eyes closed. Open them and you would believe you were eating a naked rat.

Driving by, he saw Clay sitting in shadow on his porch steps, a coffee can resting on his knees, from the distance looking much the same as the last time Buckman saw him. Again, he had the sense of nothing having changed. It was both calming and disquieting.

He pulled in the driveway, stopped the car, and got out. As he walked to the porch. Clay looked up, smiled, and spit a long brown strand of tobacco juice into the can. His face was grey and wrinkled, his hands shaking. He smiled again.

"Billy Buck. How are you?"

"Pretty good, Clay, and you?"

"Not so good." Clay's smile faded slightly, his eyes squinting at Buckman as he studied him for a moment. Finally, he wiped a drop of tobacco from his chin with the back of his shirt sleeve and shook his head.

"Billy Buck, you been away?"

"It doesn't seem like it, Clay. What's wrong, are you sick?"

He shook his head a second time, eyes on his feet. "Just age, Billy Buck. Woke up one day last winter and I was an old man. Couldn't split my firewood and couldn't take a piss. Doctor down to Graham stuck a tube in my pecker to make the water come, but he wouldn't do a goddamn thing to help me with the firewood. Doctors." He spat again.

"A catheter."

"Don't know. He could have been a Methodist."

"The tube he put in your penis. It's called a catheter."

Clay looked up, his chin again brown with tobacco stains. "I don't know. He never told me its name. He just stuck it in and I made like a waterfall."

Buckman laughed. As a kid he'd never known when Clay was pulling his leg.

"Say, Billy, you headed into town, by any chance?"

He shook his head. "I'm going down to my parents' place."

Wiping his mouth on the shirt sleeve, Clay stood up, holding the coffee can in both hands, turning it slowly. "You can't fool me, Billy Buck. You been away, otherwise you wouldn't have said you was going down to your parents' place. You don't know about your mother, do you?"

"What about her?" Buckman's heart thumped, and he lost a breath.

"Dead. She died four, five years ago. Cancer got her. They found it one day and she was dead a few weeks later. Your father's got your brother Wilfred's youngest daughter living down there with him, looking after things."

Buckman was surprised by his tears. He hadn't contacted his parents since he left Canaan. He'd thought of them often enough, usually at night, waking in the hours between two and four. Unable to get back to sleep, he would wonder how they were, what they were like after all these years. Had they grown, changed, or were things the same as they'd been when he was a boy? As bad? He thought most of his mother, a quiet, stiff woman. Cold, some might say. Cold, he'd always thought as a boy. Cold and judgmental, always saying how angry their father would be if they did this or that. Now he knew she'd been frightened, what seemed like cold judgments her only way of warning them to be careful. Not to cross Calvin Buckman. Protecting them and herself from his wrath.

He'd wondered about them, about their lives, theirs and those of his brothers and sisters. At times he had created imaginary scenarios of his return to the Old World, but he was never willing to risk finding out, to reopen the pain of his childhood, never willing to travel its twisted roads.

Now he was back, but only out of desperation. There didn't seem to be any place else to go.

Wilson Roberts

He wasn't sure if the tears were for Velma Buckman, whose cries he had heard at night, lying in bed listening as his raving, drunken father slapped and punched her, furious over some minor infraction of his endless and unpredictable rules. They might have been for Wilfred's daughter. They might have been for himself, here because he had no place else to go. Just like everyone else in the Old World.

A GRASS COVERED driveway led to his father's house. Parked on the gravel road beside the mailbox and the delivery tube for the *Graham Recorder*, he was surprised to see the house had been painted red. In his youth, the clapboard siding had been white, rarely repainted, with large sections where the paint had peeled off. He had no memories of Calvin ever having painted the building. Someone must have offered him a deal on paint left over from a barn. The place looked better than he remembered. Everything else about the Old World would turn out to be worse.

The young woman who opened the door to his father's house wore a faded cotton print dress at least three sizes too big for her. No more than sixteen, she was heavy, nearly obese, her pasty white skin mottled with shapeless brown splotches. Her hair, red as his brother Wilfred's, was pulled back in a knot. The right side of her face and her nose were covered by a raspberry birthmark. There was a bruise on the left side, the scratches in it still oozing blood.

"Yeah," she said, standing in the doorway, frightened, ready to slam it quickly if he made any move toward her.

"Are you Wilfred's daughter?"

"Yeah."

When she didn't say anything more, he smiled and held out his hand. She cringed backward, pushing the door. but not closing it.

He asked, "What's your name?"

"Velma." The name came out in a mumble.

"Like your grandmother." Buckman did not like the irony of it. The girl's eyes were dull and the few words she had uttered came out in a slow mumbling sound. She had his mother's name, lived in his mother's house, was probably wearing one of his mother's dresses, and looked as though she was getting the same kind of abuse his mother had gotten. What kind of hell had he come back to?

Giving her his best bedside smile, he held out his hand again. "Well, Velma, I'm your Uncle Bill. Your dad's my brother. I'm glad to meet you."

She stood unmoving, silent, watching him with wide, green eyes, her mouth twisting nervously.

"You don't look like my uncle."

He smiled. "What should your uncle look like?"

"Like Uncle Vaughn and Uncle Dave, like the others. They all look like Grampy Cal or Grammy. You're taller, and you got more hair. You got better clothes too. They ain't handsome like you, you know?"

Buckman knew. He prided himself on being handsome. He had his hair styled twice a month, resisting his hair-dresser's pleas to color the grey temples. He was tall, slender and his features were rugged, like his father's would have been, if he didn't drink too much and had teeth, both of which had been problems for Calvin long before Buckman left the Old World. Still, Velma's comment made him smile. Except for their height, all his brothers would look like him if they had the money to dress and groom the way he did. They'd looked alike as children.

Buckman took a step backward, to show he was no threat. "I really am your uncle. May I come in?"

She shook her head. "Grampy Cal's out in the barn. If he wants you to come in, he'll say so. He told me not to let nobody in the house, if he's here or if he ain't, unless it's somebody he says to let in."

Buckman shrugged, smiling at her. "Then I guess I'd better go up to the barn and talk to him."

Her mouth a thin, unsmiling line, she nodded silently and closed the door.

Leaving the porch, he walked toward the barn, turning around once to look at Velma, the girl watching him from behind dining room curtains.

The barn was made of rough-cut lumber, most of its red paint long since weathered away. The few remaining patches caught and reflected the fading sunlight. He'd walked to this barn thousands of times as a child. Standing at the foot of the earthen ramp leading to the main floor, he looked up at the weathervane on the roof, a coach drawn by four horses. It pointed south, the direction from which he'd come, as it had for as long as he could remember, frozen in place by rust. Beneath the vane, beneath the roof, in the dark emptiness of the building, he'd find his father. He did not look forward to the reunion.

Stepping inside, he was struck by the half-forgotten yet still familiar odor, a mixture of old hay, motor oil, pine wood and animals. He coughed once and moved across the floor where his father was working on a gray 52' Ford tractor.

Calvin Buckman looked up from the engine as Buckman walked into the barn. Wiping his hands with a greasy rag, he watched his son cross toward him, floorboards creaking underfoot. "You're a little late for your mother's funeral," he said, picking a wrench from the fender and turning again to the engine.

"I'm surprised you recognized me."

Calvin sniffed and spit on the floor. "Shit always smells the same, no matter how long you got it piled up. I said you're pretty goddamn late for your mother's funeral."

"I just heard she'd died. Clay told me." Already he could feel his childhood rage building. Just the sight of the man and his instant reproach. Forcing it down, he looked around at all the open space in the barn. He could hide the Porsche here with no problem.

"No matter. You never came back when she was alive. I guess there was no reason for you to come see her buried."

She'd been buried all her life, Buckman thought, stifling an angry response. He needed his father now. Needed the Old World's protection. As much as he resented the need, it would be stupid to argue with him. It had always been stupid to argue with Calvin Buckman. As a child it had gotten him countless beatings.

He walked around to the other side of the tractor, leaning on the fender opposite his father. Calvin did not look up. Might as well plunge into it, Buckman thought.

"I'm in trouble, Dad. I need to stay here for a while. Hide. You know?"

"All I know is how I told you not to leave. That was a long time ago. Nothing good comes to people who leave. Isaiah Toomb's boy Todd was shot robbing a liquor store in California, and both of Henry Zagorski's sons are in jail in Illinois. Now you're in trouble. What did you do? The police after you?"

"It's better I don't tell you. What you don't know, people can't force out of you, if they ever find me here."

"How long?"

Buckman looked at his father. "How long what?"

"How long you going to stay?"

He shook his head. "I don't know yet. Will you let me stay?"

Calvin grunted. "I got a choice? You're my son. You say you're in trouble. I guess it don't matter how long you want to stay. I might not like it, but if you say you got to stay here, then you can stay."

"I'll carry my own weight. I've got some money and I'll work here. The place looks like it could use another set of hands. And I can help people here. I'm a doctor, Dad. I'll bet you never expected anything like that from me."

As soon as the words were out, he regretted them. He regretted giving his father the knowledge, and he regretted the need to brag, to impress Calvin Buckman. He'd planned on keeping it all to himself, everything that had happened since he left the Old World. And at his first chance he blew it. Calvin had spoken harshly, and he'd done nothing but try to curry his admiration by bragging. Not a great start.

Calvin looked up at him, shook his head, then buried his face back in the engine. "By God, I guess I didn't expect it. I guess I didn't even expect to hear you was still alive until you walked in this barn a few minutes ago. Now you tell me you're in trouble and say you're a doctor. I don't know which is worse. It was doctors that killed your mother. She'd been real sick, the pukes, the shits, passing out. I took her down to the hospital in Graham and they took x-rays, found cancer in her and cut her open, saying they was going to take it out of her. Then they sewed her up, put her in a bed and she died."

He stood up, looking at his son over the tractor engine. "I got less use for doctors than I got for you. They killed your mother and if wasn't for Wilfred's Velma I wouldn't have nobody to do for me. Keep it to yourself around here about being a doctor. Stay, if you've got to, but while you're in my house you'll be what I tell you to be and that's a farmhand, not a doctor. You'll work six days a week and go to the missionary church with me and Velma on Sundays."

As he spoke, Calvin came around to the front of the tractor, standing two feet from his son. He was tall, heavy, wearing green coveralls splotched with grease and manure, his face covered by gray beard stubble.

"You agree to that?" Calvin balled his fists, leaned toward Buckman, and added, "Son?"

With a sour taste rising into his mouth, Buckman nodded, furious at himself for trying to impress Calvin with his accomplishments.

"I agree."

"Good." Calvin extended a grease blackened hand.

Buckman looked at it for a second longer than he should have, then put his own into it. Calvin crunched down hard, shaking Buckman's hand as he spoke.

"Then you can stay. Don't interfere with me and Velma, kick in seventy-five dollars a week for running the household, work your ass off doing whatever I tell you needs doing around here and explain yourself however you've got to when you see your brothers and sisters." He paused, looking Buckman hard in the eyes. "As long as you don't tell anyone about that doctor crap. You understand?"

Dropping his son's hand, Calvin walked to the barn door and hollered at the top of his lungs.

"Velma, you let my boy in the house anytime he wants. He's going to be staying with us for a while."

Buckman's hand ached from his father's grip, the skin covered with black grease. He shook it, wiping it clean on a rag hanging next to the hayloft ladder. Starting toward the house, he stopped, looking back at his father. "There's one more thing I've got to do."

Calvin, already back at work, leaning into the tractor, looked up.

"What now?"

"My car. I need to hide my car in the barn."

"Steal it?"

"It's mine, fair and square."

"What do you plan on driving if you got your car hidden in my barn?"

"I thought maybe your pickup, or anything else you've got around. I won't need it very often."

"Make it a hundred dollars a week and you can use the pickup now and again, when I don't need it."

Without thinking, Buckman turned on his father, eyes blazing.

"Jesus, it sure as hell's good to be home again, back in the loving bosom of my family."

The words surprised him, and he regretted them even before Calvin jumped from behind the tractor, grabbing Buckman's shirt and pushing him against the hayloft ladder, its square rungs digging into his back.

"Listen to me you snot nosed brat. I didn't ask you to come home with your tail between your legs, and I didn't push to find out what kind of shit you're into. You thought you were too damned good for us. Now you want me to put up with you and your snotty ways, hide you out in my house, hide your fucking car in my garage. I'll go along with it because you're my son. But I don't like it and I don't like you, so keep your damned wise ass mouth to yourself. You're here and you and you need us so you ain't too good for us anymore. You need us. We sure don't need you. Got me?"

Buckman nodded, arching his back away from the ladder, pushing against his father's strength.

Calvin jutted his face into Buckman's, his words accompanied by a fine spittle. "If you're worried about somebody spotting your car, you better get your ass in gear and bring it in here right now."

When his father let him loose, Buckman walked out of the barn toward the Porsche. Velma was sitting on a porch rocking chair, staring at the tops of the trees. He started the car and drove it up the dirt ramp into the barn.

"By God, I guess you'd better hide it," Calvin said as he pulled it in. "You sure as hell had to steal something or kill somebody to get a car like that." He paused for a moment, smiling with his mouth, glowering with the rest of his face. "But then that's what you doctors do, isn't it? Steal and kill and drive fine cars."

Without a word, Buckman drove into a spot under the hayloft. Taking two small suitcases and a knapsack from the trunk, he put the keys in his pocket. After a few minutes of rummaging around in the tack room he found a dirty ripped tarpaulin and carefully draped it over the car.

Calvin ignored him as he leaned rakes, hoes, a shovel, and a couple of pitchforks against the tarp, and set an ancient, mildewed saddle on the hood.

Finished, he left the barn.

Velma was still in the rocking chair as he came across the yard carrying his belongings and money.

She watched as he came up on the porch.

"You hungry?" She asked.

"I haven't eaten since last night."

"We're having Dinty Moore beef stew for dinner. Me and Grampy Cal usually eat a whole can ourselves. I'll have to open two cans of it if you're going to eat with us."

"I'll be eating with you regularly, for a while."

She nodded. "We only got one can right now. You'll have to drive down to Wesley Johnson's store and get some more if you want me to cook for you. Maybe you ought to get enough for tomorrow night too."

"Sure. Where are the keys to the pickup?"

"Grampy Cal keeps them in his pocket. You'll have to ask him for them when you want them."

Buckman sighed and turned toward the barn. He'd get the keys, asking

Calvin politely, noncommittally for them. It didn't matter what his father said, how he acted. Buckman would be an iceberg, his only worry being the possibility of something banging up against him in the night.

He looked at the barn, its door gaping before him, Calvin inside working on the tractor. It was a lousy place, the Old World, with its patterns of abuse and incest, his own history here that of victim as well as outraged and silent observer, listening as Calvin raped Buckman's sisters behind closed doors, watching and suffering as he beat his sons whenever he wished.

He had never complained. Who would have listened? Insiders and outsiders alike accepted such abuse as the way of the Old World. The Buckmans. The Thompsons. The LaTrans. All the rest of them. Many of the Old World families were clans with their own customs, often perverse to the eyes of outsiders, but ignored within the narrow valleys and dark hollows of Canaan Forks.

Taking a deep breath, Buckman walked into the barn to get the keys. Welcome home, he thought as he passed through the door.

THAT NIGHT HE sat on the floor by the window of his room, looking out at shadows of budding trees by porch light. With the recent exception of Irene, he had been a solitary person since his divorce. He knew he was a good doctor, with a warm bedside manner, able to set his patients at ease, chatting with them, visiting their hospital rooms more than most doctors would. He saw it as part of the healing process. But his social life was a void. Back at his center city apartment in Philadelphia, or at the farm in Bucks County, he was alone.

Now he was going to be living in the house with Calvin and Velma, undoubtedly subject to visits from his brothers and sisters, forced to associate at some level with people he hadn't seen or thought of in years. Even more reason to be an iceberg. To keep himself under the surface, hidden from the eyes of the Old World, waiting for whatever might come. If he couldn't be alone, he would create solitude within.

Downstairs, Calvin clicked off the porch light, the shadows disappearing into darkness. Buckman stayed by the window, eyes fixed on the stars glimmering above the tree line. He heard Calvin's footsteps as he came up the stairs, the creaking of the floorboards in the hall sounding just as they had when he was a boy. Even his father's bedroom door still squeaked as he shut it.

The memory of Clay Presnell's voice echoed in his memory.

"Billy Buck, you been away?"

Not much changed in the Old World. People aged. Died. But people here acted just as people in the Old World had always acted. And the place seemed the same. Looked the same. Sounded the same. Smelled the same.

He touched the window glass with the tips of his fingers, the surface cool and smooth. Tired, aching from the road, he was resisting going to bed. Tomorrow he would have to work with Calvin, talk with Velma, see other people, and talk with them, ignoring their stares tolerating their visits and their questions about where he had been what he had been doing and why did he come back.

Already he'd gone down to Wesley Johnson's store. By now the word had probably spread throughout the Old World, Billy Buckman's home. At the very least, his brothers and sisters would be stopping by to look at him, to probe the last twenty-five years, poking at him with sticks of questions and judgments. And he would have to keep it all submerged, not only to protect himself from whoever had been looking for him last night in Upper Black Eddy, but also to protect his life of the past twenty-five years from contamination by the Old World.

The sooner he went to sleep, the sooner it would all start. The longer he sat up, fingers against the cool glass, staring into the night, the more solitude he would have to sustain him through whatever the Old World would be throwing at him.

And it would throw things. He had no doubts.

CHAPTER TWO

Philadelphia, Pennsylvania \ Thursday, February 12

TED MATHIEU ENJOYED the visit with his parents. He and his father, Carson, talked about the Phillies, the old man griping as usual about the pitching, saying there'd never been anyone as good as old Robin had been back in the day. They discussed the weather, how hot the summer had been, was there really a greenhouse effect and if so, what did it mean for the family house on Long Beach Island? Was the Jersey Shore doomed by rising waters, overpopulation, and medical waste?

The conversation moved dangerously close to ecological and natural catastrophes. Too close, for Carson, to the reason for Ted's hospitalization, and he led it sharply away, asking what Ted was doing with the Mercedes while he was in the hospital.

"Jack's got it." Ted looked at his mother as he answered, raising his eyebrows in a plea for relief.

Brenda Mathieu broke in. "Your cousin Linda married a diver down in the islands. They're going to open a water sports shop on St. John."

"Not a great idea, Ma, there's already too many dive shops on the island. So, how are your plants doing?"

Brenda's smile was bright and forced. "The old jade tree looks kind of sad. The petals are falling off, and it's got mites. I sprayed it, but it doesn't seem to be getting any better. The spider plants look real good, though, and I've got two flats of tomato plants growing in the kitchen windowsill. I'm going to plant them in the back yard just as soon as it's spring."

Smiling, he nodded and looked out the window at what he could see of the city. Worthington Hospital was in the Northeast part of Philadelphia and the view was limited to roof tops and chimney stacks.

They were good people, his parents. Loving. As supportive of him as their Catholic morality would allow. When he dropped out of seminary, they shrugged their shoulders and said it's all right not to be a priest. When he went to law school, his father was suspicious, believing all lawyers to be ambulance chasers, or involved in equally shady doings. His mother thought he should be a doctor.

Both had been proud when he graduated third in his class at Penn, and they had bragged to all their friends when he joined Dewey, Carleton, and Pease, a large Center City firm with a revolving door to Washington and a diverse corporate and Main Line family practice.

They never questioned him about Jack, welcoming him at all family gatherings. Ted's mother always had a Christmas present for him, and last year even hung a stocking up for him on the mantle, along with Ted's and his sister Evvie's.

Ted reached over and gave his father's hand a squeeze. Careful not to touch the IV tube, Carson gave his son's hand two squeezes in return, and Ted gave his father three back. It was a quiet signal of affection they had been exchanging for as long as Ted could remember.

"I love you guys." Ted looked at both his parents.

His father leaned over, kissing him lightly on the cheek. He could see tears forming in his mother's eyes. She pretended to cough, then dabbed at her nose with a tissue, surreptitiously drying her eyes as she did.

Later, as he and Brenda were leaving, Carson turned in the doorway and stood looking at Ted, lying in the bed. He was frightened by how thin his son was, pale and covered with angry looking sores.

"Jack's all right," he said. "But he don't know squat about cars. If he has any trouble with your Mercedes, tell him to give me a call."

Ted smiled at his father and waved. "Okay Dad. He'll be relieved to know you can help."

Carson nodded, satisfied, and waved again. "See you tomorrow kiddo."

When they were gone, Ted chuckled, easing himself down in the bed and pulling the sheet up. His father hadn't worked on a car since they traded the '72 Chevy. Just looking under the hood of the Mercedes would freak him out. It was the gesture, though. Telling him to have Jack give a call. It was as close as Carson would ever come to saying it's all okay.

Tired from the visit, Ted took a nap. He woke when the nurse brought dinner, picked at a plate of chicken a la king, peas, and mashed potatoes, watching the evening news on television as he chewed the tough, stringy pieces of chicken.

Later, he looked through a file containing the final arrangements of several insurance settlements he had negotiated before getting too sick to go into the office. He'd kept the illness hidden until four months before, when he started missing two and three days a week. Then he'd made the mistake of telling one of the senior partners what was wrong. The next day he'd been asked not to come in anymore.

"You know how much we value your work," the partner had said. "You're the best the firm has in dealing with the damned insurance companies, but we need to consider the morale of the office staff and the other attorneys. The rest of the senior partners feel you should do your work at home. People don't understand. I'm thinking about them."

"What about me? When do you think about me and my needs?"

"You're a fine lawyer, Ted. We don't want to lose your contributions to the firm. We just think it would be better if you worked at home. That way you can keep your position and you won't lose your insurance coverage."

The threat of losing his insurance had been clear enough. Too tired and ill to fight, Ted arranged for work to be sent to his apartment on Society Hill.

Now Janice, his secretary, was bringing it to the hospital. She would come, stand in the doorway to his room and reach around, dropping any papers she had brought on a chair just inside the door. Still standing there, she would chat with him, mostly office gossip, who's slacking up on work, who's having an affair. Finally, she would wave and say she had to get going. Later, a nurse would come in and hand him the papers Janice had brought.

"You don't have to give me the files back," she had told him the first day he'd moved out of the office. "I'll give you copies, and I'll have everything on my computer. You can phone me, and I'll call the files up. We can talk about the changes you want me to make, and I'll bring you revisions of whatever we're working on. Okay?"

Okay hell. Nothing was okay. Nor would be again. He lay in a private room, seeing only Jack, his parents, a handful of friends, and Henry Cottman, a thin, carbuncular priest who had been in the seminary with him. Nobody from the office stopped by, except Janice, who stood in the doorway. The last several times she dropped work off for him, she'd tried convincing him to get a laptop computer. Then he could work in the hospital and email her the results. She'd be able to receive it right at her desk without wasting all the time coming down to the hospital.

It was an ever dwindling world, and he resented how it had changed. The nurses and some of the docs tried to be upbeat, but he dreaded it each time he got a new resident, or a nurse was transferred from another floor, and he had to see their nervous faces when they looked in on him. Dr. Buckman was the best of the lot. He'd visit whenever he had a few spare minutes, drop by, talk about politics, gripe about his insurance rates, always chiding Ted for his legal participation in malpractice suits.

"If it wasn't for you lawyers, we could practice a lot more medicine and spend a lot less time in court," he said one time.

Ted had grinned at him. "If some of you docs didn't make so many mistakes, and the rest of you didn't cover for the ones who do, there'd be a lot less malpractice going on. It's docs, not lawyers who make the suits. The lawyers just carry them out."

Buckman had laughed, nodding his head. "You're right but try convincing the AMA of that. Most doctors are going to cover other doctors' asses until the government sets up a real system for review and publication of information on the fuckups. It stinks."

Ted looked forward to Buckman's visits. He was the only person he could have a normal conversation with. Jack would come, sit by his bed, and try not to cry. His parents skirted the issue of how serious his illness was, and friends never stayed long enough to do either. Henry Cottman's visits were useless. The last thing Ted wanted was somebody praying over him, especially a sickly looking priest who said his illness was a visitation from God in retribution for leaving the seminary and the depravity of his subsequent lifestyle.

Buckman kidded around with him, let him talk about cancer and the genetic research being done to find cures. He'd answer Ted's questions and then go on to talk about anything which occurred to either of them. Even to the comparative virtues of Mercedes and Porsches. There were no forbidden topics. Buckman's visits were an island of normalcy in Ted's increasingly isolated and frightening world.

The evening news over, the tray with most of the chicken a la king and peas untouched taken away, Ted spent an hour reading case law for a brief he was writing in a suit filed by a client who had been injured during a road race of high performance automobiles in the Poconos. By the time he was finished, he was too tired to do anything but watch television and go to sleep. He woke once when the night nurse came in to check on him. They chatted for a few minutes, and she left.

The television was on, Jimmy Fallon doing his monologue. Ted forced himself to stay awake until it was over, then drifted off. When he woke again, some long forgotten black and white movie was running. He flicked it off with the remote, scrunched up his pillow and turned over on his side to sleep.

As he did, he saw a man's figure standing in the shadowed doorway, faintly outlined by the night lights in the corridor beyond. Without speaking, the figure glided across the room and stopped at the IV bottle, as though checking to see if it was full. Too late, Ted saw the man insert a needle attached to a syringe filled into the tubing. Before he could think to yell for help, the potassium had reached his heart and it stopped beating.

CHAPTER THREE

Canaan, Massachusetts \ Friday, May 3

THEY WERE SITTING at the kitchen table. Heat from the wood cook stove forced them to open the doors and windows. There were no screens and several barn cats jumped from the windowsills onto piles of *Grit* newspapers and farm catalogs stacked along the walls. A yellowed 1963 Surge calendar, with a faded picture of a nude girl in her late teens leaning against the control panel of a milking machine, rustled in the breeze. The month showing was November.

Velma refilled Calvin's coffee mug and looked at Buckman.

"You want more coffee?"

"No thanks." He smiled, barely able to see her face in the dim light from the bulb in the porcelain ceiling fixture.

"Give him some more," Calvin growled. "Billy Buck here probably ain't been up at five o'clock since he left here to go off and be some snot nose doctor. I don't want him getting tired on me before we got a good day's work done."

Velma poured the coffee, studying Buckman's face. "You a doctor?"

Calvin grabbed her arm, his fingers tightening into her flesh. "You don't tell that to a soul, get me girl? I don't want nobody knowing about Billy here being a doctor. Next thing everybody'll be coming here asking him to fix this, that, and the other thing. We got too much work to do around this place, without having half the valley coming in to get doctored for nothing."

"Maybe he could charge them money to do it," Velma said. "You're always saying that we don't got enough money."

Calvin's fingers dug deeper. "That won't get the new roof on the barn and the corn in the ground. That takes hard work and I finally got someone to help me out around the place for the first time since your Uncle Benny married the Silas girl down to the other end of the Black Horse and moved over to Shelburne in Franklin County. I ain't about to have it wasted with Billy Buck doing a bunch of doctoring for everybody around here that can't afford to pay him for doing it. If they need doctoring, they can damned well go over to Canaan Falls, or down to the hospital in Graham. It sure ain't going to happen at my place on my time."

Buckman sipped his coffee. "It's all right, Velma. I don't want people here to know I'm a doctor. I can't call attention to the fact I'm here. You understand?"

"What if somebody got hurt, or was going to have a baby, or something? Would you be a doctor then?"

"Maybe then, if I could stop somebody from dying, or being seriously hurt. But you've got to keep this a secret. My own life might depend on it."

Calvin loosened his grip on her arm. She moved quickly back to the stove and stood rubbing red welts raised by the pressure from Calvin's fingers, her red wet eyes fixed on the two men.

"That was stupid." Buckman shook his head, looking at his father. "You tell me not to say anything about being a physician, then you tell Velma all about it. Why don't you put a notice up down at Wesley Johnson's Store?"

"It don't matter none, her knowing. She'll keep her damned mouth shut. Right Velma?"

The girl nodded, still staring at them. "I won't say a word to anybody, honest, Grampy Cal."

"You goddamn better not girl, if you know what's good for you."

Velma's eyes filled with tears. She wiped them with the heel of her palm and snuffled lightly.

Buckman looked from her to his father, telling himself to keep his own damned mouth shut. This was a perfect place to hide for a while. He couldn't afford to blow it by having a fight with the old man. It wouldn't get him anywhere, and Velma's well-being wasn't worth his life. She'll have to figure things out for herself.

Calvin drained his coffee and stood. "Time to get your ass in gear, Billy Buck. We got a shitload of work to do this morning"

Buckman rubbed his eyes, yawing. "I'll be right along."

Calvin grunted and started out the kitchen door. Standing in the doorway, he turned back, looking from Velma to Buckman, started to say something, then shrugged his shoulders and headed off toward the barn.

Velma followed him to the door and stood watching as he disappeared in the barn. Once he was out of sight, she came back and sat across from Buckman, playing with her fingers as she stared at the crumbs on the table.

"Maybe I will have another cup of coffee." He got up, crossing to the stove.

"I'll get it for you." She jumped up, pushing ahead of him. "Grampy Cal would be mad if he knew you had to get your own coffee."

"Looks like my father rides a pretty tight rein on you."

"He ain't so bad. He lets me have my own room and only bothers me once or twice a week." She handed him the coffee and returned to the table.

Buckman walked to the window and looked out toward the barn. Just then his father started the tractor engine. "What do you mean, bothers you?'

She looked back down at the table, shaking her head.

"Nothing. I didn't mean nothing by it."

"Does he come to your room. At night?"

Buckman heard the indignation in his voice. The girl cringed at the tone, raising her eyes to his.

"There ain't nothing wrong in it. Daddy says Grampy Cal's lonely since Gram died and I'm supposed to do what he wants so he won't be unhappy and kill himself, like Uncle Amos did when Auntie Martha died. Daddy says if Grampy Cal kills himself it'll be all my fault."

Taking a deep breath, Buckman covered his face with his palms and groaned. For the last twenty-five years the Old World had existed in his mind as a concept, like something from a medical sociology study. He'd known coming back wouldn't be easy, but he'd imagined it in the abstract, removed from the reality of life where he had grown up. Now he was being slapped in the face by the place, confronting feelings he'd buried long ago, feelings complicated by the overlay of years spent training himself to look at the ethical and moral components of his actions. Even with his life in the balance he feared coming back had been a terrible mistake. In some ways what he would be facing here was as bad as what he was running from.

Velma stared at him as he sat, his face covered. Several times she opened her mouth to speak, thought better of it and stopped. Buckman moved his hands uselessly and stared back at her.

"How old are you?" He asked to break the silence.

"I'll be seventeen in July."

"Then you've been here since you were fourteen."

She shook her head. "Thirteen. I turned fourteen a few weeks after I come here."

"And Grampy Cal's been coming to your room at night ever since then?"

She grunted a yes. "It's not any big deal. I done it back home, before I come here. Lots of times. And he don't make me sleep with him. He just comes in, bothers me for a little bit, and then goes back to his own room. I get up, take a bath, and go back to bed."

He cleared his throat and looked her in the face. "Velma, you know what Grampy Cal is doing to you is illegal, don't you? You know it's a crime?"

Her eyes grew wide and frightened, her face even paler than normal. "You won't tell nobody, will you, Uncle Billy Buck? I don't want to get in trouble. Please don't tell nobody."

"You wouldn't get in trouble. You're not committing the crime. Grampy Cal is."

"I'd get in trouble. If you told anybody and they made trouble for Grampy Cal, him and Daddy would make trouble for me. I don't want no trouble, Uncle Billy, so act like I never told you."

"You never mentioned this to any of your teachers or counselors at school?"

"I ain't gone to school since sixth grade. When it comes time for me to go on the bus to the Union School down to Canaan Falls, Daddy said I didn't need no more school and I never went."

"And nobody ever came around asking why you weren't going to school?"

She shook her head again. "You won't tell nobody about that either, will you? I don't want to get in trouble about school or about Grampy Cal."

"Don't worry, Velma. I won't tell a soul."

He laughed inwardly at that. He couldn't tell a soul. He didn't need anybody asking questions around the Old World, nosing around the family. Nosing around him. That was the bitter truth of his return.

He got up, put the coffee mug in the sink and started for the door. As he was passing the table, Velma reached up tugging on his shirt.

"Are you really a doctor?"

He bowed. "Doctor William C. Buckman, M.D. Specialist in diseases of the immune system. The C. stands for Calvin. After my father. Nice touch, don't you think?"

"I think something's wrong with me, Uncle Billy Buck. I ain't had the curse in five or six months. You don't think I got cancer like Gram? I ain't going to die, am I?"

"I THINK VELMA'S pregnant." Buckman was steadying the extension ladder as Calvin set it against the barn.

"You're the doctor. Get rid of it." He turned and leaned on a rung, facing his son through the ladder.

"I don't have the right equipment and I don't have decent conditions to work under. You ought to take her to the hospital in Graham or find an abortion clinic somewhere."

"I don't believe in abortion clinics. Reverend Erskine Dye, the minister in our church says they ought to be bombed out of business."

"But you don't want Velma to have a baby?"

"I've had enough damned babies, five of you kids and two others over in Charlemont. I don't need no more. I'm too old and set in my ways to have children around. Velma's bad enough, mooning over music on the radio and giggling whenever Wilfred brings one of her sisters over here. I don't want no baby."

"But you're opposed to abortion?"

Calvin nodded. "Reverend Dye says women are running around killing babies whenever they think it's going to put a crimp in their lives. That's wrong."

"You just asked me to get rid of Velma's baby."

"Velma having a baby wouldn't do nobody no good. She ain't old enough or smart enough to raise it, and I'm too old and too smart to do it. Getting rid of it wouldn't be an abortion, it'd be a favor to her and to me."

"That's the whole purpose of abortion clinics."

Calvin pushed his face through the rungs, hissing at Buckman. "No damned abortion clinic. Besides, I don't want her going down to Canaan Falls or Graham. Might start people asking questions they shouldn't ought to be asking. And even if they didn't, I don't carry insurance to cover whatever they'd do to her down there. Hell, I don't carry no insurance, except for fire on the place. They'd probably never take her in after all the bills I ain't never paid on your mother."

"It might not matter anyway," Buckman said.

"It matters. She starts opening her damned mouth down in the towns and she could get us into a lot of trouble. It matters a whole hell of a lot."

"It wouldn't if she's too far gone for an abortion." Knowing she wasn't, he enjoyed watching Calvin's reaction.

"Damn her." Calvin stomped his feet, his face twisted with rage. "Goddamn stupid bitch, getting knocked up like some damned cow. Don't she know how she can ruin everything?"

"I don't think Velma knows much of anything."

Calvin's voice was a snarl as he spoke and turned to the house. "I'll teach her a thing or two."

Buckman's heart pounded, his fists clenching and unclenching. How had he come from this? And what had he been thinking to come back to it? Two days in the Old World and all the old childhood rage, its frustration and bewilderment were churning through him, combining unbearably with the rage, frustration and bewilderment which had driven him back here. He stood, struggling to control his breathing, eyes on his father walking toward the house, arms swinging as though ready to enter the prize fight ring.

The yelling started immediately, words indistinguishable, but the tones clear. Rage and fear echoed against the hills, mixed with the sounds of slapping and the breaking of furniture. Buckman was paralyzed. Just as he had been when he was a child, listening to his father go after his mother. He knew he should interfere before the girl was seriously injured, but doing it would enrage the old man, something he couldn't afford to do. Calvin Buckman's farm was his safety zone. Anger him and Calvin would kick him off the place.

Shaking, Buckman turned away from the house, his eyes drifting up to the south facing weathervane on the barn. He should have gone to Europe, disappeared into the Caribbean or Mexico. Hidden out in Key West, or New Orleans. The world was rich with exotic and exciting places he could have gone to, rich with exotic and exciting things he could have done. He should have. What he should not have done was come back to the Old World.

Cursing his lack of foresight, he turned and started for the house. Halfway there, the noises stopped. When he reached the kitchen, he saw Velma standing in shadow by the stove. Bleeding heavily, a thick flap of skin hanging from her chin, she held a cast iron skillet as she stood astride Calvin, who lay on the floor, the right side of his head caved in.

She raised the skillet at Buckman's approach.

"Don't come no closer."

He put his hands in the air, palms out. "I won't hurt you, Velma. All I want to do is take a close look at Grampy Cal. Be a good girl and let me see what I can do for him."

"You don't touch me."

"I won't come near you. Go on over by the door to the back parlor. You'll have the whole room and the kitchen table between us."

She moved slowly away, never taking her eyes from him. As soon as she was across the room, Buckman walked over to Calvin and knelt beside him, pressing his fingers to his father's neck. The old man's pulse was weak, his breathing shallow. Buckman stood and looked into Velma's eyes. She lowered her head and stared at Calvin, whose eyes fluttered open. He looked from Velma to Buckman, then curled his finger at his son, motioning him to come closer, his lips moving silently.

Buckman knelt again and bent over, his ear next to his father's mouth.

Calvin's breath was heavy and rasped in his throat, the words unintelligible.

"I can't understand you," Buckman said softly, stroking his father's cheek.

Calvin's eyes widened, darting wildly as his lips twisted, his face straining from the attempt at forming words. The rasping grew heavier, and his face reddened. Pulling himself up on one elbow, he leaned toward Buckman.

"Home," he said, his face contorted from the effort.

Buckman nodded, smiling at him. "What about home?"

Calvin looked at him and fell back. The breath rasped in his throat a last time. He lay still.

Buckman felt his neck for a pulse. There was none. Getting up, he looked at Velma and slowly shook his head, his voice soft. "He's dead, Velma. Grampy Cal's dead."

Velma started to cry. "He was hurting me. He was hurting me worse than he ever did. I didn't mean to kill him, Uncle Billy Buck. I only wanted to stop him from hurting me more. See, look at my chin. It hurts real bad. I just wanted to stop him. If I wanted to kill him, I could've shot him. Grampy Cal taught me how to shoot a gun real good. We used to go down to the dump and shoot the rats there. Sometimes I'd kill more of them than he would."

There was a note of pride in her voice. Then she stopped suddenly, coming back across the kitchen to where Calvin lay. Leaning down, she placed her fingers in the soft pulp of his head. "Now what's going to happen to me? What will they do to me? You got to help me, Uncle Billy Buck. I ain't got nobody else who can."

After bandaging her chin Buckman sat on a chair, his father's body on the floor a few inches away, despair coursing through his body, hammering every nerve ending. The Old World had him. Here he sat, in the house he had been raised in and run away from twenty-five years before. Kneeling next to him was his backward teenage niece, pregnant by his father, who lay dead on the floor beside him, his head crushed by a skillet Velma had swung against it.

She was sniffling and whimpering, begging him to help her. "You can't tell daddy, Uncle Billy Buck."

"Don't worry," Buckman said and threw a tablecloth over his father's body. "This'll be our secret. I'll never tell anyone, and you can't either."

"I won't, Uncle Billy Buck. I promise. Just don't tell Daddy."

"Never," Buckman said, wagging his forefinger in the air between them.

He knew what to do. After all, he'd grown up in the Old World. The natural thing would be to hide the body. Covering up Calvin's death was the only way of helping himself. Reporting it, bringing in the police, there'd be stories in the newspapers, which would surely get picked up by the wire services, maybe even the television networks. Eventually, the wrong person in Philadelphia would read about it or see them on TV and it would be all over for him.

He looked at the lump on the floor, forcing himself to think practically. He'd hold himself in check, stay his emotions, his fears. Maybe for a long time. Nodding, he forced a smile at the sobbing girl.

"I'll help you, Velma, but you've got to promise you'll never say anything about this to anybody. Not to your father, your brothers, or sisters, not to your girlfriends. Nobody. Ever. You understand?"

She sobbed, nodding her head.

"What we do is tell everybody you and Grampy Cal had a big fight and he stormed out of here and hasn't come back. Can you do that?"

"I think so."

He took one of her hands and held it gently. "You can't just think so. You've got to do it. Promise me you'll never say anything to anybody about what happened here this morning."

"I won't, Uncle Billy Buck. I promise."

"Good. Now we've got a burial to take care of."

CHAPTER FOUR

Philadelphia, Pennsylvania \ Friday, February 22

MELINDA SHOEMAKER WAS crying. She hurt all over and none of her friends would come to see her. Her mother said it was because she was sick, that her friends' parents were afraid they would catch her illness.

"Dr. Bill says you can't catch it just from being in the same room with someone."

"I know," her mother said, stroking the child's forehead.

Melinda's blonde hair was neatly combed, flaring out into fine points on the pillow. Her eyes, sunken from the disease, were still bright, even filled with tears.

"When is Daddy coming?"

Irene Shoemaker shook her head. "I don't know, honey. I've talked to him three or four times, and left dozens of messages on his answering machine. But you know how busy he is, and how his work down in Atlanta makes it hard for him to come north."

"He'll be here soon, though, won't he?"

"Sure," Irene said. "Anytime now. Maybe this afternoon, maybe tomorrow morning you'll see him walk right through your door."

"And he'll say, 'hi sugar-tater' and he'll have a present for me, right Mommy?"

"I'm sure he will."

"Then he'll come home to live with us, and everything will be just like it used to be, right Mommy?"

"It won't happen that way, Mel. He doesn't want to come back, and I sure don't want him to. But it's not because of you, honey. It's because of Daddy and me. We just couldn't make it work."

Melinda nodded, frowning at her mother. "I know. You grew in different ways. Dr. Bill says sometimes it's worse for people to live together than to split up. He says it's even worse for the kids when people pretend for them. But I don't like it Mommy. I don't like it that Daddy left us."

Irene smiled at her daughter, wondering if a child of seven could begin to understand all the things she had just said, even though her tone of voice when she spoke held all the inflections of understanding.

"Do you talk to Dr. Buckman about everything?"

Melinda nodded, grinning. "When I told him you thought he was cute he said he thought you were pretty cute too, and I said maybe he should ask you out for dinner."

Irene's face reddened, but she was smiling as she scolded her daughter. "Melinda Shoemaker. I don't want you discussing my social life with everybody who comes in and out of this room."

"I don't, Mommy. It was only Dr. Bill. He's the only one I really talk to. The others are nice, but they just come in to do things for me or bring me things. Dr. Bill comes in to talk. He's nice. He sits here and talks to me about all kinds of things. Besides, you really do think he's cute, don't you?"

Irene smiled again, nodding lightly. Bill Buckman was a good looking man, and he seemed like a nice one, humorous, thoughtful, perhaps a bit reserved except for a genuine affection he seemed to have for Melinda. Irene had thought about asking him out, and she might have done so were it not for her upbringing. She'd been raised when it was practically unheard of for a woman to ask a man for a date. The conditioning was still holding. Maybe she'd break free of it one of these days, but it was going to be tough.

She ran her fingers through Melinda's hair. "Be careful what you say. You could get me into hot water with that giant economy size mouth of yours."

Melinda laughed, had trouble catching her breath and started gasping, wheezing, holding her sides in pain.

Being careful of the IV tubing, Irene helped her sit up, then perched herself on the edge of the bed, rubbing the child's back. The spell would pass in a few minutes. Melinda would be fine for a while...if lying in a hospital bed where she was dying quietly could be called fine.

When the attack was over, Melinda lay back down and fell quickly asleep.

Irene sat on the bed for another five minutes before turning off the lights and heading to the hospital snack shop for coffee and a sandwich. She met Bill Buckman standing at the nursing station looking over a stack of papers fastened in an aluminum clipboard.

Resting it on the counter, he smiled at Irene. "How's our patient?"

"Asleep but otherwise the same. Sad and lonely."

Handing the chart to a nurse, he came from behind the station, placing a hand on Irene's shoulder. "You look tired, Ms. Shoemaker. You should go home and get some rest."

"Mel expects me to be there when she wakes up."

"It's nine o'clock. When I finish rounds, I'll sit with her and when she wakes up, I'll tell her you went home to get some sleep."

"I am tired."

"Then go. Doctor's orders. I'll call if anything happens, although I don't expect any change. She's been stable for a couple of days. I think her new medication's beginning to work."

Irene began to cry. "It's so unfair. How could this have happened to her? I thought hospitals screened blood better."

"It happens. I can't imagine a worse nightmare."

She nodded. They had been over it all before. Many times. The automobile accident on their vacation. Mel's injury. The emergency transfusion at the small hospital outside of Scranton and the child's subsequent illness. Buckman had explained the lapses in the screening system, promising they would do everything possible for her.

"Thank God for the insurance. One of the few good things I got from the divorce settlement was that Barry had to keep medical insurance for both of us. I don't know what I'd have done without it."

Buckman put his arm around Irene's shoulders, walking her toward the elevators. They were both conscious of it being more than a gesture of professional concern.

"Don't come back until tomorrow."

"Why are you doing this for Mel? You must have a home you want to get back to yourself."

Buckman shook his head and pushed the down button. "I've got a house, up in Bucks County, but it's too far for me to drive this late, this tired, and there's nobody in either of them except me. I've got nothing to go home to. No one. And anyway, I've got to be on call in the morning. Not that it makes any difference. I'd stay with her anyway. Melinda's special. I'll sit with her until I'm sure she's settled for the night, then catch some sleep in one of the crash pads the hospital keeps for interns and residents."

The elevator door slid open, and he ushered her in. "Don't worry about her, Ms. Shoemaker. I'll take care of everything."

Smiling, Irene waved as the elevator doors glided shut. Maybe she should ask him out.

Buckman watched the lighted numbers above the door as the elevator descended. He hadn't told her about the apartment he kept in the city where he stayed the nights he was on call, not that he planned on going there. He would stay here near Melinda. He was fond of her, perhaps seeing in her the child he'd never had, as well as the patient. He knew it was not wise to care about patients, that his job was to keep a calm and rational distance between himself and the people whose health he was charged to monitor and maintain. It was complicated, and he didn't think about it for long. He barely thought about how attracted he was to her mother.

Later, when Buckman went to Melinda's room, she was awake, watching a Nickelodeon rerun of *Mr. Ed*.

"Hi Dr. Bill," she said. "Where's Mommy?"

"I sent her home and told her I'd stay with you for a while tonight. She was very tired." He reached down, ruffling her hair. "Hey, I thought you were asleep."

"I pretended to be so Mommy would go home."

"You take pretty good care of your mother."

"I told her you thought she was cute."

"I thought that was just between us."

"It was, but she was talking real sad about Daddy and I thought it might make her feel better. She thinks you're cute, you know."

"You've told me at least a dozen times."

She laughed, snuggling down in her bed. "Are you going to ask her out?"

Buckman sat next to her, absently patting her hand. "You're a real Cupid, aren't you?"

"I don't know. What's a Cupid?"

"Somebody who tries to fix people up together."

"You mean like those TV advice shows?"

He laughed, a quick barking sound. "And what in the world would you know about shows like that?"

"I see them sometimes on television when I can't sleep and turn it on late at night."

Buckman laughed again, he fluffed her pillow and checked the IV flow.

"I wish I could go home and back to school."

Forcing a smile, Buckman looked at her pale skin and sunken eyes. The kid had less chance of going home and back to school than he did of winning the Nobel Prize.

He sat with her until the end of the show when Ed Clark, one of the nurses, came in to make sure everything was ready for the night.

"A lot of patients on the floor tonight, Doc." Ed wiped his brow in a gesture of overwork. "And they've only scheduled me, Anne Lambert, and a couple of aides to work it. I don't know what medicine is coming to. There's no way two nurses can properly care for all these people."

Buckman got up. Walking to the end of the bed, he tweaked Melinda's big toe.

"Good night, toots. Be nice to Nurse Ed. He sounds like he's close to the end of his rope tonight."

Ed looked at Melinda and shook his head. "It's awful here, Doc. Some people wait for more than a half hour after they ring us for help."

"Sounds like a union issue to me, Ed."

"Corporate headquarters doesn't give a rat's ass about the union. We go on strike; they'll just hire scabs and go about business as usual. That's all this place it about, doc, business, profits. There shouldn't be such a thing as a for-profit hospital."

Buckman shook his head. "It's not that bad, Ed. You're getting paid a lot more than nurses at other hospitals."

"And working twice as hard for it. I'd go over to Jeff or Penn tomorrow if I could get on, but they can hire qualified people fresh out of school for a lot less than they'd have to pay for me."

Buckman shrugged, winking at Melinda. "I guess you'd better be super dooper nice to Nurse Ed tonight."

Melinda squeezed his hand, giggling. She looked up at Ed and pointed to the TV screen. "I'll be good to you Mr. Ed."

The nurse bared his teeth at her. "Are you calling me a horse's fanny, young lady?"

She giggled again, her laughter quickly giving way to wheezing. Buckman moved back to her bedside, his forefinger on his lips.

"Shh. Don't get too excited now. It's time for sleep. Just relax and close your eyes."

Reaching up, he turned off the bed light. "You go on and take care of whatever you've got to do with the other patients, Ed. I'll stay here and settle Mel down for the night."

"Not many docs like you," Ed said.

Buckman shrugged and winked at the girl in the bed. "Not many patients like Mel."

When Ed had gone, Buckman pulled Melinda's covers up to her chin, flicked off the television and watched as her eyes closed, her breathing growing deep and regular. When she was asleep, he leaned over and kissed her softly on the cheek, then left her room, walking past the nursing station where Ed Clark was setting up a tray of night meds. The bright hallway lighting was off, leaving only the subdued lights the nursing staff needed to move around without bumping into walls or tripping over wheelchairs and gurneys.

"She's sound asleep," Buckman said.

"Thanks Doc. She's a great kid. Be a shame to lose her like we lost Ted Mathieu last week, but then you just can't tell with this damned thing."

Buckman grunted and walked down the hallway toward the crash pad.

THE FLOOR WAS hectic for the next few hours. Ed Clark took the night meds around from patient to patient, then had a panicked call from an elderly man in 1208A who told him the angel of death was sitting on his chest.

When Ed turned on the room lights the angel disappeared and the man insisted he leave them on for the rest of the night. Since the patient in the other bed had slept through the commotion, Ed agreed, figuring he'd come back in twenty minutes or so, when the man had gone back to sleep, and turn them off.

At two-thirty, the patient in 1208A rang again, crying out for help as he did, saying the angel of death was back, crushing his chest. Clark rushed down the hall, ready to give him a few more minutes of light, only to find him in the middle of a massive heart attack.

Both he and Anne Lambert were in the room, busily working with the paramedics who had come with the crash cart, as they tried to save him. Neither of them noticed the man walking down the hallway. One of the aides at the nursing station was reading a novel and never looked up. Two other aides were taking a coffee break. The figure turned into Melinda's room. She lay curled on her side, facing the door, her eyes closed, her forefinger gently rubbing the side of her nose. It took a few seconds for him to take the potassium filled syringe from his pocket and insert the needle into her IV.

Melinda never stirred.

CHAPTER FIVE

Canaan, Massachusetts / Friday, May 3 -Saturday, May 4

BUCKMAN DUG A grave deep in the far corner of an unplowed field, as Velma watched, wringing her hands, crying with a sniffling whining sound. When it was deep enough, he carried Calvin's body, wrapped in a plaid flannel blanket, to a cart he'd hitched to the tractor, hauled it out to the site and with a heavy rope lowered his father gently into the ground.

The tears surprised him, streaming down his face as a convulsive sob wracked his body. The plaid package looked small at the bottom of the hole. All the love and hate he'd ever felt for Calvin, the swirling, confused emotions of a boy become a man erased the years of self-exile from the Old World.

He hated his past. He hated thinking about it. In the years away he rarely thought about Canaan Forks and his life there. It was a closed chapter and only the present had seemed important. He was sure his focus on the moment was what made him a good doctor, attending to the immediate situation with all his being, the past and future insignificant, only his full attention and action in the moment counting for anything.

Now, looking into the grave where Calvin lay immobile, forever incapable of touching him, the past snuck up, filling Buckman's moment. As a boy, the only time he had spent away from Canaan Forks was in high school, and that didn't count for much since he was regarded as just another kid from the Old World, viewed with the prejudices people from Canaan Falls and the surrounding farms had for kids from the Forks. Still, being at school was better than staying at home, watching his parents, working the farm's rough land, and playing around with cars like the rest of the boys he'd grown up among, most of whom had dropped out of school the second they turned sixteen.

He went to the community college in Graham without any plans beyond than having a safe place away from home a little longer. In his second semester, one day in early February, he and Nelson Thibault, who commuted to school from Brattleboro, Vermont, were driving up Route 5 to Nelson's house where they were going to spend the weekend. Thibault's car hit a patch of ice just north of Bernardston, spun across the road and hit a telephone pole.

Buckman's shoulder was dislocated. He blacked out from the pain. A few minutes later, he opened his eyes and saw Nelson Thibault struggling for breath, the steering wheel jammed against his chest, blood pouring down his face.

Forcing a buckled car door open, Buckman made his way to a small gas station and package store half a mile up the road. The owner called an ambulance and soon the boys were in the emergency room at the Wessex County Public Hospital. Within minutes Buckman's shoulder was back in place, the pain nearly gone. He watched as the nurses and a doctor worked on Nelson, setting, and wrapping his broken ribs and taking care of the cuts on his head.

He had been impressed by the order and cleanliness of the emergency room, the efficiency of the nurses and doctor, their concentration and impersonal caring. The next week he applied to the nursing program at the college.

There should have been no problem. His grades were high, and he was enthusiastic, but the head of the program, Jack Varner, didn't approve of men in nursing, claiming they were not submissive enough to physicians. Buckman was rejected. He went on to major in biology, earned top grades, transferred to the University of Massachusetts, and was pushed in the direction of medical school by his professors. It had all come easily to him. Studying, with its intense immediate demands forced him to throw all his concentration and intellect into the task before him, ignoring his past and the Old World.

Shaking his head at the flood of memory, he stared into Calvin's grave for a long time before he dropped the first shovelful of dirt onto the blanket. Small pieces of sod and stone landed on the body, Buckman imagining them coving Calvin's eyes, soil filling his nose and mouth. He almost wished he had not covered the body.

Velma, watched for several minutes before running back to the house. Buckman took little notice until she returned with a handful of blue and red plastic flowers, their stems bent and broken, their colors faded from sunlight hitting them on the windowsill where they had sat since before he left the Old World, one of his mother's few attempts at brightening up the dark house where she had lived and suffered Calvin's endless abuse. Velma tossed them into the grave and they landed over Calvin's heart.

"He should have them," she said. "It's going to be dark in there when all the dirt's put back in."

"He won't know, and he doesn't deserve them anyway."

"He should have them," she said again and looked up at him, her face twisted with puzzlement. "Uncle Billy Buck, how come you didn't bury him out in the woods? On the television, they're always burying people out in the woods. There's shadows and bears and Daddy says there's mountain lions in the woods and people get scared to walk around in dark woods, so they stay away."

Buckman dropped a second shovelful of dirt on Calvin's plaid shroud, pebbles rattling as they rolled from the metal surface of the shovel.

"There's also a lot of roots and rocks in the woods. They make it almost impossible to dig a hole deep enough to bury someone so they won't be found. You don't want somebody's old hunting dog, or a coyote or a bear to dig him up, do you Velma?"

She shook her head, wiping a hand across her teary eyes. "It would be real bad if somebody found Grampy Cal, wouldn't it, Uncle Billy Buck?"

"It would be very bad, Velma, but nobody's going to find him. He's buried deeper than he would be in a cemetery, and as soon as I finish filling in his grave, I'm going to plow the field and start planting corn. There won't even be the trace of a burial by this evening."

She was quiet for a few minutes, watching as Buckman slowly filled the grave. When she spoke again, her voice was small and frightened.

"Will it make the corn go bad with Grampy Cal rotting away down there under it while it grows?"

Buckman smiled and shook his head. "Your grandfather won't ever harm anything again, not even the corn growing above his grave."

"How about his ghost? Will Grampy Cal's ghost haunt us?"

Buckman looked at the girl's face. Her eyes red, her cheeks stained from tears and dirt, she was wringing her trembling hands and staring at the pile of earth and stones growing on the plaid covered lump that had been Calvin Buckman.

He shook his head. "Not if you never tell anybody what happened here. If Grampy Cal's ghost knew you were talking about him and telling people how you'd killed him for beating you, it would be angry and might come after you, so be very, very careful not to say anything about any of this."

She started crying again. He disliked frightening her any more than she was already frightened, any more than she had been terrorized all her life by his brother and his father, but there was too much at stake. Calvin's death had to remain a secret. No investigations, no publicity. Nothing to give the outside world any clues as to where he might be. Terrifying Velma by threatening retribution by Calvin's ghastly remains seemed to be one way of ensuring her silence.

Whimpering, she asked, "I can't even tell Daddy?"

"Especially you can't tell him. Grampy Cal's ghost would be extremely angry if it thought your father knew anything."

Snuffling, she wiped her nose on her arm. "I won't tell, Uncle Billy Buck. I won't even tell myself about it when I go to sleep at night. I'll make myself forget all about it, just like it never happened."

He smiled at her. "You think you can do that?"

She nodded. "Daddy taught me. He said you can forget anything you want to forget, like taught me to forget the things he done with me before I come to Grampy Cal's."

"But you remember them."

"Not mostly. Mostly I forget them and only remember them if there's something important to remember them for. Like just now, when I remembered them so I could tell you how I forgot them."

Buckman laughed. Standing over his father's freshly filled grave, in the middle of a cornfield in the Old World, he laughed until the back of his head ached and his throat was sore. Velma watched, her face looking even more frightened than she had been a few moments before.

BUCKMAN SPENT THE afternoon plowing the field, the little Ford tractor running as smoothly as it had when he was a boy. Whatever else the old man was, he'd been a good mechanic. A doctor for machines.

He smiled, struck by an old, long forgotten pleasure in driving that gray and red machine through the field, towing the plow and making furrows in the soil behind him, but it was a childhood pleasure, and he felt it only in a moment of naïve nostalgia, a false memory of a pastoral childhood he knew only from books he had read under his covers at night with a flashlight, a wistful reminiscence that would vanish if he had to stay in the Old World forever, work the land, drive that tractor year after year, forced to keep it in operating condition by banging grease blackened knuckles against its engine block until they bled. There lay a major difference between his father and himself. His father worked on things that couldn't talk back to him. Machines. The earth. Plants and cows. Buckman couldn't work on things unless they did talk back. How do you feel? Where does it hurt? Any other symptoms?

Horseshit. The difference was greater. Those were just the signs of difference. He was nothing like his father. Couldn't be. Wouldn't be. If he hadn't run away from anything else when he left the Old World, he'd run away from that. From Calvin. From Calvin's ways.

He and Hannah had been at a restaurant in Philadelphia when she told him she was leaving him, that he was too cold and she was leaving, getting a divorce, and moving away from the area. She said he never got angry, but he was never loving either. When he replied, telling her he thought they had great sex, she'd laughed sadly, nodding her head. Great sex, she told him, sure they had great sex, but he'd never made love to her. He'd said he didn't understand what she meant.

She'd reached across the table, stroking his cheek. "That's the problem, Bill. You're bottled up. I don't know what you're sitting on, and I don't think you know, not really. You're as good in bed as you can be, but you never make love. You're as good in life as you can be, but you don't do anything with love. With pride, sure. With care, absolutely. With love, never. I don't think you feel it. Know what it is."

And then there were times, she said, when she was afraid he was going to hit her.

He was shocked. "I'd never hit you, Han, I've never hit anybody."

"It's the way you look at me, like you're ready to slug me sometimes. It frightens me, even though I've never even seen you get mad. I know you're angry, even if you don't."

"That's ridiculous. If I was angry, I'd feel anger."

"Something inside you is boiling."

He'd argued with her, told her he loved her, he'd try harder.

"You don't have to try to love," she said. "You either do it or you don't."

"I love you."

She shook her head. "You're fond of me. You feel affection for me. You like being seen with me. But you don't love. I don't feel love from you. Kindness. Pleasure, certainly. Not love."

They discussed the lack of love calmly and the next day she was gone. Her clothes gone from their closets, her jewelry and make up gone from the bathroom and dresser, her furniture gone from the house, her car gone from the garage, her gentleness and laughter gone from his life.

In the ensuing years he'd thought a lot about love. Read about it in philosophical works, psychiatric studies, poems, novels, studied it in the people around him, practiced it in his work. But he'd never felt it until Melinda Shoemaker came into the hospital, and he'd ached for her and for himself all the way through her dying.

And with Melinda had come her mother, Irene. He'd never felt before the way he felt with her. It was a whole new start for him. And now there was this. He was back in the Old World, cut off from Irene. She must think he abandoned her. Hell, she'd have to think he was a creep, running off without a word.

He stopped the tractor in the middle of the field and pounded his hands on the steering wheel, howling into the sky, tears running down his cheeks.

At supper time, Velma heated a can of Dinty Moore beef stew and they sat in the kitchen, spooning it out of bowls. She had put a bouquet of dandelions in a cracked coffee mug in the center of the scarred oak table and the water was seeping out, pooling and running toward Buckman's lap. Getting a yellowed linen napkin from the sideboard, probably untouched since long before his mother's death, he wiped it up. Velma cringed as he did, her eyes wide, her breath coming hard.

"I'm awful sorry, Uncle Billy Buck. I'll be more careful next time, really." She grabbed the napkin, taking it to the sink where she wrung it out, rinsed it and wrung it out again before hanging it on the handle of the oven.

"It's all right, Velma. No big deal."

"You ain't going to hit me?"

He shook his head.

"Grampy Cal would've. He would've hit me good."

"I'm not like Grampy Cal."

"I know. You're a doctor, right Uncle Billy Buck? You help people when they're hurt or sick."

"I want you to forget you ever heard I was a doctor. Can you do it for me?"

She nodded quickly. "Just like I forgot I killed Grampy Cal with that old skillet when he was hurting me so bad, and just like I forgot the things Daddy used to make me do." She smiled proudly at him. "I could forget everything if I wanted to."

THE OLD WORLD

THE NEXT MORNING after his breakfast coffee Buckman got in his father's pickup and drove down the road to his brother Wilfred's place.

"Heard you was back, Billy Buck." Wilfred came from his porch as Buckman got out of the pickup. "I'd've given you a call, except Calvin's too damned cheap to get a telephone."

Buckman was shocked by the change in Wilfred. His brother's teeth were gone, his red hair turned white and thin, his pale pink scalp showing through the strands. There was little trace of the once hard muscular body Wilfred had when he was a star left tackle. Moose Buckman, the terror of Canaan Central School District, as the local newspapers used to call him, was nothing but soft fat.

"News travels fast," Buckman said, reaching for Wilfred's hand.

"Clay Presnell don't have much to do these days except carry news around. He came over here soon as you left his place yesterday to tell us you was driving down to Calvin's place in some fancy little red car. Didn't think we'd ever see your ass in Canaan again. By God, I haven't even thought about you in twenty-five or thirty years. If your car is anywhere near as fine as Clay says, I guess you been doing all right for yourself since you left."

"It's twenty-five years, and I haven't been hungry in a long time, Moose." He took a deep breath and started the lie. "Look, I'm not here for a visit and a chat about old times or what I've been doing with my life. I'm trying to find Calvin. Have you seen him last night or today?"

"I don't see much of him at all, not since my little Velma moved in down there to take care of him. Why?"

"He and Velma had a fight last night. Calvin got on one of his high horse rages, yelling and screaming curses at her, and then he stormed out of the house. He hasn't been back since."

"And you got the pickup, so he's on foot. Jesus, Billy Buck, you been back a day and already you've got the old man so riled up that he walks out of his own house."

Buckman stared his brother in the eyes. "The girl's pregnant, Moose. Your daughter's going to have a baby."

Wilfred snickered. "Bet Calvin's tickled shitless over the news. Hell, he probably walked down to Wesley Johnson's Store, picked up a cigar and a couple of bottles of wine and got drunk up in the hayloft celebrating, toasting his pecker, telling it what a fine thing it's done."

"I already checked the barn."

Wilfred shrugged, waving his hands in dismissal. "Well then, he's drunk in somebody else's barn. Don't worry Billy Buck, the old man's gone off and gotten drunk plenty of times before, and he'll go off and do it again." He paused for a moment, then gave Buckman a dark toothless grin. "Pregnant, hunh? Looks like I'm going to be a brother and grandfather all rolled into one."

He turned back to the house. "Hey, Charlotte, Velma's going to have a baby."

Buckman followed him into the front parlor. It hadn't changed since their Uncle Amos and Auntie Martha had lived there. In the half light, he could see the threadbare overstuffed furniture sitting where it had always been, the same curtains hung over the windows, thin, gray with smoke from firewood and cigarettes. The paint by numbers picture Auntie Martha had done of a hunting dog pointing at a pheasant was over the fireplace where a rusting Ashley woodstove sat on the hearth. The house looked as though his uncle and aunt had transformed into Wilfred and Charlotte, leaving everything else as it had been, even the case containing Uncle Amos' fiddle propped in the corner by the doorway to the back parlor.

Buckman had never heard Amos LaTran play, but his mother, Amos' sister, always said he was the best French Canadian fiddler in western Massachusetts.

Buckman's cousin, Charlotte, came out and nodded distantly to him. She weighed well over two hundred pounds and wore tight pink acrylic slacks and a loose, white sweater, the front of it covered with grey splotches of grease and dirt.

"Must've surprised your father when you showed up to his place." Her smile was as dark and toothless as Wilfred's.

"Your daughter's pregnant, Charlotte." His voice was abrupt, vacant of any sound of greeting, despite the twenty-five years which had passed since he saw her last. He didn't have to work at the empty tone.

She shrugged, looking at him with dull eyes.

"It happens. Maybe someday things will be different, but that don't change today. Calvin didn't kick her out?"

Buckman shook his head. "He got furious when she told him and took off early yesterday morning. We haven't seen him since."

She shrugged again. "That happens too. One day they're going to find his dead body alongside the road, or down some godforsaken gorge where he's fallen when he's been drunk on his tail." She looked at Wilfred. "And like father like son, I always say."

Walking toward the kitchen, Wilfred gummed a smile at her, told her to go fuck herself and looked at Buckman with raised eyebrows.

"You want a beer, Billy Buck?"

Buckman shook his head. "I better get looking for Calvin. You want to help me?"

Wilfred yelled from the kitchen. "By God, I don't think so. He'll sober up and come home, or he'll fall and kill himself, like Charlotte says. Either way, there ain't much point in looking for him. He's either alive or dead. Helping you look for him won't change it much, and when he does die, I don't guess that'll change anybody else's life much either."

"Finding him might keep him alive."

Coming back with a beer, Wilfred fell into a faded red chair and spread his hands, shaking his head.

"Well then, Billy Buck, if you think it matters so goddamn much, you'd better start looking. You don't want anything bad happening to old Calvin now, do you? By god, find the old bastard, and you might even get one night's worth of thirty years family responsibility taken care of."

"What about Velma?"

Wilfred snorted. "What about her?"

"She's pregnant. Surely you don't want her staying down at Calvin's"

"Surely?" Wilfred mocked Buckman's tone. "Surely, eh? Surely, I don't want her back up here with me and Charlotte. It ain't no baby that belongs up here she's carrying, not that I'd want any goddamn baby up here. There's been enough of them here over the years and I'm surely not wanting to have no more around. Sure as hell Charlotte ain't going to have one. You see how fat and ugly she is, ain't no man in his right mind going to poke it to her no more. That enough sures for you Billy Buck?"

Charlotte, who'd been standing by the woodstove, lit a cigarette and sat on the arm of Wilfred's chair, her right buttock hanging down on the top of his thigh.

"And you ain't been able to find your pecker under that gut of yours in years. I'd just as soon fuck a dog as dig around there looking for your pecker."

Buckman cleared his throat. "What about Velma?"

Charlotte knocked a cigarette ash to the floor and looked at him. "Now you're living back down there you'll see she's well cared for, won't you, Billy Buck? See Calvin don't hit her too much or do nothing else mean to her."

Buckman walked to the door. "I'll do my best."

Charlotte smiled, her teeth jagged and rotting. "Velma's my baby, the youngest of twelve. I worry a lot about her."

Wilfred shoved her, nearly pushing her off the chair arm. She pushed him back, knocking his cigarette to his lap.

Brushing the ashes to the floor, he yelled at her. "Jesus Christ woman, all you worry about is having enough cigarettes and potato chips and beer. Last you worried about Velma was the time Calvin beat her up and she come around wanting to move back into her room. You was more worried I might let her do it then you was about how beat up she was."

Buckman interrupted him. "You think Calvin might have gone to see any of the other brothers or sisters?"

Wilfred picked up the cigarette, breaking up the ashes with his foot, grinding them into the rug. "Vaughn lives in one of them trailers down to the other side of Wesley Johnson's store, and Dave's got one up near Devil's

Gorge. Neither of them are sober more than an hour a day, so he might have gone down to get skunked with one of them. Benny lives in Franklin County, over to Shelburne, up near the Audubon preserve on the High Ledges. He tenant farms on Chuck Mallison's orchard and thinks he's too goddamn good to have much to do with the rest of us, like some other goddamn people I could tell you about."

"What about Judy and Barbara?"

"What about them? They ain't about to take the old man in, drunk or sober, you know?"

Buckman knew. Calvin was one of the reasons he'd left the Old World and never come back. Calvin Buckman and the Old World way of life.

"You'll let me know if he shows up?"

Wilfred nodded. "If he does, but I don't expect he'll show up here. He'll come home soon as he's sober. Hell, he's got Velma and Dinty Moore beef stew waiting for him there."

Buckman waved and went out the door.

"Billy Buck." Wilfred got up and came after him, emptying the beer can as he walked.

Buckman was on the lower porch step when Wilfred reached the outside. His brother was grinning at him.

"Don't feel too bad if anything happens to Calvin. With him out of the way you'll get to have Velma and her Dinty Moore beef stew all to yourself."

HE WANT BY Vaughn's trailer, a rusted and battered relic of the Fifties. No one was home. He left a note, then stopped at Wesley Johnson's store. Johnson didn't recognize him and Buckman didn't bother to reintroduce himself.

Did he know, he asked, where Calvin Buckman might be? No, Johnson hadn't seen Calvin for several days. No, he was sure he hadn't come in last night for anything to drink. And no, he didn't know where Vaughn was.

Thanking him, Buckman got back in the pickup and drove home. He didn't feel good about having to do it, but he'd planted the seed. They'd all remember he'd been the first one to be concerned when Calvin didn't come back. When Calvin never came back, no one would even think to suspect Buckman of having done anything besides look for him.

Velma wasn't in the house when he returned. He looked for her in the yard and the barn, finally finding her standing in the middle of the freshly plowed cornfield. He started out to meet her. Halfway across, he noticed she was carrying a small bouquet of dandelions.

She looked terrified when she saw him.

"Don't hit me Uncle Billy Buck. I just wanted to give Grampy Cal some flowers, but I couldn't find where we put him. There ain't no harm in doing that, is there?"

"I thought you were going to forget all about what happened with Grampy Cal."

"I was, just as soon as I left him some flowers, but there ain't no grave out here. Does that mean I forgot it already?"

"I suppose it does." Buckman took the flowers and cupping her elbow in his other hand, gently turned her around and began easing her back toward the house. "Now, why don't you do whatever it is you do during the day. I've got a field of corn to get in the ground."

He was surprised how quickly he remembered how to do things. The corn planter attachment was in the barn, sitting in the same shed it had been in when he was a boy, working the farm with his father and brothers. He hooked it up to the tractor, filled it with seed corn which he found stored where seed corn had always been stored, and started out to the field.

Driving over the furrows, the warm sun softened by a breeze, he looked at the surrounding trees and hills. Dark as it was, the Old World was a beautiful place, if you could overlook the cramped and twisted lives its people endured. Thirty feet beyond the edge of the field, Buckman's Brook rushed down from Dog Mountain, headed for the North River which ran down from Vermont, ending up in the Deerfield River west of Greenfield, in Franklin County. The air was heavy with the scent of maple blossoms.

By midafternoon, he finished planting. Parking the tractor near the brook, he took off his shoes, rolled up his pants and waded upstream. The cold slippery rocks surprised him. He struggled to keep upright as he found his way over the uneven footing. Surely it hadn't been like this when he and Wilfred used to race Dave and Vaughn through the water to its source on Dog Mountain. He remembered how easily they'd run, the wind in their hair, while Benny, the baby of the family, would stand watching them, clapping, and laughing for the winner.

Three hundred feet farther on, the brook entered the woods. Following it, he came to a pool at the foot of a sloping rocky falls. Nothing had changed. The trees might have been bigger, but there was no way he could tell. It could have been twenty-five years ago, thirty-five. He almost expected to see Wilfred, Vaughn, Dave, and himself come sliding down the falls and splashing into the pool. Sitting on a boulder, he watched the water fall rush into small eddies filled with leaves and sticks, and swirl them into circles, catch them in foam pockets, then shoot them downstream.

He tried imagining what was happening in Philadelphia. How many people were involved? What did they know about him? Who was looking for him? He sighed, thinking of the perverse need that had driven him back to the Old World. At the time he decided to come, it had seemed a logical thing to do. But why? What quirk in his psyche made it seem logical that, in his greatest crisis, the most intensely dangerous time of his life, he'd feel safer here than in Mexico, or the Caribbean. He could have rented a house on one of the remote small outer islands in the British Virgin Islands, Cooper, Jost Van Dyke. Even Anegada. Instead, he fled to the Old World and in running away from his present, he'd run smack up against his past. The shock from the impact had him reeling.

The early shadows stretched across the ground as he drove the tractor around the field toward the barn, the unmoving weathervane outlined against the sky. Unhooking the planter, he pushed it into the shed, shot grease into the fittings and covered it with a tarp. He gassed the tractor at a pump under a nearby oak tree and drove it up the ramp to the barn floor. He greased it, wiped the dirt off its grey body and red wheels, and hung the key on the nail where his father had always put it.

Velma had supper ready when he got to the house, hamburger fried in butter with onions and potatoes, covered with canned onion soup.

"I rode my bicycle down to Mr. Johnson's store. I thought since you'd been working so hard, you'd like a fancy dinner."

"Thanks," he said, picturing her on the bike.

It was time to tell her.

After eating, he carried the plates to the sink, ignoring her protests that to do so was woman's work. Then he told her to sit down. "You know how you were worried you might have cancer like Gram, and I said you didn't?"

"Because I ain't had the curse for so long?"

He nodded. "Do you know why you haven't had a period?"

She looked at him, her mouth hanging open. "Is it something bad? Am I going to die from it?"

"You're not going to die. You're not even sick. You're going to have a baby."

Shaking, she got up from the table and walked to the window by the front door. She stood there for a moment, then turned back to him. "I'm going to get a beating now. Oh God, I'm going to get an awful beating."

He smiled at her, talking softly and evenly. "Nobody's going to beat you, Velma. Who would want to beat you for getting pregnant?"

"Grampy Cal. Grampy Cal will give me a beating."

"You know Grampy Cal isn't going to beat you, don't you? You know where Grampy Cal is?"

Shutting her eyes, she shook her head. "I ain't supposed to know. I promised you I'd forget."

"That's all right, Velma. You know he's where he can't hurt you, don't you?"

"But his ghost can, if I don't forget all about how I hit him with the skillet, and it killed him. His ghost will be real mad when it hears I'm going to have a baby."

"His ghost can't get you. There are no such things as ghosts, so you stop worrying about Grampy."

"But you said earlier it wouldn't come get me just if I didn't tell nobody what happened. You said if Grampy Cal's ghost knew I was talking about him and telling people how I'd killed him for beating me, it would be real angry and might come after me."

Startled by her near perfect recall of his words, Buckman shook his head, reaching for her hand. "There are no ghosts, Velma, unless you imagine there are. They exist only in your mind."

"And Daddy'll give me a beating. He give my sister Gladys a beating when she got pregnant, and she was planning to marry Jeff Shippee before it happened. She told me she'd marry the first guy that asked her just to get away from Daddy." She spread her hands along the tablecloth, straightening it out. "Ain't nobody asked me to marry them. Now I don't guess they will. I been ruined."

"Nobody's going to beat you and you haven't been ruined, Velma. I'll take you down to Canaan or over to the hospital in Graham and we'll find out if you still have time to get an abortion. If you do, then get it and you can go on with your life."

She started to cry. "You mean get rid of the baby, like Reverend Dye talks about down to the church? I couldn't do that. It's a sin to kill a baby. I already sinned by killing Grampy Cal, but I figure Jesus'll forgive me because Grampy was trying to hurt me so bad. But if I kill the baby, Jesus will throw me into the lakes of burning shit they got down in Hell."

Buckman repressed a smile. All through his childhood he'd heard his father talking about the lakes of burning shit down in Hell and how they were bubbling there, waiting for Calvin's children if they disobeyed their father. It was one of his favorite threats.

"Do you want to have a baby, Velma?"

She scratched her head and started fiddling with the saltshaker.

"With Grampy Cal gone, I don't know who'd take care of me so I could take care of the baby, but it would be somebody to love me. Babies got to love you, right Uncle Billy Buck?"

Buckman was about to reply when he heard a car pull up and stop outside the house. A car door slammed and a few seconds later, Wilfred came up on the porch and called through the door.

"I hear you got yourself knocked up." He snarled the words at Velma as soon as he was in the room.

She looked at Buckman, then back at her father, cringing from his twisted face.

"For chrissakes, Moose, leave her alone. It's Calvin's who's to blame." *And you, you deadbeat fuck*, he thought, looking at his brother.

"You keep out of it, Billy Buck. I'm going to have everybody around here saying my daughter's a slut whore, and I don't need you butting into things while I tell her what I think of her myself."

While he was speaking, Velma darted from the table and ran upstairs. They heard the door to her room slam.

Wilfred grinned at Buckman. "What the fuck. I didn't come over here to get into it with Velma anyway. I'll deal with her later."

"It's not her fault, Moose. If you have to take it out on somebody, take it out on Calvin when he gets back from his spree."

"Fuck Calvin. He was just doing what a man's supposed to do. Ma died and he got horny. What'd you expect him to do, sit around and jack off?"

"It would be better than screwing his granddaughter, don't you think?"

"Hell no. If he wasn't fucking her somebody else would be. What's the big deal?"

Buckman swallowed hard. He needed the Old World too much to fight with it. "If you didn't come over to see Velma, what do you want?"

"I got a phone call for you a little while ago. I figured I'd stop by and tell you, seeing as I had to pass by on my way down to Wesley's Johnson's for some beer."

Ice water ran through him, his breath stopping in his throat. They've found him. For the first time in his life he was glad his father was a gun nut. He'd have no trouble arming himself here, although shooting another human being would be a violation of everything he stood for.

Wilfred watched his brother's face. Baring his gums, he spoke in a mocking sing-song tone. "What's the matter, Billy Buck? You look sick. What'd you do, knock that broad up that called you?"

"Broad? It was a woman who called?"

Wilfred nodded. "Said her name was Irene and said it was a matter of life and death for her to get ahold of you. I figured she was knocked up and was after you to marry her or give you some other kind of trouble."

"What did you tell her?"

"Shit. I told her that you was a snot who thought he was too fucking good for Canaan, Massachusetts and lit out of here as soon as you finished high school. I said we hadn't heard a goddamn word from you since, and we didn't give a shit if we never did. Said we didn't give a shit if you was lying dead along the road somewhere with the goddamn dogs eating your rotten fucking flesh."

Buckman smiled. "It's a bit picturesque, but I appreciate you covering for me."

"Shit, Billy Buck, there's nothing to it. The only lie I had to tell her was that we hadn't seen your ass since the day you left town."

CHAPTER SIX

Philadelphia, Pennsylvania / Tuesday, February 26 -Friday, March 1

CHRYSTAL FLARE, RICHIE McChesney and Elroy Parker died at Worthington Hospital within a four day period. All were suffering from the mysterious disease that sickened Ted Mathieu and Melinda Shoemaker, and all died of heart attacks.

Crystal, an exotic dancer who turned a few tricks for extra cash, had been at Worthington for six months, her condition steadily deteriorating. Three times Buckman had thought her close to dying and each time she rallied, hanging on to life with stubborn will.

"I've never seen anyone quite like her," Buckman said at a review meeting with Donald Craemer, the hospital's chief administrator for patient affairs.

"She's killing us," Craemer said. "No insurance. No money. No family. She's a fucking money pit. What's the point of keeping somebody like her alive, anyway? What good is she? A stripper and a hooker. It's a waste of hospital resources if you ask me."

"There must be some reason she's hanging in there the way she is. People don't fight like she's fighting unless they've got something to live for."

Craemer sneered. "Probably wants to turn a few tricks in here and spread her goddamn disease a little farther."

Buckman stood up, gathering his papers. "I think there's a little more to it, Don."

He left Craemer's office, shutting the door noisily behind him. Crystal

Flare intrigued him. The last time he'd been in to see her, she'd been reading a collection of poetry by Denise Levertov, which she quickly hid under the covers.

He'd caught her reading other books and noticed the same response. Each time she'd hidden whatever she'd been reading and made some wise remark in a Bugs Bunny voice.

"What's up Doc? Ain't you got any carrots with batteries around this place? A girl can't have any fun at all on your ward."

"Hey Doc, what happens if I bite one of your nurses?"

"Geez Doc, you're pretty cute. Wanna vibrate my germs?"

After his meeting with Craemer, he made rounds of his patients. Elroy Parker was sleeping. He checked the IV and monitors, then quietly left the room.

Tom Martin was well enough to go home for a few weeks, but already scheduled to return for more tests and treatment. He was expecting to be released by noon. When Buckman stopped by his room he was busy packing, whistling, and talking to his wife, who sat in a leather armchair by the window.

"Dinner at the Brick Hotel in Newtown," he said, folding his pajamas and putting them in a duffle bag. "I want a good meal and I want to be around people who think I'm just another guy out for dinner on the town."

"Sounds good to me," Buckman said, leaning on the jamb with both hands.

"Thanks, Bill. Franny thinks I ought to go home and stay in bed until I come back in for the rest of the treatment."

"You need lots of rest, and you can't forget to take your medication, but it's perfectly all right for you to go out to dinner, see a few shows. Just don't wear yourself to a frazzle."

He visited with the Martins a bit longer, then walked down to see Richie McChesney. He lay in his room, the blinds pulled, his open eyes staring at shadows on the ceiling. He turned when Buckman came in the room, giving him a limp wave.

"How are you feeling, Richie?"

"No good, Doctor Buckman. I ache from my toes to my teeth. I got the sweats. I feel sick to my stomach. I need a fix, doctor. Just one. Please."

Buckman shook his head. "I'm sorry, Richie. I can't do it. Even if I wanted to, I don't have access to what you want."

"Access, shit. I can get access. All you got to do is tell that fucking nurse not to watch everybody who comes to my room. I'll have access."

"The nurse is following my orders. No fix."

Richie slapped his mattress with both palms, his eyes filling with tears. "This sucks, man. I got fucking disease that nobody knows what it is, I can't get no dope and my girlfriend won't come see me here in your goddamn hospital. This is worse than AIDS."

"Sorry," Buckman said.

"Sorry don't cut it. You got to do something for me. I feel like hell. Hell, I feel like I'm going to die."

He stopped, then grinned. It was the kind of grin he must have had as a kid, wide, amused at the discovery of connections, ironies. Buckman hid his sadness behind a return grin.

"I guess there's a good reason why I feel like I'm going to die, right?"

Buckman nodded. "It's called drug withdrawal."

"Drug withdrawal, shit."

"You're nowhere near dying."

"Are you telling me I got time to get my shit together, go to college, be a doctor and live in a fine house like some folks I talk to everyday?"

Buckman sighed.

"You ain't telling me that, man, then help me get something so I don't feel like a walking piece of shit. What in the fuck are doctors for, if they can't make you feel better, even if you're dying?"

It was a question Buckman often asked himself, recently. He liked being a doctor. It was the one given in his life, like air and water. Like the shape of his face in the mirror each morning. And he had busted hump to get here.

None of it had been easy, but he'd loved every minute. Each day, each new piece of knowledge, brought him farther away from his roots. Freed him from them. As the Old World receded, as he pressed it into corners of memory, he became increasingly the product of his current life. The farmhouse in Bucks County. The Porsche. His clothes. His position. All defined Dr. William Buckman. He dropped the C from his letterhead and office door. He worked hard at projecting warmth and caring, at last almost feeling them.

When AIDS came along they had dealt with it, at last reducing it to a chronic condition that people could live with and have near normal lives. Now there was this disease, insidious. Deadly. A truth to be hidden. A blight on human joy. It was like the silent bruises on his mother's face, the looks of fright and memory in his sisters' eyes as they watched their father move about the kitchen each morning.

It opened all the old questions about the nature of certitude, of liberty and freedom, of love and guilt. It was the shadowy world of monstrous beings and horror novels miniaturized into medical reality.

And Richie McChesney was the monster's host. So were Crystal, Tom, Elroy, and the ones already dead as well as the host of others dying or waiting for the monster's invasion.

He took Richie's hand, looking down into his eyes. He saw pain there. Pain and fear mingled into desperation.

"I'll order you a shot of Demerol. Okay?"

Richie smiled, then turned to look out the window. Buckman gave him a thumbs up, stopped by the nurses' station to give the order for Richie, then walked down the hall to Elroy Parker's room. He looked in and found his patient sleeping. He passed the rooms of other patients on the floor, waving to them as he went by, exchanging greetings and wisecracks. They were a cross section of the city. Junkies, lawyers, hookers, insurance executives, shopkeepers, dock workers, kids, parents, raging queens and closeted bankers, university professors, high school athletes, housewives and small children. The waste was overwhelming.

Crystal Flare's room at the far end of the hall was filled with potted plants, some sitting on the dresser and windowsill, others hanging from the drapery rod in front of the window. She waved as he walked in and quickly slipped the book she'd been reading under her top sheet. Buckman caught the name of it just before it disappeared, *Tragic Ground* by Erskine Caldwell.

"Hey Doc, how're you all doing?" There was no Bugs Bunny crack, her soft voice showing its southern roots.

"Tired and hungry, how about you?"

"Depressed."

"What, no happy hooker routine?"

She shook her head. "Not today."

"What's so special about today?"

"I turned forty this morning, my roommate called to tell me my son was joining the army, and for the first time in twenty years I'm homesick for North Carolina." She bit into an imaginary carrot, chewed it for a minute and gave him a buck toothed smile. "Ehh, so what d'ya think of them carrots, Doc?"

"I just learned something."

She bit the carrot again. "What's that, Doc?"

"I never knew you were from North Carolina."

"A mountain community called Sugar Grove. Mamma and Daddy have a thirty acre farm there. They've got a small tobacco allotment and raise most of their own food. Daddy sells cordwood to the folks in Boone and drives a truck part of the year. Good country folks. I miss them and I'd be ashamed to have them see what I'd become. As far as they know, I'm just Hattie Jean Haskell. They wouldn't even let Crystal Flare set foot in their front yard."

Buckman looked at his hands. They were clean and smooth, his fingernails trimmed to the quick.

"If I had stayed in Sugar Grove I'd've probably have married Bobby Triplett and be teaching Sunday School at the Sugar Creek Free Will Baptist Church where my granddaddy used to preach when I was a girl. Can you imagine me teaching Sunday School? What a laugh, right Doc?"

"I can imagine you doing anything you want to do."

"You think I want to dance naked in front of a bunch of drunks, and then take one or two of them upstairs for a quick jump on my bones?"

"You do it. You must get something out of it."

He saw the anger which flashed quickly in her eyes at his words, then saw it flicker out as she looked at the air in front of her. She was quiet for a long time. When she finally spoke, it was with a dull calm.

"I used to like making men horny, watching them nudge each other and make silly groaning noises when I started taking my clothes off and dancing like I wanted them all to fuck me. But the scene grew old real fast."

"You still do it."

"Did it. I did it until I got sick. It was what I knew how to do, so why stop? It paid the bills, fed the kid and me. Sometimes a nice john would come around regular for a while, slip me a few extra bucks because he liked me, or I made him laugh with my Bugs routine, you know?"

"But you didn't like it."

"I always felt dirty. There were nights when I'd go home and stand in the shower for an hour, rub soap all over myself, scrub hard as I could, rinse it off and soap up, sometimes three of four times, until my skin hurt."

"Why did you keep doing it? There are other ways of making a living, you know. You did have choices."

"Maybe I couldn't see them. Maybe I didn't want to. Maybe once you disgraced yourself in your own eyes you don't want to change anything because it would mean admitting the disgrace and doing something about it. Maybe it was just easier to keep on doing what I was doing. Maybe it seemed better than thinking about it."

She fell silent again. Her hair, unbleached since she entered Worthington, had nearly an inch of brown and grey growing from the scalp, and Buckman was struck by the smoothness of her skin. With the bleached look completely gone, he could imagine her teaching Sunday School in an improbable place called Sugar Creek.

Her voice was nearly a whisper when she spoke. "You know, Doctor Buckman, sometimes I almost think getting sick was the best thing that could have happened to me. I'm not dancing, I'm not hooking, I'm not scared shitless about getting beat up, or murdered by some crazy serial killer. I'm getting lots of rest, reading good books and I don't have to worry about how I'm going to provide for my old age. How many people do you know with that kind of peace of mind?"

"Only the very rich and the terminally ill." He regretted his glibness the minute he spoke.

She laughed. Reaching for his hand, she gave it a squeeze. "You're a good man, Doc, and I haven't said that too many times in my life."

When she was sure Buckman was gone, Crystal pulled her book out from under the covers, returning to her reading. She hadn't been trying to hide it from him. She wasn't ashamed of reading, and she wasn't ashamed of the books she read. It was a matter of sharing them with other people. Once somebody knew she was reading something they'd read, then they'd want to talk about it with her.

Then she would lose it. The book wasn't just hers anymore. Talking about books with other people robs them of their specialness. When she read a book, she created the world in which its events took place just as much as the author did. Talk about it with other people and the secret world she shared with the writer would be gone, as wide open and violated as she was with a john. It was a world she guarded jealously.

Like this one. Her friend Mary had picked it up in a used bookstore and brought it to her, thinking she'd like a story about the south. It was a good book, and she was enjoying it, although she knew it didn't have to be set in Georgia. The things Erskine Caldwell was telling about in it could happen anywhere. Did happen anywhere. He just set it in the south because he wanted to.

She read until her eyes began to close, then slipped the book into the drawer of the bedside table and fell asleep. She never stirred when the killer entered the room and injected death into her IV.

Elroy Parker died the next night. He'd spent the evening playing chess with his business partner, interrupting the game long enough to exchange a few pleasantries with Buckman, introducing him to Linda.

"Best landscaper in the city," Parker said.

She laughed. "He just says that because I don't mind driving out into the country and picking up a load of cow shit to dump all over peoples' gardens."

Parker shuddered. "Everybody needs a partner like Lin. It's a good balance. We do the design work together, and I don't mind hauling rocks around, lifting things, doing the heavy work. At least I didn't used to mind, back when I could still do it."

"You'll do it again," Linda said. "They'll find out what's wrong with you and next thing you know you'll be back out there getting your rocks off."

"Let's keep the conversation on shit and off rocks. When are they going to find a cure, Doc? Monday? Or am I going to have to wait another week?"

"At least another week, Roy, maybe two."

Parker shrugged. "Yeah, well the way Lin's playing this game, it'll take at least two weeks to finish it."

Buckman smiled and left.

Linda stayed another hour, neither she nor Elroy concentrating much on the chess game. Parker nodded off several times, and each time he opened his eyes he was sure she'd moved both their pieces to her advantage. When visiting hours were over, she leaned down and kissed his forehead.

"I'll come back day after tomorrow."

"Bring some pictures of the Northeast Plaza job. I want to see how the gardens around the fountains look."

She promised she would and left. He watched television for a while, did the crossword in the *Philadelphia Inquirer*, pushed his IV pole out to the solarium, where he thumbed through a three year old copy of the *Reader's Digest*. It was after midnight when he returned to his room. The bed had been made and the covers neatly turned down. He lay down, called his brother in San Diego chatting with him for an hour. He had been asleep for less than twenty minutes when the killer slipped out of the shadowed hallway into his room.

For Richie McChesney it was different. He was lying in bed, his pain and vomiting worse than ever. Buckman had cancelled the order for the Demerol the day after letting him have it. He was groaning and crying when the killer came in. The killer asked, "Feeling pretty bad, Richie?"

"Terrible. I never felt so bad. You come to help?"

The killer smiled. "You're going to love what I have for you, Richie."

"Only thing I'd love right now is a fix."

The killer reached a rubber gloved hand into his pocket and pulled out a clear plastic bag filled with white powder along with a loaded syringe and needle. He put the bag into Richie's hand and closed his fingers around it.

"Is that what I think it is?" Richie asked.

"It's whatever you want it to be," the killer said. He brought the needle over to the side of the bed, giving Richie a good look at it. "And so it this."

Richie smiled. "I love it."

"Then you're going to love this," the killer said, injecting an overdose of heroin into the IV tube.

CHAPTER SEVEN

Philadelphia, Pennsylvania \ Friday, March 12

IN THE DAYS following Richie McChesney's death four more patients died at Worthington Hospital. All deaths except Richie's were diagnosed as cardiac arrhythmia. With Richie, the staff members believed they had somehow missed seeing one of his friends sneaking him a fix.

Buckman was uneasy. Despite his urging, Charlie Blanchard, CEO at Worthington had not authorized anything beyond the most routine autopsies.

"For chrissakes, Charlie," Buckman said in a meeting with him. "So many patients dying like this, almost one right after the other, must be able to tell us something, give us some new information to go on."

Blanchard twisted his mouth, seemed to think for a minute, then shook his head.

"It's just too damn bad, but the Worthington-America Medical Group isn't designed for or meant to do research, and Worthington Hospital isn't a research institution. We've got to think about the bottom line for the investors. We can't waste resources doing detailed studies of unrelated deaths. It's not just this place, for Christ's sake, Bill, we've got to think in terms of the entire corporation, the other hospitals in Atlanta, Charlotte, Baltimore, and Pittsburgh, as well as the HMOs and the Worthington-America insurance programs. We're talking major corporate responsibility here."

Buckman shook his head in disgust. “Major corporate responsibility should include getting Worthington in on the cutting edge of this thing, Charlie.”

“Maybe, maybe not.” Blanchard was silent for a moment, his fingers drumming on the top of the desk. When he finally spoke, his voice rasped the words out. “Goddamn it, Buckman, it doesn’t matter. As I keep telling you, Worthington isn’t a research or public service institution. The bottom line in all our operations is profit. We don’t turn a profit here, and I’m out the door. Hell, they could close the hospital, and everybody could be out the door if the home office decides to reallocate resources. And let me tell you, if we start fucking around with your crazy ideas about some new and mysterious disease we’re going to cut into profits.”

“It’s not a crazy idea, Charlie. It might be wrong, but it’s not crazy, and we’re not going to know if it’s wrong unless we research it.”

Blanchard shook his head. “It’s out of the question for us.”

“You’re making a mistake, Charlie.” Throwing his arms in the air, Buckman snorted in exasperation.

Blanchard got out from behind the desk. Leaning against the front of it, he smiled at Buckman, his voice low and soothing. “Look, Bill, whatever this is, somebody at one of the research and teaching hospitals will spot it. They’ve got grants and other kinds of money out the old wazoo to deal with things like this. It’s part of their mission. Worthington Philadelphia is barely turning its profit. The home office has been talking drastic cost cutting measures already, partly because of the way this damned disease, if it is a singular disease and not just a bad series of events, has been bleeding every part of our operations. Between the expense to the hospitals of treating indigent patients under the Hill-Burton Act and the shots to the gut the insurance and HMO branches have been taking, Worthington-America is hurting bad. If the home office makes big cuts, I could be out of a job, and so could a lot of other fine administrators. I’m not going to throw the corporation’s money and my career down the drain just to investigate what may end up being unrelated deaths. It’s not our problem. Our problem is treating patients and making money.” Seeing that Buckman was about to argue with him, Blanchard put his hand out in the motion traffic cops use to stop traffic. “Sorry, Bill. My mind’s made up.”

“Maybe it is, Charlie, but I’m going over your head on this one, directly to headquarters. This is a hospital, for chrissakes, not a money mill. Maybe I can get Mark Davis to go along with me. Somebody’s has to listen.”

Charlie Blanchard poured himself a cup of coffee. “Don’t be an asshole, Bill. You’ll be swinging out there on your own. Nobody wants to waste hospital money. Not the board of directors, not headquarters, not the administration, not most of the docs, and certainly not Mark Davis.”

“Mark’s been your patsy since he became chief of staff, but if he’s got any guts he’ll listen.”

“Don’t count on it, Buckman. Davis is part of my team. If he wasn’t I’d have never recommended him for the position.”

“He’s still a doctor. When he hears me out even Mark Davis would be hard put to ignore me. I’m on to something, Charlie, and you’re a fool not to see it. Hell, if you played it right, this could make Worthington’s reputation as a major hospital, as a major national medical resource.”

“Or destroy it.” Blanchard shook his head. “You’re on your own if you decide to fight me, Bill. It could get dangerous.”

“I’d hardly call being on the outs with a hospital president dangerous. What would be dangerous is to ignore what’s happening.”

Blanchard pushed himself off the edge of the desk. Crossing the room, he opened the door to his office. “Just think about it, Bill. I hate to see you take unnecessary risks for the sake of a little false glory.”

Buckman walked out.

Blanchard shut the door behind him and stood listening for a moment. He heard the mumble of Buckman’s voice as he said something to the receptionist, then heard the door to the outer hallway slam.

He paced the room. This was bad shit. Noticing his MBA diploma from Duke hanging crookedly, he straightened it, then saw the photograph of his Cessna was also crooked and straightened it.

Goddamn doctors like Buckman made the work of a hospital administrator into a pure hell. Never concerned about costs unless they affected their salaries. Buckman didn't realize what a crisis this disease could bring about. It could destroy the entire health care system unless something was done about it. And, if the public health care system was in trouble, the for-profit operations, like Worthington-America, were close to disaster. The bleeding hearts would pump tax money into the public and not-for-profit sectors as long as there was tax money to pump. Obamacare---if they ever get the bumps out of it and Congress finally really gets behind it---is bad enough, but W-A's top thinkers were afraid that unchecked, things could lead to a strengthening support for a single payer system. Nobody was going to do any favors for the outfits in it for the money, for-profits, like W-A. For them it was sink or swim, and Charlie Blanchard was damn well not going to sink.

It was all bad shit, and Buckman was bad shit. He had a bug up his ass that could ruin everything. It was time to do something about him.

He picked up the phone and called Mark Davis, telling him of Buckman's suspicions, filling him in on his own thoughts on the matter.

"Of course, when I nominated you for chief of staff, I knew you were the kind of man Worthington-America needed in its corporate ranks. I'm sure you'll know how to handle Buckman when he comes in to see you."

He smiled as Davis' assurances crackled over the phone. "Wonderful, Mark. I knew you were a member of the team. I'll see to it that corporate knows it too. You're a real asset, my friend."

Hanging up, he grabbed his coat. On his way out, he told the receptionist he'd be gone for several hours, then headed for the little red Mercedes two seater convertible waiting for him in the hospital parking garage.

BUCKMAN SAT AT the desk in his office thumbing through Melinda Shoemaker's autopsy report. The desk was a mess. Folders and charts on the patients who had died since the second week of February lay open, their contents scattered over the work area.

None of it made sense. Ted Mathieu's and Elroy Parker's deaths he could almost understand. And Crystal Flare, given the way she had lived. Maybe some of the others. All were adults in weakened conditions resulting from disease, susceptible to opportunistic infections and failing hearts. Yet none had died from infections and not in one case had there been any warning, not a single early symptom of cardiac problems.

Melinda's death didn't goddamn make sense to him at all. It really didn't figure. She been sick, but she hadn't been skirting the edges of death as closely the others. And her death hurt the most. He still could see her grin, hear her teasing him about how cute her mother thought he was, urging him to take her out on a date. He was angry at her death. Furious.

After years of dealing with sickness, this disease had gotten to his core. Melinda had been special. And her mother was special too. He had not asked her to dinner as he'd intended to since Melinda first began teasing him about it. His relationship with Irene amounted to little more than talks about Melinda's condition, although more than once Buckman had fretted over her, telling her how tired she looked from worrying about her daughter and urging her to get more sleep, eat better.

The focus of their conversations was never personal, although he sometimes thought about her at night, envisioning her deep red hair, wondering how the straight lines of her face would look in laughter and passion, instead of lined with the constant worry and fear he nearly always saw when looking at her.

Damn Blanchard with his crap about Worthington-America Medical not having the resources to investigate these deaths. They had the bucks, they had the skilled personnel, and they had the equipment. He'd talk to Mark Davis. Patsy or not, Davis was a fellow physician and as chief of staff he was the hospital's medical director. He and Buckman had little in common beyond work and their few brief conversations were limited to mundane discussions related to work, but Davis had a reputation of having been a fine internist before going into administration.

A tall, bony man in his middle sixties, he gestured at a pile of papers on his desk looked up as Buckman entered his office, speaking before Buckman could say a word. "I'm busy."

"We need to talk."

Davis moved slightly backward, as if to ward off an attack, his eyes avoiding contact with Buckman's. "I'm too busy to make time for you now. Make an appointment with my secretary. I'll have her find a few minutes for you in the next day or two."

"I need five minutes right now. It's important."

Davis sighed. Shaking his head, he picked up a handful of papers and waved them in the air between them. "What about I'm busy don't you understand?"

Buckman understood. "Blanchard called you."

"Charlie Blanchard and I speak regularly."

"About unexplained deaths in the hospital?"

Davis blinked quickly and Buckman noticed a light tic in his right cheek.

"You're upset," Buckman said.

"Nonsense. I am, as I said, busy."

Buckman said, "I want to talk about what makes me nervous."

The tic in his cheek increased as Davis pulled back a few more fractions of an inch and turned to look at his medical school diploma hanging on the wall. It was crooked and he rose, walked over, and straightened it.

"I'm not nervous. I'm busy. Very busy."

"I'm not leaving."

"Five minutes, then you're out of my office."

Without bothering to sit, Buckman outlined his ideas, concentrating on the pattern of cardiac failures he'd seen over the last month. Davis sat as his desk, pulling at his small white beard and nodding, each movement of his head threatening to dislodge the shock of thin grey hair parted just above his left ear and pasted over the top of his head to hide the baldness.

When Buckman finished, Davis leaned forward, making a tent with his hands, elbows resting on the desk. "Not even remotely fascinating, Dr. Buckman. Charlie warned me you'd be coming in with some alarmist crap. He told me you'd be trying to convince me to waste the hospital's resources on foolishness."

"Charlie's priorities have nothing to do with medicine and everything to do with Worthington-America's finances. This is about medicine, about our patients, and I need your support, Dr. Davis."

Sucking his lips over his teeth with a wet sound, Davis squinted at Buckman. "Charlie's got his fingers on the pulse of things around here, Dr. Buckman. I'm sure, if you presented him with a sound argument, he'd probably be glad give you some support."

Buckman's laugh was sour. "You're sure he probably would, eh? That's quite an unequivocal statement. I'd be careful about going out on a limb like that if I were you."

"You're the one on the limb, Dr. Buckman. Now leave my office. I have hours of paperwork to do."

Buckman slammed the door behind him.

Back in his office he called Irene Shoemaker, asking her to have dinner with him.

"It's important," he said when she sounded hesitant.

"This sounds more than dinner," she said.

"I'd rather wait and talk about it in person."

There was a long pause before she agreed.

"I'll pick you up around seven," he said.

She gave him directions to her house, then asked, "Why dinner, Dr. Buckman. Why didn't you ask me to meet you at your office?"

Buckman felt as if his tongue was stumbling around his answer. He could have asked her to come to his office. Why hadn't he? "I thought coming to the hospital might be difficult for you."

"You mean given how recently Melinda died?"

"Right." He did not know what else to say.

When she replied she understood perfectly, Buckman thought her voice had a peculiar tone, almost as though she were smiling.

BLANCHARD NODDED, PASSED the receptionist and made his way to an office down a dimly let side hallway, set far apart from the other offices in the suite where Worthington-American's Philadelphia branch had its offices. The door, unmarked except for a number, was shut and locked. Inside he could hear music, symphonic, he guessed.

He knocked.

There was no response.

He knocked again, calling out as he did.

"Chris, it's Charlie Blanchard."

When the door opened, Blanchard was struck, as always by how powerful a man Christopher Koenig appeared to be. No wonder headquarters hired him, he thought, looking at the two hundred and ten pounds of muscle on the six foot frame. Christ, he looked like a battleship with arms. Dressed in a pair of dress slacks and a white shirt, unbuttoned at the collar, a red and black necktie knotted and hanging loosely, Koenig's sleeves were rolled up three turns, black hair springing out like wire from his arms and around his thick neck. The hair on his head was thin and cropped to a quarter of an inch in length. It always looked the same and Blanchard was sure he ran clippers over it every morning. He had a thick black mustache which hung down over his top lip.

"You're a pain in the ass, Blanchard. You just blew Mozart's Thirty-eighth for me, right at the peak. I could kill you for that."

Blanchard shrugged a silent apology. Any response he could make would be useless in dealing with Koenig, the coldest man he had ever encountered, which made him perfect for the work Worthington-America hired him to do. Following him into the office he stood, arms hanging loose at his side as Koenig glowered and sat in a leather easy chair next to the window, crossing his legs.

Reaching over, he flicked off the stereo, took out the CD and returned it to its case. "No sense wasting good Mozart on you, I'll start it again later."

Koenig spoke in a soft voice, almost a whisper. It reminded Blanchard of Jack Palance in *Shane*. "I'd ask you to have a seat, but the only other chair is my desk chair. You'll just have to stand."

"No problem." Blanchard's words barely escaped his lips. His mumbled reply went unacknowledged.

"What's so important that you broke discipline and came here?"

The man frightened him. Blanchard studied the tips of his fingers as he spoke. "There's a problem at the hospital that could end up being a problem for all, for the entire program, a big problem for you, Chris."

Koenig got out of the chair and stood inches from Blanchard. Blanchard could feel his breath as he spoke, his voice, softer, lower.

"My name is Christopher. I like it and I like to hear people use it."

Blanchard reddened as he felt himself cringe. "Sorry Christopher. I didn't come here to argue with you or cause any problems. I've got a big enough one without fighting you."

Koenig smiled and returned to his chair. Making people like Blanchard back down pleased him almost as much as the irony of his name. Christ Bearer. It was a good joke. He often wondered if his parents had appreciated it when they gave it to him.

Blanchard tried hiding the way Koenig made him shudder.

Swinging away from Blanchard, Koenig spoke. "I'll decide if your problem is one I should bother with or if it's another example of an inferior mind incapable of dealing with an ordinary situation."

"A doc at the hospital is pressuring me to authorize research into the heart attack deaths of patients over the last few weeks. He thinks it may be the start of a new phase of the disease."

"Did you tell him he's right?" Koenig smiled. "It is a whole new phase, wouldn't you say?"

Blanchard ignored Koenig's taunting tone. "I told him Worthington-America isn't a research institution. I warned him that corporate is looking for ways to cut costs, that it isn't going to pour money into a sinkhole of research."

"True. And?" His mouth closed and smiling Koenig stared at Blanchard who, after a long and awkward silence, walked over to the window, looking down at the street.

"People look insignificant from this height," he said.

"They are insignificant. If people had the slightest significance, you and I wouldn't be in this office having this discussion."

"That's different. Of course, people have significance."

Koenig was still smiling. "To whom? Did those patients who died in the hospital have any significance to you? We both know they were a drain on Worthington-America's resources, a threat to its profits, but did they have any meaning to you beyond their inconvenience?"

Blanchard didn't answer.

Koenig's smile widened, his lips parting over the gold tooth. "Now, tell me more about this doctor you think is such a problem."

OVER DINNER AT the Brick Hotel in Newtown, Buckman told Irene about his thoughts on the cardiac deaths at Worthington-Philadelphia since the middle of February.

Sitting across from him, dressed in a blue brushed silk dress, her red hair pulled back in a loose bun, she asked, "And you think I can help you in some way?"

"I want you to write a letter to Charlie Blanchard, the hospital administrator, telling him how your daughter died and saying you're aware of my concerns. Urge him to go to the chairman of the board, Donald Castile, asking him to authorize Worthington-America to begin research into sudden cardiac deaths among our patients."

"Okay," she said. "I'll do it."

"Just like that?"

"Just like that. I've been thinking about Mel's death; how strange it seemed."

Buckman nodded, cutting a piece of steak. "I loved your daughter, you know, Ms. Shoemaker."

"Irene, call me Irene, and I'll call you Bill. And it's all right to say Melinda's name too. She was very fond of you. She wanted me to ask you out on a date." She dabbed at her eyes with the end of her napkin.

"She was always talking to me about it too, saying I should ask you out."

They ordered desert, drank their wine, and Irene talked about Melinda.

"Young as she was, she never came into a room without people feeling better because she did."

Smiling, Buckman nodded. "I know what you mean. I always felt better after having been with her. She was a special kid."

They talked on about Melinda, Irene often wiping her eyes with the napkin. After a while, she fell silent, her eyes wandering around the room.

Buckman sipped from his glass, then changed the subject. "You know, Irene, I don't have the slightest idea what you do. You're obviously educated, intelligent. I can't imagine you being a homebody."

"I teach linguistics at Penn."

"Sounds pretty rarified."

"It gets more rarified. I specialize in dialect variations and dialect change."

"I thought a dialect was a dialect. I never thought about them changing."

She nodded. "It happens all the time. A lot more rapidly now than it used to, a result of how much people move around and influence one another's speech patterns. I do computer mapping of the changes and key them into the *Linguistic Atlas of the U.S.*"

"I didn't know there was such a thing."

She laughed. "Most people don't. My work isn't going to change the world."

"It sounds interesting."

"It is. Take you for example. You're from western Massachusetts."

He breathed in sharply. "How do you know? I make it a point not to tell people where I'm from."

"You make it sound mysterious."

"No mystery, just a miserable childhood. I don't like talking about it."

They were silent as the waiter brought dessert. When she left, Irene took a bite of cheesecake, washing it down with coffee.

"Things were that bad in Canaan?"

This time Buckman started. "Canaan? I've never told anyone that, except for my ex-wife."

Irene laughed. "An educated guess. I knew you were from Wessex County, but your speech patterns were Shelburne, Colrain or Canaan. I finally settled on Canaan because of the way you pronounced the ng at the end of thing. There's a nasality in it that's probably the result of the large French Canadian settlement in the western part of Canaan during the late Nineteenth Century."

Buckman laughed. "That's amazing."

"It's no more amazing than your ability to diagnose a strep throat or hepatitis. You took your doctorate in medicine, I took mine in linguistics and I did my dissertation on patterns in the Connecticut Valley region of Massachusetts. We both learned the diagnostic tricks of our trades. I specialized in dialects; you did it in internal medicine."

"It's still amazing, at least to me. My mother is of French Canadian extraction."

"Was your childhood really bad?"

"I grew up in what medical sociologists delicately refer to as an incest community. In Canaan that's a whole section geographically isolated from the rest of the town and it has a community wide pattern of all kinds of sexual abuse."

She nodded. "I know the area."

He finished his desert and signaled the waiter.

"Now, if you don't mind, I don't want to discuss it anymore. I put Canaan behind me a long time ago and I haven't talked about it since I left. I don't even really think about it, so let's drop it for this evening, okay?"

"Dropped. What would you like to talk about?"

Buckman leaned toward her. "How about we try figuring out what we're going to do on our next date?"

CHAPTER EIGHT

Philadelphia, Pennsylvania \ Friday, March 12

KOENIG SAT IN the leather chair long after Blanchard left. From the main hallways beyond his office, he could hear people leaving for the day, secretaries, assistants, and corporate executives saying goodnight, doors closing, keys rattling in locks.

He didn't join them. Except for Castile and Blanchard, no one at Worthington-America knew Koenig's name. Only two of Castile's hand-picked vice-presidents at corporate headquarters knew there was someone using this office, and they had only been told he was a consultant on a very confidential deal Worthington-America was exploring. Castile and Blanchard alone knew why he was there.

And Blanchard was a problem. Castile he could deal with. At least for the present. The man was cool and distant, sure of himself and smart as hell, almost as competent as Koenig regarded himself as being. Almost. Almost to Koenig meant a big difference, resulting in the only worry Koenig had with the job. The entire operation had been Castile's idea. Koenig's involvement was the result of a long and discreet nationwide search. The almost came once Koenig was on board and Castile insisted on bringing Blanchard in.

"I need my own man on the inside, someone I've worked with and trust."

"Someone who can take the fall if there's an exposure," Koenig said.

"Blanchard's a good man," Castile told him.

"I don't like it. I don't like him. You and I are firm. You hired me; I work for you. Blanchard could be a weak link between us."

"I need someone at the hospital making sure no one gets close you. Think of him as your in-house shield."

"It's a bad idea," Koenig had said. "The concept was yours, so you'll protect it. I'm the operator in the field, so I'll protect it. Blanchard's a wild card. He has no part in its planning or operation. If something goes wrong, he'll be the one to bargain immunity in exchange for information."

"He owes me for his job. I picked him and I placed him, and I pay him more than he'd get anywhere else. I own the sonofabitch. He'll do what I ask him to do. The plan depends on having someone inside the hospital, at least in the test phase. Worthington-Philadelphia is the pilot. If things go right here, I'll move you around the country, to all our hospitals and HMOs, maybe even into other hospitals where we have under-insured patients. You'll be safer at that point than you will be during the test program here, when there are going to be more deaths in one place over a shorter time than there will be later."

Koenig argued, Castile insisted. Since he was paying the bill, the biggest bill Koenig had ever presented, he went along with it. It made him uncomfortable, and sometimes, late at night, he wondered why he'd agreed to go along with it. The money was good, but at times, most often late night, he thought perhaps he'd been a fool. It was the most bizarre undertaking of his life. Mostly he worked for one person on one kill at a time. Once he'd had three kills for one employer. Maybe half a dozen times there had been two kills. But never anything like this, an indeterminate number of kills in an open-ended job.

At those late night times, the red numbers of the digital alarm clock glowing in the darkness, questioning his judgment for getting involved with Castile's scheme, he wondered about his grip on reality. Not that it was high risk. Castile was too smart for that. Too careful. But something was wrong. Maybe not with the job. With him. For taking it. It wasn't his style.

And then there was Blanchard.

The man had rubbed him wrong from the first. Arrogant, intelligent without being clever or witty, he was narrowly trained instead of broadly educated, as vain about his masters in hospital administration from Duke as a Ph.D. in philosophy from Harvard might be.

And calling him Chris on top of it, for chrissakes. He was the type who would have called Faulkner "Bill" at first meeting.

'Hiya, Bill,' he would have said.

And Faulkner would have looked at him through those ice blue eyes of his, the mouth set thinly beneath the trim mustache, hands resting on the keyboard of his metallic grey Royal typewriter.

He'd have spoken in soft tones, *Hidy, Mr. Blanchard*, a reproach Blanchard would be too thick to understand, and he would have replied, *Just call me Charlie*, forcing Faulkner to be more direct.

We haven't been acquainted long enough to assume the terms of friendship, Mr. Blanchard.

He knew it would have gone that way had Faulkner ever been unfortunate enough to meet Charlie Blanchard. It was a blessing for the old Mississippi author that he was long dead, would never have to deal with Charlie Blanchard. Koenig had been to the house in Oxford, seen the neat rooms, the shoes by the bed, the place's gentility washing over him as he walked through its halls and gardens, listening to the leathern flapping of the magnolia leaves. He'd stood in the doorway of the study, looking at the chapter outlines of *A Fable* written on the walls, muttering thank you Mr. Faulkner, over and over.

Faulkner, Dostoyevsky, Ellen Glascow, Conrad, Jane Austin, Henry Fielding, he'd read all their works many times. He liked other writers, admired many, but those six were his favorites, the quality of their minds approaching his own titanic intellect. Each created a fully realized world and took him into it, showing him what Faulkner had described as the human heart in conflict with itself.

Koenig knew what that phrase really meant. Knew Faulkner was talking about the writer's heart in conflict with itself. The best writers were solipsists, like he was a solipsist. Their art lay in creating worlds and people, then choosing to let them wither and die, pathetic creatures at the mercy of the creative mind. Koenig's art lay in choosing people in the real world to suffer and die. Men and women of flesh and blood were the pathetic creatures at the mercy of his brilliance and creativity.

Wilson Roberts

From high school and the first two years of college, Christopher Koenig had been headed for success, determined to become one of the top criminal lawyers in the country. He was a scholar, an accomplished pianist, a star athlete, a three letter man all through high school, a soccer and baseball star during his first year at Drew University. Because of his strength and build, his teammates and associates had always called him Ape Koenig. Late in the second semester of his freshman year, he came across Eliot's *The Waste Land.* After reading the part about Apeneck Sweeney, he refused to allow anyone to call him Ape, insisting on his full first name.

Eliot's poem had an even more profound influence on him. Its description of vast mindless hordes of people surging over the plains of Europe, the lament over the fading of the elite traditions of the West, changed Koenig's vision of himself. It helped him understand the uniqueness of the superior mind and see how wasted his talents would be if spent providing legal defenses for the criminal activities of others. Better to find some way of improving and purifying the world than to contribute to its impurity by aiding those who embodied impurity.

From then on, he distanced himself from other people. Majoring in philosophy and literature, he read the nihilists and understood the emptiness of human existence. He read Nietzsche and accepted the implications of his superiority, Sartre and accepted the futility of striving toward transcendent realities, as well as the importance of living in good faith with himself.

During the spring break of his senior year at Drew, while many of his classmates were going to Florida and the Caribbean to spread themselves on beaches and waste their money in casinos, Koenig wandered the streets of New York City, watching winos and junkies lying in doorways, the mindlessly bustling executives in the financial district, the fluttering and ineffectual average citizens working in stores, or shopping in them. He had found nothing but flurries of meaningless activity, hordes of lives contributing nothing but pollution and waste to the purity of the world.

His first kill was in an alley not far from Washington Square. There had been no risk and nothing to gain. He had been passing the alley when he stopped to light a cigarette. In the flash of the match he saw a man sleeping a few feet away, several empty wine bottles on the pavement beside him.

Moving in to look at the sleeping man, Koenig had been revolted by the stench of vomit and urine. Instead of backing away, he stepped closer, leaning down to look at his face. The jaw was slack, the chin sunken, the lips parted to show jagged, rotting teeth.

With his foot, he had tentatively poked at the man's leg. He hadn't stirred. He picked his arm, held it for a moment and dropped it to the pavement. There was still no reaction. Curious as to the degree the drunk had anesthetized himself, Koenig kicked him in the ribs, as hard as he could. He felt them give, heard the sound, but the drunk only groaned and rolled over. He kicked him two more times. There was still almost no reaction. Finally, as though it were the most natural thing to do, he took out his pocketknife, knelt and drew it slowly across the man's throat. Standing in the alley off Washington Square, watching the blood spread over the littered sidewalk, shivering with the thrill of what he'd just done, Christopher Koenig knew he had found his life's work.

AFTER GRADUATING SUMMA from Drew, he traveled the country, exploring its cities, killing once or twice in each of them, always someone on the fringes, drunks, petty thieves, prostitutes. With each death he felt purer, stronger. Soon he understood how the purification of the world by the elimination of those he killed was related to his own purity.

He decided on a life of celibacy after killing a prostitute and her client in Seattle.

It was hours after midnight. Dressed in a black cloak and hat, whistling in the fog, imagining himself as Jack the Ripper, he saw a woman and man get out of a taxi. Standing in shadow, he watched, listening as the man paid the driver. He was leaning on the woman as the taxi drove off, his voice loud, the words slurred.

"I expect a lot more for a hundred bucks than a blow job in the back seat of a taxi." He lurched backward, toward the street as he spoke.

"Oh honey, of course you do. And don't worry about it for a minute. You're going to get everything you paid for, just as soon as I get you up to my room."

"That's good, sweetie, because Barney Thompson always gets what he pays for. You got anything to drink up in that room?"

She had laughed, patting him on the shoulder. "Sure do. Whatever you want. A little beer, some vodka, gin, whiskey. You'll love the service at Betty's place."

Koenig watched as she led him up the steps to the front door of a three story brick tenement building. When it shut behind them, he followed. The door had been unlocked and he slipped into the hallway, listening as they climbed the stairs.

"I'm not complaining about the blow job. Blow jobs are great. It just wasn't worth a hundred dollars. A hundred dollars should get a man a lot more than a blow job in the back of a taxi, you know?"

"You're going to get a lot more. And you'll even get it to music. Have you ever gotten laid to Mozart?" Koenig heard her voice fade slightly as they rounded the landing and started toward the third floor. "By the time I'm finished with you, you're going to say, 'Betty, how much more money will you accept for such fine service?' and I'll just laugh and tell you to give me whatever extra you want. How's that sound to you?"

Koenig had been unable to hear the man's muttered reply. Carefully, quickly, he began climbing the stairs after the two, reaching the top just in time to see the door to the woman's room close behind them.

Looking at the latch, he had smiled. It was an old affair, easily opened once the molding was pried from around the door jamb. Reaching under his cloak, he took out a heavy knife, jamming it under the molding. It moved easily. All he had to do was wait for them to quiet down. Then, if he felt the risk of breaking in was worth it, he'd kill them both. His hands trembled with the excitement of it. This would be his first double killing and the first time he had killed inside a building.

He heard them talking, their sounds muffled by the door. The man's voice was low and whining, the woman's punctuated by laughter. He heard the rattling of ice, the clinking of glasses, followed by the strains of Mozart's Twenty-fourth Symphony. The music was superb, pure, out of context with the sordid goings on in the room where it played. Listening to its perfection erased any misgivings about what he had to do. He was encouraged to act, thinking of the two people rutting as Mozart's music played, of their lust-filled breath degrading air filled with the symphony's perfect sounds.

It had taken less than fifteen minutes for them to stop talking. He waited another half hour. The music ceased and there was silence inside the room. Careful not to make any noise, he pried the molding away from the door jamb and slipped the blade behind the latch. The door swung open, revealing a small room, most of it taken up by a Murphy bed which swung down from a closet. The man and woman were asleep. She was curled up as far from him as she could get. A candle on a nightstand guttered in the draft from the open door.

Shutting it softly behind him, Koenig had walked to the side of the bed and blown out the candle. He killed the woman first, slicing her neck to the bone with his carefully sharpened knife. Her eyes had fluttered open. She stared at Koenig as she died, her mouth working in silent words. Koenig had stared back, expressionless, fascinated by the way her body slowed down and stopped, for the first time wondering, as he would often do during subsequent kills, how it would feel to fasten his lips to the bleeding throat and drink his fill. He never tried, repressing the urge, even the memory of the urge, to the deepest caverns of his psyche. It would not resurface for a long time.

The man died without waking.

Koenig relit the candle and placed the stylus on the recording, re-starting Mozart Twenty-fourth. He sat by the bedside studying the room. It was filled with cheap and tawdry gimcracks, five and dime clothing scattered on two chairs and piled on the floor. Listening to Mozart by candlelight, two cooling bodies on the bed beside him, was like nothing he had ever experienced. The music soared, filling the room, moving him beyond himself, into a dark smooth place where he was alone and powerful, sailing on a sea whose waves rose and fell around him, an invincible pilot on a ship of self.

He realized those who knew how to take others' lives as he did were priests of a rare and elite order. Their profession would be desecrated by rutting between the sheets as these two had been doing before the kill, participating in the act which creates life, either in sham, as the dead man and woman had been doing, or in the illusion of love.

With the Twenty-fourth Symphony filling the room he took a silent vow of celibacy, as well as a vow that he would no longer waste his calling by creeping around in shadows killing simply because he found his victims revolting in their mediocrity. The vow had elevated him. It had codified his superiority and given it the dignity he had earned during his time perfecting the art of striking without detection. He had apprenticed himself to death and was now a master. The woman had seen it in his eyes as she looked into them while dying. No doubt the words she had been trying to say were thanking him for releasing her from the meaninglessness this room so obviously represented.

He had come here in the final stages of his apprenticeship, his novitiate. He was leaving a seasoned professional, ready to command a wage for his talent, supplicants for his calling.

HE HAD A marketable skill. His next step was to learn how to manage the money it would make for him. The following two years he spent doing a master's in business administration at the University of Pennsylvania's Wharton School, at the same time proving himself to members of Philadelphia's underworld.

Things went smoothly for Koenig after that. Over the years he made millions as a contract killer. He also published a large body of poetry in both small literary and mainstream publications. Some of his works had been anthologized in college texts, and he was gathering a reputation as a visiting teacher of poetry in MFA programs around the country. He enjoyed having graduate students looking to him for inspiration. Those who flocked to him saw him as a giant of the second half of the Century. Picking up Eliot's banner and pointing in verse to the restoration of privilege and the place of the elite.

"You must have a vision," he would say as they sat taking notes in seminars, all the while knowing the best their narrow lives would translate to were constricted little droplets of words, published only in those pathetic journals teachers of literature edit and publish for other teachers of literature and their graduate students.

"You must understand your place in the world and be able to celebrate that place in words and images."

By the time he was fifty, he was wealthy from his secret profession and well regarded in his public one. Several times he thought of retiring, concentrating solely on the poetry, and once he tried, only to find himself roaming the streets a few months later, seeking random victims. It was not the way he wanted to end up, so desperate for a kill he had to stalk the night like a paperback vampire.

Besides, an irreplaceable thrill lay in the balance of his two lives, a poetry of language and a poetry of action, realms which never interacted except in his dreams and poems. But realms which could come together. He walked a tightrope between his public and private lives. A misstep on his part, the appearance of a knowledgeable reader in the wrong place, any number of unpredictable and seemingly meaningless events could sway the wire and he would fall. In the unpredictable lay the thrill. Koenig was confident he could outwit anyone, but he could not outwit chance. If chance led to discovery, it would take all his intelligence, all his skill and ruthlessness to survive.

Still, he played with the idea of retirement. Then Donald Castile showed up.

"They tell me you're the best," Castile had said to him at a summer cocktail party on the lawn of the Berkshire estate owned by Rebecca Churchill Endicott, a mutual acquaintance, who was on the board of Worthington-America as well as a trustee of Hillsdale University, where Koenig had been a University Presidential Fellow, teaching poetry writing for several semesters.

Koenig had shrugged. "There are many poets."

"I'm not talking about poetry, Mr. Koenig."

Nodding politely, Koenig took Castile's elbow, leading him to a quiet grove of sugar maples.

"Rebecca said you have been asking to meet me."

Castile cleared his throat. "Worthington-America is in trouble, Mr. Koenig. Long term care of patients is wasting our resources, threatening our reserves, and undermining profits."

"And you think I can help?"

"I'm sure of it, Mr. Koenig."

"And why should I get involved in your corporate affairs, Mr. Castile? I have no need for money beyond the quite satisfactory wealth I have already accumulated, and the intricacies of business bore me, quite frankly."

Castile had laughed softly. "I'm not asking you for your business expertise, Mr. Koenig, although I've been told it's quite extensive and unique."

"Then what are you proposing?"

The gentile politeness was gone from Koenig's voice, its tones cutting through Castile like a knife.

Looking around at the people scattered across the lawn, laughing, drinking, making business and social arrangements as they partied, Castile shook his head.

"I hardly think this is the place to go into details, Mr. Koenig."

"This is the perfect place, Castile. The only bugs in these maples are the flying kind, although I'm sure you'll permit me to check you, just to be sure you're not wearing any kind of wire or electronic bug yourself."

Once he was sure Castile was clean, Koenig told him he was ready to listen.

Castile cleared his throat again. "I want to run a pilot program in the Philadelphia hospital of the Worthington-America chain. If it works there, we'll extend it through the entire system."

Koenig's expression didn't change. "What kind of pilot program? What will you extend through the entire chain if it works?"

Castile laughed awkwardly. "I guess I got a bit ahead of myself."

Silent, Koenig waited for him to continue.

For a third time, Castile cleared his throat. "Health care is a perilous business. Government interference, new diseases, severely ill patients, all make unnecessary demands on our resources that threaten the bottom line. Especially the patients. We give them long term care in our hospitals and through our HMOs, and we finance their long term care through our insurance programs. After all the expense, they die."

"Everybody dies, Castile."

"Not as expensively, Mr. Koenig. That's where you would come in."

"You want me to reduce the expenses of their deaths?"

"A nice way of putting it."

Koenig's smile was an unpleasant sight. "You want me to kill long term patients before their time. You think it will cut your losses."

Castile nodded. "It will cut our losses."

"I do not work cheaply. Your losses may be cut, but they will not be eliminated."

"Any savings will be significant, especially on the scale we're looking at."

"Why me, Castile? Why not do it in-house, through some of your medical staff or your other employees?"

"It took me two and a half years of careful searching to find you, Mr. Koenig. You're discreet, professional, and expert."

"I've been around all that time."

"You're also invisible."

"I have many skills."

"I had this idea three years ago. Six months later, I decided Worthington-America was facing enough of a crisis to put it into effect and I needed to find someone to handle it, a single, professional accountable only to me. I started investigating possibilities. It wasn't until a year and a half later that your name even came up. I spent the last year finding you and checking you out."

After more talk, they agreed, details to be worked out later. Koenig was still uneasy, and it wasn't like him to take a job he was uneasy about. His real self-questioning would come later.

Now Blanchard was on the edge of panic because one doctor at the hospital thought the cardiac deaths might be signaling a new development in the puzzling illness plaguing the medical world. For Koenig, all they signaled was the need for a little undetectable potassium to be injected into a few bloodstreams. Although, Koenig was pleased with the irony of his variation on the McChesney kill, giving the useless scum an overdose. Of all the kills at Worthington- Philadelphia, McChesney's had been the most amusing. None had been really satisfying. After successfully taking care of Mathieu, the others had been routine, almost boring. McChesney had been a game, a bit of a relief.

He'd keep an eye on the doctor Blanchard was concerned about, but he would do something about him only in the most extreme emergency. The hospital deaths weren't extraordinary. The death of a doctor who was agitating for the investigation of the others would raise an alarm. Koenig's entire career had been spent without raising alarms.

He turned out the office lights and stepped into the empty hallway. He was growing increasingly uncomfortable. He liked cleansing the world and he liked the money Worthington-American paid him. He liked the way Castile deferred to him. He liked the image of being a corporate consultant, which is what he was in the minds of the few people who were aware he was around. Such things should have made everything seem new again, exciting.

They didn't. A nag at the back of his mind kept cautioning him. Get out. Away. This is foolishness. It had been warning him since the beginning and he had been ignoring it since the beginning. Maybe it was time to start listening.

What he didn't like most was Blanchard. He didn't like his style. He didn't like the way he called him Chris. He didn't like the man's fearfulness. He was the weak link in the operation. Castile had insisted on including Blanchard, and Koenig had gone along with him. But he knew Blanchard was trouble. He'd known it the first time he'd seen him, heard him speak through his small, twisted mouth as he played with his fingers, his eyes darting around the room, the fingers of his right hand incessantly drumming against the knuckles of his left hand. Eventually, he'd have to deal with him. Indeed, there will be time, he thought. Now he wanted to get back to his apartment and take a long hot shower.

CHAPTER NINE

Canaan, Massachusetts \ Saturday, May 4

CANAAN FALLS DID not look like the town Buckman had known years before. The elm trees were gone from the main shopping district on Franklin Street, replaced by young maples and hybrid poplars. Parking meters lined the sidewalk where a well-meaning town planner, working with Federal money, had placed several small brick malls. There were benches filled with unemployed teenagers, listening to boom boxes, smoking cigarettes, and jostling one another, sharing the space with middle aged men and women released from state hospitals, then left to fend for themselves sitting there staring vaguely at passersby, cringing from the busy activities and loud music of their teenage companions.

Arcade Hall, one of the oldest wooden structures in the commercial area, was gone. In its place an awkward looking white stucco and glass building housed the local branch of a Boston bank. Across the street, in a storefront, was the Canaan Insurance Agency, the sign in its window advertising Aetna, Northwestern Mutual, and Worthington-America.

Next to the insurance office, Eileff's Store had spread over an entire block. When Buckman left twenty-five years before, it had been a small general store, selling everything from freshly ground hamburger to wheelbarrows to work clothes and used cars. Now it had an ugly salmon pink enamel plate facade attempting to unify the appearance of several Nineteenth Century brick buildings, the name, Eileff's written in black script sprawled across the front. Zagorski's Hardware Emporium was gone from the corner of Franklin and Hill Streets, replaced by Henry David's Men's Shop in one half of its old space, a pizza restaurant in the other.

Buckman sighed. The Old World might not have changed, but the rest of Canaan had kept up with the worst of the times, unplanned development sprawling over its once lovely hills, the roads leading into the center littered with fast food restaurants and small strip shopping malls, a Wal-Mart and Home Depot sitting on the land where the Pratt farm had once been, the 200 year old house and barn gone, paved parking lots covering acres of Hadley loam, some of the most fertile land in the valley.

Parking the truck in front of the police station, he fed the meter and walked down the street, salivating at the odor of pizza. Velma had probably never eaten pizza. He thought of Dinty Moore beef stew and hamburger fried in butter with onions and potatoes, covered with canned onion soup. As soon as he'd made his phone call, he'd pick up a pizza and take it back for their dinner.

He'd been surprised when Wilfred said Irene had tried reaching him. Then he remembered how easily she'd picked up on his speech patterns the first time they went to dinner. It had been a simple deduction for her to figure out where he'd gone. His alarm gave way to puzzlement. Why had she called him? When he left Philadelphia on Thursday, he hadn't told anyone he was leaving, especially Irene. If he stayed it could cost them both their lives. He was no hero. It had been time to go, and he was determined to get out with his skin, and Irene had become too important to him to let anything happen to her. The best he could do was leave with no word to her and hope she would shrug her shoulders and eventually forget about him.

He hadn't been gone long enough for her to become alarmed and try to find him. She should have barely reached the miffed stage, wondering why he hadn't called for the last several days. As far as she knew, nothing drastic had happened. Miffed. That's all she should be. What would drive her to look for him in Canaan?They had seen a lot of each other in the weeks since he told her of his fears about possible mutations in the virus. Mutation, horseshit. He was glad he hadn't known then what he knew now. She was safer not having any idea what was going on at Worthington, or where he had gone.

He wished he didn't know any of it. Wished he'd never walked into Castile's office two days ago, asking again for him to authorize the research he wanted done. When Castile refused for the fifth time in as many similar conferences, he muttered some offhand comment about the sooner more of these goddamn patients died the better Worthington-America's financial picture would look.

Buckman had sneered at him and turned on his best sarcastic style. "You might just as well finish the lot of them off yourself and save the corporation all the time and money. Just get a good hit man and go for it."

He hadn't been prepared for Castile's response. The man's face had whitened, his hands visibly shaking as he quickly looked up at Buckman, then pretended to bury his attention in the papers on his desk. Buckman stood, arms at his sides, looking at him.

Castile glanced up. "Stop being an asshole and get out of here. I'm too busy for your nonsense."

The response startled him. It was inappropriate, unless Buckman had accidentally hit on the answer. He looked at Castile, needles of ice stabbing his stomach.

After several long minutes, the fact registering, Buckman choked. "My god, that's what you're doing, isn't it? You've been killing these people."

Castile turned red; his face stiff as he slammed a fist on the top of the desk. "I've had it with your goddamn asininity, Buckman. Get out of here and let me get my work done."

Numbed, he left, walking down the hall, arguing against himself. Castile was right; he'd been an ass. Castile wouldn't, couldn't, be behind anything of the sort. Buckman had gotten too involved with the lives and deaths of his patients. He needed a break.

Driving to his home along the Delaware in Upper Black Eddy that night, his mind racing, he had gone over the events of the past several months. He replayed the meeting in Castile's office, one minute wondering if he'd been right about what had been going on at the hospital, the next convinced that he was tired, confused and totally off the wall. Slowing his thoughts, he tried sorting things out. Every time he thought of a new fact, it seemed to be another link. Things were fitting together. By the time he got home he was sure he'd been right. He wanted to call the police but there was nothing to prove any accusation he might make. If he was right, he didn't know who or what he was up against, aside from Castile. There was his life to think about. Anybody who would put together something like this could easily decide to eliminate him.

He did not sleep that night. As he lay in bed tossing and thinking about Castile's reaction, trying to convince himself he'd been wrong, he heard the car in his driveway. He'd known instantly what it meant. Castile had ordered his death.

That was when he'd made the bed, so it would look as though he hadn't slept at home that night, then gone out the back window and hidden in the woods the rest of the night, crouched behind a low clump of rhododendron, watching, waiting for the intruder to leave, so he could pack a few clothes and head for the Old World.

Thank god there hadn't been time for him to tell Irene, although she was bound to be pissed at the way he left. Both had been working on the assumption their friendship was leading to a more complex relationship. They'd been discussing it in just such terms until Buckman took her to a drive-in movie one night, left her in the car while he went to the food pavilion and came back with a large order of popcorn and two Cokes. Handing them through the window to her, he got in the car, turned down the speaker and told her he was in love with her, damn it.

She had laughed. "Damn it, too," she said.

REMEMBERING THE SOUND of her voice, Buckman smiled as he walked past the Canaan police station toward a drugstore with a public telephone sign over its door. He went in, got ten dollars in change from the clerk and closed the folding door of an old fashioned wooden phone booth behind him. Wilfred had offered to let him use his phone, but he needed more privacy than prying family members and an Old World party line would provide.

He dialed Irene's number. An answering machine clicked on, her voice saying she couldn't come to the phone right then, but if the caller would leave a name and number she'd call back as soon as possible.

Clearing his throat, Buckman spoke awkwardly into the phone. "This is Bill, returning your call."

He was about to tell her he'd try back later when Irene picked up her receiver.

"Sorry, I was screening my calls just in case that horrible man called." Her words rushed out.

Buckman asked, "Horrible man?"

"He came asking all sorts of questions about you. He frightened me, Bill. Everything about him was frightening. I didn't know anything, of course. I didn't even know you were gone. But you are, you bastard. I tried calling your office, and then I tried your house. Where are you?"

"You don't want to know."

"You're in Canaan, right? Your brother told you I'd tried to reach you. I've tried everything I could to find you. Your office didn't know where you were. No one at the hospital knew. There wasn't any answer at your house, or your apartment and I was scared. That man is death walking. It's in his eyes, and he was looking for you."

"Did he hurt you?"

"Scared the shit out of me. I looked for you everywhere and finally called information for Buckmans in Canaan and got your brother. I asked him for you and could tell he was lying when he said he hadn't seen you since you left. It was in his voice."

Buckman laughed. "Is that part of linguistics too, knowing when someone's lying?"

"It's part of common sense listening, hearing the hesitation in someone's voice, picking up little quavers and unusual phrasing. Tell me I'm right. You're in Canaan."

"I'm in Canaan." As he spoke, there was a loud screeching sound over the receiver.

"And that man has something to do with your leaving?"

"What did he look like?"

"Big. Mean. With hair all over his arms and sticking out of his collar. I think he was wearing a false beard and a wig, although I'm not positive about that. If they were fake, they were first class fake, but the color wasn't quite right for the hair on his arms and the clots of it sticking out of the collar. Know him?"

"No, but I think I know who he is, what he is anyway."

"He said you'd disappeared, and it was important he talk to you. When I told him I didn't know you'd gone away, he got furious and said it was critical for him to get in touch with you, to find out what you knew and why you'd gone off somewhere. I told him I didn't know where you were. I prattled on like an idiot, he had me so unnerved. I told him doctors of medicine knew all kinds of things, then I told him I was a Ph.D. in linguistics and that doctors of linguistics knew all kinds of things which doctors of medicine didn't have any idea about. I was so frightened, I said anything that came into my mind."

"How did he react?"

"It was strange, extraordinary. He started talking about language theory, different kinds of meaning constructs, and other kinds of technical concepts only linguists are interested in. Then he suddenly stopped and got cold, frightening, like he was chagrined at himself for getting sidetracked and asked me again why you'd left the city."

"What did you say?"

"I said I didn't even know you'd left. I told him that you were a bastard if you'd gone away without saying anything to me. I meant it, too, Bill. I thought we had something going, that our drive-in movie confession was as important to you as it was to me."

"Did he tell you what he wanted from me?"

"No. All he said was he'd be back and if I heard from you, I'd better tell him where you were. He said it was a matter of life and death."

"It is, Irene, and I don't want you involved in it. That's why I left."

"What kind of trouble are you in?"

"Big trouble. Bad trouble. Don't ask about it. I don't want you involved. It's bad enough I'm in it."

"I'm already involved if that man's going to come around harassing me about you."

"Just keep telling him you don't know where I am."

"But I do know."

"Forget me, Irene." The words sounded foolish and melodramatic as soon as he uttered them.

"Horseshit. I'm coming up there." Her tone was brusque. She was probably as annoyed by the melodrama of his tone as he was feeling foolish.

"Don't. There's nothing you can do." Christ, more melodrama again. How could being in real danger result in his sounding to silly?

"I'm not going to stay here. If that man comes back and I have to lie to him about where you are and he can pick up lies as easily as I can, I'd be in trouble by trying to fool him. It looks as though if you're in trouble, I'm in trouble."

"Don't come here, Irene."

"I'm leaving this afternoon. The University didn't give me any classes this semester because of Melinda's illness, just committee assignments and approval to work on a research project. I don't have any hard schedule keeping me in Philly. Where's a good place for us to meet in Canaan? It shouldn't take me more than six hours to get there, including packing a few things to bring along."

Buckman groaned, banging his fist on the shelf below the telephone. "There's nothing I can say to stop you?"

"Nothing."

He took a deep breath, both relieved and terrified that she was coming. "You'll come into town on Franklin Street. There's a little pizza joint on the same side of the street as the police station. I'll meet you there around eight tonight."

"We'll get through this together, Bill."

"You don't have a clue what this is."

"I know your life is in danger. That man who was here looking for you doesn't want to sell you insurance."

Buckman laughed. "Wait till you hear all of it."

THE PICKUP CAB was filled with the smell of the pizza he was taking home. Bouncing down the Windybush, he lifted the cardboard lid, picking at cheese and pepperoni. He was worried. The last thing he needed was Irene coming to town, and it was the thing he wanted most. He didn't want to face this thing alone, and he didn't want her getting in any deeper than she was.

He thought about the man she described. Big. Mean. Now, worse, according to Irene, he was smart. Very smart. Great. He was being stalked by an intellectual murderer.

Driving past Wilfred's house, he was struck with amazement that he was suddenly taking responsibility for his brother's daughter. None of this was what he had bargained for when he returned to the Old World. A little privacy, yes. Hiding out, absolutely. Now, in addition to the threat from Philadelphia, he was caught up in the family again. It was as messy as he remembered, maybe worse, but at least the family mess wouldn't kill him.

He turned left on the Black Horse Pike and a few minutes later pulled into his father's drive. A rusted 1970 Valiant, the left rear shock obviously broken, sat in the shadows by the house. As he shut off the engine and opened his door, a bony man in green work pants and a flannel checkerboard shirt came out of the kitchen door. He carried two cans of beer. Velma followed him, sitting on the back step as the man walked toward Buckman.

"That you, Billy Buck? If it is, I got a beer for you, if it isn't you then whoever you are still ought to drink it before it gets warm."

Buckman nodded, shading his eyes with his right hand, trying to place the man.

"It's me, Vaughn," his brother said, seeing Buckman's confusion. "It's been a long time, right brother? By God but it's good to see you, Billy."

Vaughn Buckman smiled, holding out his hand. Buckman reached for it, receiving a startlingly warm and strong clasp in return.

"I come over soon as I got your note about Calvin. The old bastard's still not back, ay?"

"I guess not. He hasn't been to your place?"

Vaughn shook his head.

Buckman studied his brother. He'd been his favorite when they were young, sledding together in the winter, sliding down the falls on Buckman Brook in the summer. He and Vaughn discovered the cave on Dog Mountain, entering the dark opening, heavy with odors of bats and other animals who found shelter there. They spent summer days pretending to be Indians holed up in the cave against encroaching settlers. It was Vaughn who had taught him how to shoot a gun. Vaughn had been one of the best hunters, one of the best shots, among all the kids they'd grown up with. Now he looked like an old man. Buckman guessed Moose was right. Vaughn was a juicer. The ravages of alcohol had stained his eyes and pushed his face into early aging.

"Life's been hard." Vaughn's voice was matter-of-fact, without the whining self-pity Buckman found in many drunks. "It's good to see you, Billy Buck. Calvin gave you up for dead twenty years ago, and so didn't the others. Nobody gave a shit, but I figured you was doing all right and just didn't want to be held back by the Old World. Hell, look at all the good staying here has done for me."

Vaughn laughed, holding out his arms and gesturing inwardly, toward himself.

At the sound of the laughter, Buckman smiled at his brother, seeing the boy he'd known underneath the hard skin and bleary eyes.

"You don't look well, Vaughn."

Vaughn shook his head. "I'm a fuck up, Billy Buck. No work. No money. Just a check from the State every now and then, enough to make the payments on the trailer and keep up with my food and liquor bill at Wesley Johnson's Store."

He handed Buckman the beer, then turned and sat on the opposite side of the steps from Velma, sucking down his own.

Buckman took a sip. Sitting between them, he looked at his brother. "What happened, Vaughn? Next to me, you did better in school than any of the rest of them."

Vaughn sighed, sucking down more beer. "Velma, go get me another brew from the fridge, will you?"

When she got up, he leaned his elbows back on the porch floor and sighed again. "A couple years after you left, I was working for the railroad as a brakeman. It was a damn good job, good pay. I liked riding the trains, drinking beer with the other guys, smoking a little dope along the way, sometimes doing a run over to Albany, or east to Boston, every now and then getting up to Montreal. It was fun, you know, and kind of an adventure. Then the Boston and Maine was bought out, bunch of us were laid off and I couldn't find another job."

Velma returned with his beer. Lighting a cigarette, he popped the top, took a long swig, and belched. "Canaan's not the town you left, Billy Buck."

"I could see that."

Nodding, Vaughn grunted. "Down to the Falls the mills have all closed down. Hell, only Canaan Tap and Die's left, and it's owned by some outfit from Florida that just runs a skeleton crew over there. Times are tough here, Billy Buck."

He took a deep drag on the cigarette, another long swig from the beer and sat forward, resting his face in his hands. "I could have taken a job in town, either in the Falls or down to Graham, working at McDonald's, Wendy's, something like that, but they pay shit and besides, those aren't jobs for grown people like us. The damn places are crawling with high school kids working for next to nothing. Then I had the accident and haven't been able to work since."

Buckman asked, "What accident?"

"I was coming back from town one night about nine years ago. Me and Dave had been drinking at a couple of the bars there and I was going down the Windybush just as Roger Peck was coming up in his truck. We come together right at the bend by Bob Shippee's place. The car was totaled, and my head went through the windshield. It ain't been right since. I stand up fast, I get dizzy. I lean over to pick something up, I get dizzy. Sometimes, maybe two or three times a year, I get fits, pass out and bite the shit out of my tongue."

"What do the doctors say?"

Vaughn laughed through his nose. "What the fuck would you expect them to say, Billy Buck? Take these pills and learn to live with it, pal. Doctors. Fuck 'em. Rich Haskins had a stomachache a few years ago, went down to the hospital in Canaan. They gave him some pills and sent him home. Two days later he started shitting blood. Nancy got him in the car and drove him down to the hospital again. He was dead by the time they got there. Doctors. Fuck 'em, Billy Buck. Doctors ain't going to do people like the Buckmans a damn bit of good. Hell, look at what they done for Ma."

He smoked and drank again, then grinned at Buckman. "So, Billy Buck, what kind of trouble you in?"

CHAPTER TEN

Philadelphia, Pennsylvania \ Saturday, May 4

KOENIG WAS RIPSHIT. Buckman had blown town and the Shoemaker woman had thrown him off base with that goddamn talk they'd had about language. All he'd wanted was some information on Buckman, the doctor Castile wanted killed. Where had he gone? How much had he told the woman?

From her reaction, it was clear she didn't know a thing. She'd been angry when he asked where Buckman had gone, obviously feeling surprised and abandoned. Then she had suckered him into that discussion of linguistic theory.

He lit a cigar, throwing the match into the kitchen sink.

Wrong.

She hadn't suckered him.

He'd suckered himself.

Koenig had to take the blame for that one on his own. Besides, people didn't sucker him. He'd gone to her for information, been thrown off track by his intellectual interests and discovered nothing. Probably because she didn't know anything, didn't have anything for him to discover.

What if the woman and Buckman had gone out together a few times? You don't tell casual dates everything on your mind, especially the kind of stuff Buckman had on his mind these days. You don't tell them when and when you're going to ground to save your neck, and only if you're a total fool would you tell them where you're planning to hide.

And Buckman had gone to ground. Of that he was sure. His life depended on Koenig not being able to find him. There was no other explanation for his leaving without telling the Shoemaker woman. He'd just barely missed

Buckman. When he went to the house in Upper Black Eddy, it showed all signs of having been used earlier in the evening, but the bed was made and the lights were off. Buckman must have come home, packed, and gotten out.

Bastard.

Castile wanted him dead. Koenig had to have him dead. He needed to be eliminated. Soon. He'd figured too much out. A little more time to think and nose around and Buckman would have a full picture of what Koenig and Worthington-America were all about.

Had been all about. Past tense. Koenig was out of it now. He walked away yesterday, the minute Castile told him about his meeting with Buckman. Damned idiot. He'd blown everything. Castile should have cooled Buckman out. Instead, by getting freaked when Buckman started asking questions, he gave himself away. Now Buckman had to go. Blanchard too. And probably Castile. Only then could Koenig cruise away from this mess. He'd made good money from the operation so far, not the maximum he and Castile had agreed on, but still, good money. His work was undetectable, unless Buckman's rising suspicions led to investigation of Castile, and Castile freaked even more and told everything.

He would. Castile was basically a coward. Why else would he have hired Koenig? People like Castile were the necessary weakness of his profession. The men and women who hired him were almost exclusively the types to break down in the face of determined interrogation, people who couldn't face the direct and indirect results of their actions. They hired him for his cool. For his ability to do the jobs they wanted done without involvement. Without hesitation. They used him to shield themselves from the results of the actions their desires set in motion. They thought of themselves as the generals and of Koenig as their foot soldier.

He smiled to himself. The truth was, he used them to finance his mission. He was a perfectionist always doing his work invisibly. No seams. Let a cop find a seam and the cop is going to find a motive. Let a cop find a motive and the cop is going to find who was motivated. Let a cop find the mover and the mover is going to point the finger at Koenig, use him as a bargaining chip to make things easier if it looked like prosecution was on the horizon. Koenig had become as expert in covering himself as he had at killing.

Goddamn Castile. Buckman waltzes into his office begging for him to authorize research into recent cardiac failure among patients and Castile telegraphs everything to him. No doubt about it. Castile had to go. Then he'd find Buckman if he had to put bamboo slivers under the Shoemaker woman's fingernails to it.

Koenig had never been close to being found out before. He worked cautiously. Aside from the joyous abandon of his earliest days, he killed without flair, only occasionally indulging his unfulfillable thirst for the slit throat. From a professional point of view, the best kills were those which seemed to be accidents or natural deaths. The next best were those which mimicked ordinary street crimes, a druggie's mugging gone sour. The sweetest were the slit throats. Those he did for himself. Taunting himself with the sheer pleasure he had known since his earliest days, watching the blood flow, wondering about its taste, imagining what it would be like to bury his face in the victim's neck.

But in the normal run of things, he didn't need sensational results and mutilated bodies. He didn't want headlines giving him some catchy name, the papers and TV news bleating about the such and such murderer striking again. He had disdain for killers who reveled in headlines, who taunted police and reporters, giving rise to headlines. *The Panty Hose Killer Stalks Albany. The Hillside Strangler Kills Once More.* Cheap, trashy, crap. Men who needed that kind of sick publicity were among the scum he waged his personal war against. Koenig's satisfaction lay in the cleansing effect of the murdered person's absence in the world. In his power to cleanse. Flair led to suspicion on the part of the police. Suspicion led to collection of information. Collection of information led to the visibility of patterns. The visibility of patterns established the existence of a series of killings.

And that could lead to the end of everything, just when life was good. The poetry had taken off and the killing had become extremely professional. Koenig was at the peak of his powers. He wasn't about to lose out because of some jerk doctor's offhand comment to Castile and Castile's over-reaction to it.

IT WAS EARLY May and already Philadelphia was as steamy as summer. A late afternoon thundershower had glazed the streets, knocking out several power transformers in the northeast section. Worthington-Philadelphia, like many institutions and manufacturing plants in the area, was operating on its standby generators.

In his eleventh floor office at the hospital, Charlie Blanchard had just finished going through the weekly purchase orders for the hospital. Basic supplies had gone up in price again, for the third month in a row. When was it going to stop? Inflation, increasingly difficult state and federal regulations, and now this shit. Even with the Feds paying the bill for medications with a series of temporary grants, the cost to insurance companies of treating patients dying from a mysteriously rising epidemic threatened to undermine the system. Worthington-America was feeling the heat, and as its insurance profits went down, the pressure on its hospitals and HMOs to cut costs increased.

Blanchard had been holding the line as best he could, laying off nurses, making do with skeleton crews whenever possible and buying the cheapest non-essential products available. It wasn't enough. Castile's program was helping, but the hospital business just wasn't what it used to be. Not what Duke's graduate program had prepared him for.

Opening his lower right desk drawer, he took out a bottle of Cognac, poured himself a drink and sat looking through the window. A pigeon sat on the sill, pruning its feathers. Grabbing a fistful of sunflower seeds, Blanchard eased the window open, scattering them on the concrete ledge. The pigeon watched and when the window closed it began pecking at them.

Blanchard smiled. Easy life, bird. No shit. Eat free sunflower seeds, flit around over the city catching the breezes and soar whenever and wherever you want, shit wherever you want. Sighing, he decided to bag it for the day, drive home to Meadowbrook, stopping to pick up a couple of thick steaks to barbecue on the gas grill he'd finished putting together last night.

Barbie would like that. She'd just gotten home from a buying trip for Macy's, and he knew she was still wiped, even after having a full Saturday to recover. He'd get a bottle of wine to go with the steaks, and some salad from the salad bar at the Acme. All that and a little candlelight on the patio. They'd send Ruby, their housekeeper, to the movies with the children.

He and Barbie could relax, get a little tipsy, forget all about the hospital and Barbie's job at Macy's. Later in the evening, once Ruby got Kimberly and Michael settled for the night, maybe they'd even get it on for a while. It had been a long time since either of them had felt like having sex. They deserved a good time. And on top of it, today was Saturday. He'd done extra duty at the hospital by coming in on a weekend.

It wasn't like Worthington wasn't getting its money's worth out of him. No matter what, Charlie Blanchard paid his dues.

He polished off the Cognac, locked his desk and file cabinets, left a message with the operator that he was leaving and headed for the parking garage. Koenig came walking down the hall at the same time. Both men headed for the elevator. Koenig pushed the down button.

"Hi, Chris." Blanchard smiled at him. "What are you doing here today?"

Koenig nodded, ignoring the nickname. Blanchard was already dead as far as he was concerned. He might be walking around, but Koenig had condemned him. It was just a matter of time before he carried out the sentence. He could stop the elevator between floors, snap his neck and stuff the body out the trap door at the top of the car and leave it there until somebody found it. He pictured the process.

Blanchard grinned, remembering Koenig's earlier fury at being called Chris. "Sorry, I meant Christopher. Old habits are hard to break, right? Sorry, I really am. Busy week? Down here looking for future clients?"

Koenig glared at his trivializing tone, looking forward to the moment when Blanchard knew Koenig had killed him, the moment of dying recognition. It was one of the prime rewards of his work. The Worthington job had allowed for almost none of it. Blanchard would begin to make up for the loss.

The elevator bell dinged, the door sliding open. It was empty. Blanchard entered first. Koenig followed. Moving to the rear of the car, he stood, eyes focused on the wall beyond as the doors slowly closed.

"You are an idiot," he said to Blanchard when the car began its descent.

Blanchard started and turned, looking at the man in the elevator with him. "I said I was sorry."

"Sorry you're an idiot? Don't apologize, Blanchard. It would be like a dog apologizing for drooling. It's your nature to be an idiot. I simply dislike you as much as I dislike dogs."

"I meant I was sorry about the slip up with your name." Giving him a weak grin, Blanchard shrugged and turned to face the front of the car. With the sound of Koenig's breathing behind him, the elevator car seemed unbearably small, crowded beyond capacity by the two of them. He didn't understand why Koenig disliked him. Aside from screwing up his name, he had done nothing to offend the man. He'd cooperated with him, giving him access to the hospital, supplying him with records of patients so he could take care of his business in the most natural appearing manner.

He ought to confront it directly, just ask the son-of-a- bitch why he was so fucking nasty to him. Let him know that Charlie Blanchard was a man of some substance, and not just some jerk he could push around, bully. He turned, about to say something, when he saw the look in Koenig's eyes. He'd never seen anything like it. Cold. Devoid of life. Dark eyes. Unfeeling as space between the stars. Blanchard stiffened, terrified beyond reason for a moment. He almost sighed with relief when the elevator bell dinged, signaling their arrival at the hospital lobby.

The doors opened and he hurried out, making his way toward the hospital's front entrance through a crowd of Saturday visitors carrying flowers, candies and other gifts for sick friends and family members. Once on the street he looked behind him. Koenig emerged from the hospital and looked each way, as though searching for someone.

Blanchard's heart pounded. Stupid goddamn reaction. Why would Koenig be looking for him? If he was pissed about Blanchard slipping and using a nickname, why was it a big deal? Koenig frightened him. The man existed outside any parameters he had ever known. Blanchard was an administrator, used to manipulating people by giving them any version of reality they might want to hear. If result was to his benefit he could withhold facts, bend them, stretch them, or fabricate them. He had fired people without compunction, disregarding the conditions of their lives. Profit was his bottom line. Profit for Charlie Blanchard via profit for Worthington-Philadelphia Hospital. It was a system which provided a good life for his family. Of course, Barbie's buying job for Macy's helped.

In Meadowbrook he was president of the neighborhood association, sat on the board of the United Way, dedicated one weekend a month to the local youth center, participated in other valuable community affairs. All were possible because of his position at Worthington. Whatever he had to do there in the name of profit was more than returned in service to his family and community.

Koenig was different. He killed people. Blanchard liked to think of himself as part of the process of keeping them alive. He looked at Koenig's position with Worthington-America as a temporary glitch in the system, eliminating a few people for the benefit of the many. Keeping the health care system from breaking down.

But he could never do what had to be done. That took Koenig with his empty eyes. Koenig was the tool necessary for Worthington-America to keep afloat. Blanchard suspected there were many insurance companies, HMOs and hospitals throughout the country using similar tools. What else could they do, threatened as they were? It was a pure necessity for the business. For the people who used the business. Let the health care system break down and you might as well let civilization break down.

When he looked again at the hospital entrance, Koenig was gone. Blanchard was relieved, although he had no real focus for his feeling, other than his gut fear of Koenig. The man thought nothing of human life. He remembered the time back in March when he'd come into Koenig's office. *You're a pain in the ass, Blanchard. You just blew Mozart's Thirty-eighth for me, right at the peak. I could kill you for that.* No doubt about it. Koenig could kill for that. Perhaps had. Blanchard shivered briefly, looked around again, then headed for the parking garage.

There was little traffic. He barreled along Huntington Avenue, the car stereo blaring. It was a clear day, crisp early spring air and a deep blue sky. Perfect for thick steaks on the gas grill. He reached home singing to the lyrics to Creedence's *Bad Moon Rising.* The garage door opened, and he parked the Mercedes next to Barbie's van. Pushing the remote to close the door, Blanchard rested his head back against the seat until the song finished playing. Before the next song came up, he turned off the sound system. Closing his eyes, he breathed slowly and counted to sixty, allowing time for his heart to slow, his shoulders to relax.

Taking a few last deep breaths, he grabbed the grocery bag and started for the house, stopping as he walked through the breezeway separating it from the garage. Barbie was sleeping on a chaise next to the pool in the back yard, Kimberly and Michael splashing in the water beside her. Grinning at the children, he placed his forefinger on his lips and bent over the pool, gathering a handful of water which he held above her stomach, letting it drip slowly down.

She woke with a screech.

He backed away before she could swat him with her towel. "A little early in the season for the pool, isn't it?"

"I couldn't stand it," she said. "It got so hot this afternoon, I took the cover off and started the filter up. The water's a little green, but I had to do it, and the kids have been having a ball."

"You had to?"

She gave him a kiss on the cheek. "Absolutely had to. You ought to go for a swim. The water is surprisingly warm for this time of year."

He nodded and told her he would think about it, but after reaching down and feeling the water with his right hand, he shrugged.

"It's warm, but I'd rather drink and take a quick nap." He walked into the house, filled a glass a little over halfway with gin, dropped in four ice cubes and a dollop of tonic.

The evening went according to plan. Ruby took Kimberly and Michael to supper and a movie. The wine was perfect, the steaks tender, delicious after marinating for an hour in teriyaki spiced with sweet basil and rosemary before being covered with a Cajun blackening powder and slapped on a red hot grill. The sex went well, a little too quickly for him, but nice. They both dropped off to sleep as soon as it was over, a buzz from their drinks curling around the corners of their brains.

He awoke to a hand over his mouth, the sharp blade of a knife at his throat.

Koenig whispered in his ear. "Don't move except as I tell you. Say nothing. Get out of bed quietly and go downstairs. I'm moving with you, the knife at your throat. If I think for a second that you're trying to get away, you're dead. Your wife's dead. Your children are dead."

Blanchard started to speak but at the first movement of his throat muscles, the knife tightened almost to the point of breaking his skin.

"Be quiet and get moving." Koenig's breath was moist in his ear.

Slowly, Blanchard eased himself from the bed and walked naked toward the door.

"Let me put on a bathrobe," he whispered.

Koenig's response was another tightening of the knife against his throat.

They moved in tandem through the hallway, down the stairs and across the living room to the French doors leading to the back yard.

"Get in the pool," Koenig said when they were at the water's edge.

Blanchard put his feet on the top step under water.

"Why?" He asked.

The answer was another tightening of the knife. He started shivering, then felt urine running down his leg, heard its soft splash in the pool.

"You'll never know why, Blanchard. All I'll tell you is that you're going to be dead very shortly. The only choice you have left is whether you are going to die quietly or noisily. The only guarantee you have is that if you die with a scream, your wife and children will be dead five minutes after you are."

"And if I'm quiet?"

"I might not kill them."

"How do I know that?"

"You never will. I might kill them anyway. But I will kill them, quite unpleasantly, unless you're dead quiet. Now, get all the way in the water. If you're lucky, this will look like an accidental drowning. I'd be more inclined to let your family live if it appears as though you had trouble sleeping, got up and went for a dip, got in trouble, and drowned. The appearance of an accident may save the rest of your family. At least you can die thinking it possible."

As Koenig pushed, Blanchard moved down the remaining three steps until he was chest deep in the pool. The water, which had felt so warm a few hours earlier, now felt cold. His shivering increased, teeth chattering. He felt his bowels loosen, then let go.

Koenig whispered. "You're disgusting."

They were the last words Blanchard heard. Koenig forced his head under the water and held him down, the knife against his throat until he was completely submerged.

Struggling briefly not to breathe, to keep alive as long as possible, he looked through the water at Koenig's face, a dark blur against the night sky. Keeping quiet was the last unselfish act of a selfish life. In his panic, he consoled himself with the idea as his body lurched forward, fighting against the surrounding water. Koenig pushed harder. His fingers were tight, painful against Blanchard's face.

As consciousness began to fade, spots flashing before his eyes, Blanchard knew he could not hold back the reflexive gasping insuck of pool water any longer. In a last gesture of rage, he forced his hand above the surface, middle finger extended. It brushed Koenig's upper lip, knocking the false mustache askew.

He did not hear Koenig's laughter.

CHAPTER ELEVEN

Canaan, Massachusetts \ Saturday, May 4

BUCKMAN PARKED THE truck in the driveway, motioning for Irene to put her car next to it.

"We'll hide it in the garage with mine in the morning," he said, getting out and opening her door.

"Things are that bad?"

He nodded, leading her toward the house.

Velma stood by the kitchen sink, her face barely visible in the weak light from the ceiling fixture. Her features creased into a frown as Irene came in.

"Velma, this is my friend Irene, the one I told you was coming."

Velma's eyes widened and her throat tightened, the words coming hard. "She's pretty, Uncle Billy Buck."

Irene smiled and walked across the room. Gently, she took Velma's hand and lightly patted it. Velma pulled away, cringing near the stove.

"We've got a lot to talk about," Buckman said to Irene.

She nodded. "I can see that."

Leading her upstairs, he took her into a small bedroom with three iron army cots lined against the wall. One of them was made up and covered by an old army blanket. A small lamp sat on an orange crate beside it, giving off barely enough light to read by.

"I used to share this room with my brothers Vaughn and Dave. Velma fixed it up for you. Once you're settled in I'll explain everything."

He left her alone. Ten minutes later she came downstairs, wearing a pair of dungarees and a light sweatshirt.

"You grew up sleeping in that bed?"

"One of those three, anyway. They're all alike. My father got them from a boy's camp down in Falltown that went out of business. He used to brag about paying fifty cents apiece for them."

She shook her head. "It's a wonder you don't have a permanent curvature of the spine."

"Kids can put up with a lot. If it's too soft and sunken for you, I'll get some plywood from the barn and put it under the mattress."

"I'll try it tonight, and let you know."

"Good." He walked to the door and stood looking out quietly. Then, turning, he went to the refrigerator. "Want a beer?"

"I'd love one."

He got two, twisted the caps off and handed her one. "It's a beautiful evening. Let's take a walk. I'll tell you everything I know and suspect."

Taking a flashlight from a shelf next to the door, he went out, holding the door for Irene. She followed as he led her up an old logging road into the woods behind the house, the beam from the flash cutting a narrow path through the night. They walked and he told her about his suspicions, ending with the break-in at his house in Bucks County and his flight to the Old World, Calvin's death, Velma's pregnancy. Everything.

When he finished, she sighed and was silent for several minutes. Finally, unable to stand the quiet, he asked, "Does anybody know where you've gone?"

She shook her head.

"Good. Velma's the only other person who knows you're here."

She turned to him, breaking her silence. "Your brother Wilfred doesn't know?"

"Only if he saw you following me down the road when we came in. There's a strong possibility he did. I imagine he looks at every car that goes by. He thinks you called because you're pregnant."

She laughed. The sound was not one of amusement, but rather a sharp release of tension. "What kind of stories have you been telling about me?"

"None. He can't think of any other reason for you trying to track me down. My brother Vaughn knows I'm in trouble because there's no other reason I'd come back. I stalled him when he asked about it and tried convincing him I was here to make peace with my family. He didn't believe me, but he knows something's wrong, that I'm in trouble, and he backed off. If things end up getting tough, if whoever's looking for me finds me, I'll be able to rely on Vaughn. He used to be the best shot in the family."

Standing against a huge maple, Irene rubbed her hands over her face. "This is all a nightmare. Why hide here? Why didn't you go straight to the police? Why don't you?"

"Worthington-America is big business, and I don't have any proof. It's a major corporation for crissakes. Its top executives are always going through the revolving door in Washington, working directly for, or as consultants with Health and Human Services, and for various agencies, in and out of government. Members of its board sit on the boards of other major corporations and universities. They're big time contributors to the Republican and Democratic parties. I start charging them with killing patients and I'm a dead man. Hell, I was almost murdered two nights ago. If I had been asleep instead of fretting half the night, whoever was coming for me would have ended things."

He ran a shaking finger across his throat, rolling his eyes and sticking out his tongue as she did.

Irene laughed and shook her head. "You're not going to find proof here in Canaan."

He nodded. "And how am I going to start looking for proof in Philly without being seen and killed?"

She was quiet for a minute. When she spoke, her voice was soft, a look of deep resignation in her eyes. "You're not."

"I'll stay here for a while and when I can't stand it another minute, I'll find a new place to hide."

"All the time hoping they don't track you down?"

"All the time."

"Doesn't sound like much of a way to live."

In the darkness of the woods, she couldn't see him shrug. "I've made a fair amount of money over the years. If I sell everything I've got I could disappear and live comfortably into my old age."

"Hiding?"

He nodded. "Hiding."

"It still doesn't sound like much of a life."

"Oh, I don't know. I could go to Australia, New Zealand. Maybe I could buy a place on a small Caribbean island. There are lots of lovely places where I could live quietly and safely."

"And what about me? What about our possibilities together? How do they fit in? And what about Worthington-America? You just going to turn your back on what you know? Walk away from it?"

He didn't have an answer. He'd told her on the phone he didn't want her getting involved. Now she was here. Things had happened too fast for him to have studied their implications.

"You've got to fight back," she said.

"How?"

"I don't know, but we'll think of a way."

"We?"

"I'm in this with you. If you're right, these people killed Melinda, along with the others. Do you think I'd stay out it?"

"It's not just Worthington-America now, you understand. I've got problems here in the Old World to deal with too."

She reached for his hand in the darkness, brushing his thigh as she did. "I'm here with you on those too."

He pulled her to him, kissing her. Their hunger amazed them both.

VELMA LOOKED UP from the stove when they returned to the house.

"I put extra butter in the Dinty Moore beef stew to make it taste even better than usual, Uncle Billy Buck."

"What about the pizza I brought home this afternoon? I thought we could heat it up for dinner."

"There ain't much of it for three people, so I cooked up the Dinty Moore to go along with it. You got to be sure to eat right, Uncle Billy Buck."

Buckman's stomach roiled as he forced a smile. "That's nice, Velma." He put his arm around Irene's shoulder. "Velma cooks a mean can of Dinty Moore."

"Sounds wonderful." She smiled broadly at Velma. "Since I'm going to be staying for a while, maybe I can help you with the cooking."

Velma shook her head. "Uncle Billy Buck already said he'd help, but I want to do it myself. You're my company while you're here." She caught herself, gasped lightly, then added, "Mine and Grampy Cal's company is what I mean. As soon as he comes home from his drunk. Did Uncle Billy Buck tell you how Grampy Cal and me had a fight and he went off to get drunk and hasn't come back yet?"

Buckman looked from Velma to Irene. "It's all right. I've told her everything. She knows all about Grampy Cal."

Velma frowned. "Why'd you tell her, Uncle Billy Buck? You won't let me tell nobody, and you tell this stranger all about it." She put down the spoon she'd been using to stir the beef stew, her eyes filling with tears.

"Irene's not a stranger, Velma." He paused, looking from Velma to Irene, throwing Irene a kiss. "She's my girlfriend, so you be nice to her."

Velma smiled, nodding. "I'll be real nice to her, but it still ain't fair that I don't get to tell nobody. Did you tell her I was going to have a baby?"

"I left that for you," he lied.

"I am. I'm going to have a baby, Miss Shoemaker."

"That's wonderful, Velma. And call me Irene. It looks like I'm going to be here for a little while, so maybe I can help you with your pregnancy. We could go into town and get some nice clothes for you, and maybe some things for your baby. Wouldn't you like that?"

"I've never had no new clothes."

Irene touched the girl's shoulder. "They make some really nice ones."

"You won't find much fancy in Canaan," Buckman said.

Irene shushed him with a movement of her hand. "Then we'll just have to go somewhere else. I passed Springfield when I was driving up Route 91. It looked like a pretty big town, and I saw a shopping mall right next to the highway. Velma and I will go down there."

"I never been to Springfield," Velma said. "I been over to Graham a few times, once to the County Fair, but Daddy and Grampy Cal always done their shopping in Canaan Falls. Sometimes they'd let me go with them."

Irene smiled at her. "Then we'll both be going to Springfield for the first time. How's that sound?"

Velma smiled back, her face flushed with excitement by the thought of adventure.

They were finishing dinner when Wilfred's truck pulled into the driveway.

Buckman's brother honked his horn and yelled from the cab as Buckman came out on the porch. "Hey, Billy Buck, hear you got company. That right? That woman you got into trouble come here looking for you?"

"It's my brother," Buckman said to Irene.

"It's my father," Velma told her. She ran to the door and yelled out, "Is Mommy with you?"

"I'm here," Charlotte yelled back.

Buckman groaned. "If Charlotte and Wilfred know you're here, everybody in the Old World's going to know it, if they don't already. Let's hope whoever's looking for me isn't as resourceful as you are."

CHAPTER TWELVE

Bucks County, Pennsylvania \ Sunday, May 5

KOENIG REACHED OVER and shut the alarm off. Sunlight slanted through his window blinds, forming a striped pattern on the wildflower designs of the wallpaper. Stretching with a yawn, he forced himself to a sitting position on the edge of the bed. He'd had his best night's sleep in a long time, dreaming of body surfing in the waves off Long Beach Island on the Jersey Shore. Turning his bedside radio on to the local classical music station, he pulled himself out from under the covers, got up and started exercising to Dvorak's Slavonic Dances.

Half an hour later he was in the shower, hot water stinging his body as he thought of what he'd accomplished the day before. Blanchard had been satisfying. Koenig had fallen asleep last night thinking of the man's eyes staring up at him through the water. He relished the moment Blanchard knew he was dying.

And his last pathetic gesture.

Shooting him the bird like some grade school kid.

Koenig had already begun a poem on the frailty of birds flying through a storm. When it was finished, he'd read it before an audience of university students. He laughed out loud, thinking of how they'd applaud his sensitivity. They would be seeing images of birds struggling against water and wind at the same time he would be remembering Blanchard's terrified eyes and extended forefinger.

God, he loved poetry.

It was a piece of rough luck that he had to let Blanchard's family live. Children bearing the fool's genes had no business cluttering the world, befouling the genetic pool. He'd had to spare them to create the appearance of an accidental drowning. He smiled at the irony of his self-interest interfering with his self-indulgence.

Now he had to take care of Castile and find Buckman.

IT WAS A lovely Sunday morning. He drove with gloved hands along the Delaware in the rental car he'd taken out in the name of Henry Lafferty, using one of his many forged driver's licenses. Looking at the river on one side, the canal on the other, grass just starting to green up along the towpath, he thought how odd it was that so many people liked this part of the country. Buckman's farm was in Upper Black Eddy and Castile lived in Solebury Township. It was pretty enough out here, thick woods, huge old sycamore trees and a few surviving elms, the air heavy with honeysuckle and mock orange, but the area was too manicured, its rich farmlands made over into park-like estates for wealthy New York and Philadelphia exurbanites.

He supposed it had been nice once, when the land had been covered with working farms, before their rambling old fieldstone houses were redesigned and expanded into small manor houses for executive estates. He wondered what the eighteenth century farmers who had struggled to build homes and raise crops here would think of the current state of their land and houses.

Driving past them he had visions of destruction, of flying low in a small plane dropping napalm in crowded swimming pools, of storming the countryside with an AK-47 firing at people who ran screaming from his snarling figure. Laughing, he decided to work on a poem which would save these feelings for him, letting him re-experience the vision as students and professorial readers struggled to render his images in mythic patterns of rebirth and eternal return.

Several years before, an editor at *Poetry* had published an article on Koenig's work in a journal from the University of Michigan, praising the delicacy of a series of five African poems containing the imagery of hunting lions. "A major innovator of ecological poetry," the editor had called him, going on to say, "Christopher Koenig understands the totality of life, its rhythms and images underlying and giving meaning and power to the rhythms and imagery of his unique poetry."

Koenig pasted the article in his scrapbook, on the same page with photographs of the five Black Panthers he had killed years before, while working for a government agency.

He stopped the car, watching a group of fox hunters in full regalia cross the road. Soon he was driving through New Hope, then on north, passing the bridge carrying Route 202 into New Jersey. A few minutes later he crossed into Solebury, and after driving and searching, found Castile's home on Chancellor Road. He pulled off the pavement, parking near the end of Castile's driveway, a long winding gravel lane passing among ancient sycamores.

There was no practical reason for coming here. It was a tease, exciting himself with the foreplay of death. Mozart's Divertimenti filling the car, he stared at the gravel over which Castile drove each day on his way into his office in Philadelphia. He looked at the name on the mailbox. Craning his neck to see through the trees, he could catch glimpses of the house, half hidden in the woods. People lived regulated and orderly lives behind those walls. It must be comfortable. Koenig thought with pleasure of the deregulation and disorder he was about to bring to this little plot of Solebury Township. He sighed and drove off.

Back in New Hope, he stopped at a small restaurant, ordered lunch and a cocktail. After gulping them down, he called Castile.

As soon as the man was on the line, Koenig asked, "You heard about Blanchard?"

"A terrible accident," Castile said. "According to the paper, his daughter found him when she went to skim the pool this morning."

"And if it wasn't an accident?"

"What else could it have been?"

"Suicide. Perhaps he couldn't live with the knowledge of what he was helping us do at the hospital."

"The reports in the papers and on the television said nothing of suicide."

Koenig laughed. "Of course. If he killed himself, and left a note explaining his reasons, you certainly don't expect the police would release it to the press until they had us all in custody."

Castile took a deep breath. "Surely you don't think it's something like that. Blanchard wouldn't betray us."

"I hope not, Castile, but I warned you he was a weak link. An inferior specimen. You never should have brought him in."

"I did what I thought best at the time. What do you think we should do now?"

"We'll just have to sit on it for the time being. I need to see you this evening. Whether or not Blanchard left information implicating us, we should assume he did then go ahead and make plans to ensure there is nothing lying around which can prove any such claims."

"Where do you want to meet?"

Koenig liked the quaver in Castile's voice. He'd have some fun playing this one out. "I'll meet you in New Hope at eleven this evening, at the Canal House."

Castile agreed and Koenig hung up, amazed, as always, at how easy it was to convince people to cooperate fully in the making of their deaths.

AT TEN-FIFTEEN he parked the car in a turnaround along River Road, less than a hundred yards from the intersection with Chancellor Way. Turning the lights off, he stuck a CD of The Marriage of Figaro in the stereo and sat waiting for Castile's car to come down the road. The night was quiet and still, heavy with the odor of honeysuckle.

Two cars and a pickup truck passed heading north. There was no southbound traffic until a car pulled up to the stop sign on Chancellor Way and slowly pulled onto River Road. Koenig got out and stood on the pavement. Once he was sure it was Castile's Jaguar, he stepped into the light, waving his arms. Castile pulled over, rolling down his window.

"What are you doing out here? I thought we were meeting in town."

Koenig gave him the closest thing he could muster to a sheepish grin. "I changed my mind. We need more privacy than we'd have in the Canal

House. Leave your car here and come with me. We'll ride and talk."

Once in Koenig's car, Castile started to light a cigarette.

Koenig grabbed it from his mouth, throwing it out the window. "No smoking in my car. If I wanted the stink of smoke in here, I'd have a cigar."

Castile shrugged and put his lighter back in his pants pocket. "I've been listening to the news all day. There's still nothing about Blanchard leaving a note or anything of the kind. I think the operation's safe."

"Nothing about it's safe, given Blanchard's involvement. It's best for us that he's dead."

Castile didn't answer. Koenig knew he was weighing his comment about the advantage of Blanchard's death, perhaps beginning to wonder vaguely if it was an accident, a suicide, or if Koenig had something to do with it. The idea would begin gnawing at the back of his mind. He'd shuck it off, but it would come back, chewing harder, steadier. All Koenig had to do was feed it a little at a time, sit back, drive, and watch the fun.

"It's just the two of us now, Castile. Nobody else knows a thing."

"There's Buckman. Buckman knows." Castile spoke quickly, a quaver beginning to edge into his voice.

"Buckman knows nothing. All he has are his suspicions. He may have ideas, but ideas prove nothing. He has no evidence. Nothing he can go to the police with. That doesn't mean he's not a problem. He is, but we don't need to worry about him right now. I'll find him when the time's right and take care of him."

They rode in silence along the Delaware. After several minutes, Castile spoke again, his voice almost squeaking with tension during the first word or two. Koenig was pleased by the sound.

"Where are we going?"

"To Buckman's farm. I didn't get a chance to look it over thoroughly the other night. Maybe we'll find something that'll give us an idea of where he's gone."

Neither of them spoke much during the twelve mile drive to Creamery Road in Upper Black Eddy. They had stopped at the end of Buckman's driveway to empty the mailbox when Koenig reached over, putting his hand on Castile's shoulder.

"Penny for your thoughts."

Castile started, then forced a laugh. He didn't want Koenig to know his thoughts. Didn't want him to know how much of a liability he'd realized he was to the killer. If Koenig hadn't started thinking in such terms, Castile certainly didn't want to get him started.

He tried changing the subject. "You think there's any chance Buckman will be here?"

Koenig shook his head. "None. I'm positive he's in hiding. This is a safe place for us to talk while we look for leads to where he's gone."

Once inside, Koenig turned on the lights. He read through the mail they had brought in. Nothing. He looked through Buckman's desk, telling Castile to check out the bedroom. Might as well get a little work out of him before finishing him off. He was teasing himself as much as Castile. Building anticipation to increase the delight of the kill.

The desk was a dead end. Bills, checks, medical journals, and brochures from drug companies. Nothing pointing to where Buckman might be. Castile came down the stairs just as Koenig began rummaging through a stack of mail Buckman had left piled on the dining room table.

"Nothing up there. I looked in his bedroom, the bathroom, all over. Nothing."

"Look through the stuff piled up on the kitchen counter." Koenig continued sorting through the mail.

Castile sat at the kitchen table, a pile of magazines and papers in front of him. The house seemed quiet, empty. There was a frying pan with congealed grease on the stove, a cup of cold coffee on the table beside him, mold already forming on its greasy surface. In the next room he could hear the rustling of papers as Koenig paged through them, looking for anything that might give him an idea of where Buckman could be.

He wished hadn't agreed to meet Koenig. He wished he'd never met Koenig. Ever. He wished he'd never thought of the idea of killing patients.

It seemed like a good idea, sound, profitable for the corporation. He hadn't counted on having to deal with a person like Koenig. In the abstract, during the planning stages, he'd imagined no trouble. But then Koenig appeared, a flesh and blood human being, capable of killing other human beings with as much equanimity as Castile balanced books and made deals. Suddenly, the bottom line was no longer profits and the well-being of Worthington-America.

Bottom line, Castile was frightened. Terrified. What if Blanchard's death hadn't been an accident? Or a suicide? Could Koenig have killed him? No, not could, did he? Of course, he could have. Koenig could kill anybody. He'd killed that little girl in the hospital, hadn't he? And all those other people. He could easily have killed somebody he disliked as much as he disliked Blanchard.

The question was, did Koenig kill him? And what were his plans? For Buckman? For the operation? For Castile?

The plans for Buckman were clear. Koenig would find him and kill him. There was only one way to find out his plans for the operation. Ask.

"What are you going to do about our deal?"

Koenig came into the kitchen. Crossing to the stove, he took off his right glove, picked a knife from the magnetized holder on the wall, running his thumb across the sharpened blade as he leaned against the counter.

"The deal's too risky," he said. "Buckman's on to it. He's on to you. He still doesn't know jack shit about me. Did you find anything helpful in here?"

Castile shook his head. Small tics of nausea rippling through his stomach, he looked at the clock on the wall. It was after one.

"I'd better be getting home," he said. "Gloria will start to worry."

"What should she have to worry about? You went out for a business meeting. Does she always worry about you at business meetings?"

"I don't usually have them at eleven on a Sunday night."

Koenig nodded. "Afraid she'll think you're out with another woman?"

Castile gave him a weak laugh. "I've never given her any reason to suspect that. I've been faithful to her since we were married."

"You're such a nice man, Donald." Koenig's tone was sing-song and mocking. He pushed himself away from the counter and came over to the table, standing behind Castile. He was quiet for a few moments, then spoke again.

"So, why would Gloria be worried?"

Castile shrugged.

"She doesn't know anything?"

"About this? Christ no. Nobody knows except you, Blanchard, and me. You and me, now." His intestine rumbled. "And Buckman, I suppose."

Koenig patted his back. "Then I don't understand why she'd be worried. You don't fool around with other women, and she doesn't know anything about what we've been doing at Worthington-Philadelphia. I'll be damned if I can see what she has to worry about."

He walked around Castile and sat at the table, still running his finger across the knife blade.

"Maybe you're the one who's worried." He smiled widely. Castile thought Koenig's teeth looked as though they had been filed to fine, sharp points. He blinked his eyes and the imaged faded.

"What would I have to worry about?"

"Me. Maybe you've been thinking I killed Blanchard."

Castile gave him another weak laugh. "Why would I think something as ridiculous as that?"

Koenig was still smiling. "It would be a logical conclusion because it would be a logical thing for me to do. Buckman stumbles on to what we're doing and we're suddenly in danger of being exposed, with an idiot like Blanchard being the weakest part of our structure. Why wouldn't I kill him?"

Castile shook his head. "Because he was one of us. He was part of the operation. Now, I've really got to be getting home."

Koenig swished the knife through the air. "Blanchard was not one of us. I am not one of us. Blanchard was one of you. A group of two. I am not part of anything you and he might belong to. When I wish to work, I work independently. I form no associations with those who hire my services.

Blanchard was always a liability. He became a threat and I killed him. I drowned him in his pool. I held his head under water and forced him to watch me, to stare at my face as he died."

"You didn't." Castile's words choked in his throat.

"I did." Koenig nodded; his smile wider than before. "Why would I lie to you about such a thing? What would I have to gain?"

Castile stood up, the room swimming. For a minute he thought he was going to fall. Then he felt as though he was about to throw up.

"I must get home."

Koenig shook his head.

Castile headed for the door.

Koenig blocked him.

"Please," Castile said.

"Please what?"

"Please don't."

Koenig laughed. "Please don't what?"

Tears welled up in Castile's eyes and ran down his cheeks. His breath was hurried, his heart pounding in his chest like one of his horses kicking against the side of its stall, pounding as though it wanted to burst free of him.

"Please don't kill me. Please." He could barely choke out the words.

Shaking his head, Koenig continued smiling. "Sorry, Castile. You're as much of a liability as Blanchard was."

Castile screamed another plea as he ran toward the kitchen door. Koenig caught him easily, grabbing his left shoulder and spinning him around. Castile's yells grew louder. Koenig slapped him across the face with the flat side of the knife, then drew the edge of the blade across his cheek, cutting a thin two inch gash.

"We're way out in the country, Castile. I'm the only person who's going to hear your screaming, and it really annoys me. Shut up and you might live another five minutes. Piss me off with your screaming and you're dead right now."

Trembling, fighting to control his bowels, Castile breathed heavily, quickly, trying to focus on Koenig's face through tear splotched eyes.

He tried reasoning with Koenig, unable to suppress the panic in his voice. "When the police find my body, they'll think it's too much of a coincidence that Blanchard and I both died so close to one another, especially when it's obvious I was murdered with a knife. That'll make them question Blanchard's suicide, you know."

"They won't find you for a long time. Buckman lived alone. I'm going to put your body in the basement and lock up the house. Who comes here? He doesn't have any family. He stays at the hospital, or his apartment in Philadelphia more often than he does here. When they do come looking for him, they might find you and they might not. If they do, they'll probably figure Buckman killed you and ran off somewhere. If they do find him, he'll be facing a murder charge. One he'll probably have trouble defeating."

Castile tried pleading, blood from the cut on his cheek running down his chin, over his lips. He wiped it away with the back of his hand, but the stream kept coming, dripping off his chin onto the front of his shirt.

"Please don't kill me. This whole operation was my idea. It would be insane for me to turn you in. I'd have to turn myself in at the same time. Please, Koenig. I've got a family. Friends. So much I want to live for. Please."

"But I want to kill you, Castile. You're a liability to me. You contribute nothing to the earth. You contribute nothing to the human condition. You're simply another form of pollution. Human pollution."

He tried to escape. Twisting out of Koenig's grip, he ran again for the back door. He tripped over a chair and fell, sprawled across the kitchen floor. As he began pushing himself upright, Koenig stepped on his right hand, breaking several fingers.

He tried crying. Lying flat on the floor, tears ran down his cheeks, his body racked by deep, heavy sobs. Gasping for air between the wrenching sounds exploding from his chest, he turned over, looking up at the blurred Koenig who knelt beside him, dish towel in his hands, he started drying Castile's eyes.

"There, there, Castile. Don't cry. Just relax. Everything will be fine. Do you hear? Everything will be just fine."

Castile took the towel in his left hand and daubed his eyes, listening to the soothing tones of Koenig's voice, relief washing over him as he pulled himself to a sitting position. He didn't know why, but Koenig had changed his mind and was trying to make him feel better, relaxed. Or maybe it had all been a test, Koenig trying to find out how Castile would do in a pinch. That had to be it. A test. Thank god. In half an hour he could be home in his own bed, the whole evening nothing more than a nightmare.

"Thank you." He smiled, wiping the tears from his cheeks, he blew his nose.

When his eyes cleared, he looked up at Koenig who was smiling back at him.

"Feeling better, Donald?"

Castile nodded, breathing deeply as he fought to regain his composure. "I'm going to be all right. I acted like a baby. You were testing me, and I blew my cool and fell completely to pieces. I'm sorry. It won't happen again. I'm all right now."

"Good. A man shouldn't die without his cool."

Grabbing Castile's hair, Koenig pulled his head back and sliced his throat, evenly and quickly. Castile blinked, moving his lips in silent words, flecks of small bubbles forming at the edges of his mouth as Koenig let him slip backward toward the blue linoleum floor.

"Sorry," Koenig said. "I can't hear you. That's the nice thing about slitting a man's throat, you can watch him die, knowing he's looking straight at you, and he can't even tell you what a son-of-a-bitch he thinks you are for killing him. That's why I wanted your eyes dry and free of tears. It would have ruined the moment if you hadn't been able to see me."

He went to the refrigerator, poured himself a glass of cold seltzer water, then came back and stood over Castile.

"If it's any consolation to you, I'll write a poem immortalizing your death. Not that anybody other than I will understand it, but it'll be about you, nevertheless."

Standing over the dying body, Koenig watched the man's neck, looked at the blood pouring from the wound. He knelt, touching his finger to its warmth. Holding it up, he moved it around, letting the blood catch and reflect the light.

Why not just a taste? Lick it off the finger? What would be the harm? He brought it close to his mouth, then quickly jerked it away, wiping the blood on a paper towel.

Castile was still alive, his body jerking, struggling for breath, when Koenig put his right glove back on and grabbed his feet, dragging him down the cellar stairs. He was dead by the time he reached the basement floor.

After taking Castile's keys and wallet, he stuffed the body behind the oil burner. Back upstairs he went through the house again, still searching for clues as to where Buckman had gone. Finding nothing, he cleaned up the kitchen and removed all traces of his presence from the rest of the house, turned off the lights and left, locking the door behind him.

It had been a frustrating evening, as far as finding clues to Buckman's whereabouts. Nothing in the house had told him anything about Buckman, except that he was a doctor, given the alumni publications from Jefferson, and what his current tastes and avocations were. He played golf, there were several golf magazines and an expensive set of clubs in the garage. He liked to dine out, evident from the number of credit card stubs and billing sheets Koenig found in his desk. He read good literature. The library off the living room was filled with first editions of major American writers, from the present back to the Colonial period. And they were obviously read. A first edition of Moby Dick, a bookmark in it, sat on a table beside a chair. There was even a first edition of Koenig's second collection of poetry.

But there was nothing anywhere in the house giving him the slightest idea of Buckman's past. It was as though he materialized at Princeton University as a graduate student. He drove down the River Road toward New Hope. When he reached Castile's Jaguar, he pulled in next to it, checked the rental car to be sure he hadn't forgotten anything, then left it parked in the turnaround and drove the Jaguar back to Philadelphia.

He parked in the hospital lot next to his own car. When Castile's family reported him missing and his car turned up at Worthington Philadelphia no one would think to look for him at Buckman's house in Upper Black Eddy, or anywhere else in Bucks County.

Back at his apartment he stayed up until dawn writing poetry, so absorbed in meters and images that a vague unease about the night's activities never fully surfaced. It played around below his consciousness, and later, when he finally went to sleep, it plagued his dreams. He saw Blanchard looking through the water at him, only in the dream Blanchard was laughing, not Koenig. He felt his fingers tightening against Blanchard's face, pushing, digging into the skin. Still Blanchard laughed. He could hear it bubbling to the surface, filling his ears, loud and taunting as each bubble burst.

When he awoke, the dream was gone, but the unease remained. He'd never felt like this before. Things were wrong. Coming apart?

CHAPTER THIRTEEN

Canaan, Massachusetts \ Sunday, May 5

WITH IRENE'S CAR concealed in the barn, Buckman and Irene spent the morning walking around the farm as he filled her in on the details of his childhood, explaining the complicated family structures of the Old World, where the taboos most people lived by did not apply. They explored the woods and fields, the outbuildings Calvin had ignored over the years, sills rotting, roofs with missing shingles, in places bare rafters open to the weather.

He took her to the caves, the brook, the sliding falls, and his old trout pools. Twenty-five years after fishing the area with his brothers, he still could find them, still feel the old thrill as he saw trout in the dark waters, resting by rocks and fallen trees whose sunken branches provided sanctuary where they lurked, waiting for their insect prey to fly close enough to the surface for them to leap and devour.

Sunlight edged its way between the steep hills and thick trees, turning the maple blossoms a bright, translucent yellow green, their delicacy highlighting a cardinal perched near the brook. His song carried through the air with the sweetness of the blossoms.

"It's lovely here." Irene reached for his hand as she spoke, giving it a squeeze.

Buckman nodded, squeezing back. It was lovely. He'd forgotten how lovely, remembering only the horrors he, his sisters and brothers had suffered at Calvin's hands, the dark, shadowy secrets children from the Old World were always hiding from their teachers and classmates in the Canaan schools.

He pointed to a patch of new growth beside a clump of mountain laurel. "There's a jack-in-the-pulpit."

Irene knelt. Reaching for the plant, she ran her thumb and forefingers along its fresh new leaves. "It's lovely here and the season is so far behind ours in Philly that it's like getting a second spring."

Buckman looked at the spring leaves, the small plants pushing through the dark forest floor. He smiled. It was beautiful, the spring woods lacy and warm, yet holding patches of gravelly snow hidden behind boulders and in the gnarled hollows at the bases of the largest tree trunks. He ached with the bittersweet longing the Old World had raised in rare dreams, a longing he successfully buried during the days, and most of the nights, of his years in exile.

To the west, the hills at the edges of the river valley rose toward the Berkshires, where spring came even later than in these fertile lowlands, only to slowly laze into the short summer, where fall came early and ended sharply in the fierce winters. Western Massachusetts was not easy country in which to live. Many years people kept fires burning in their wood stoves well into June, and often had them stoked again by the end of August, when sudden frosts could wither tomatoes, tinging meadows with brown tipped plants.

As a boy he believed the harsh climate had twisted the lives of those who lived here. In fleeing twenty-five years before, he had left the land as much as he had left the people. In college and medical school, his studies had showed him Canaan had no monopoly on incest and abuse. Now he knew these deep hills and hollows, the gorge separating them from the rest of Canaan, had attracted the people, promising a haven from the prying eyes of those who would condemn them for their ways of living. The knowledge changed his vision of the land, softened it. It was in no way a place where he would choose to live, even without its people, but it seemed less dark, less ominous.

Leading Irene back down to the farm, he took her to the edge of the cornfield where Calvin was buried. Standing in the grass, the toe of his left boot jutting into the plowed earth, playing with a clod, he broke up the dirt. Smoothing it over the ground, he nodded toward the corner of the field.

"That's where I buried him."

Irene stood silently beside him, her eyes following the straight furrows he had made with Calvin's old Ford tractor. Three large crows circled down, landing in the middle of the field, picking at the seed corn he'd planted.

"When we were kids we'd shoot them with our twenty-twos. Calvin gave us each one on our tenth birthdays. Told us it was our first test of being a man, to go out and shoot crows in the cornfield. After we'd killed them, he'd make us pick them up and hang the bodies from poles scattered around the field. Said it was the best kind of scarecrow there was. He'd leave them there until they rotted away and fell off."

"Did it work, keep the crows away?"

Buckman shrugged. "Who knows how many crows would've been around if we hadn't done it. It didn't matter. Calvin said shoot crows. We shot crows. Calvin said hang them in the field to keep other crows away. We hung the crows. Calvin said it worked. It worked. We didn't argue or ask questions unless we wanted the belt buckle on Judgment Saturday."

"You call him Calvin. Never dad, or father, even."

Buckman looked out over the field, his eyes resting at the corner where Calvin's body lay. "Calvin says it all."

Stooping down, Irene picked up a small clod, crushing it in her hand and letting the dry soil run out, back into the field. "It was that bad when you were a kid?"

Buckman grunted.

"You don't want to talk about it."

He looked at the dark spot in the field from which she had taken the dirt. "I don't want to talk about it. Not now, anyway."

"Then later. But sometime. You've got to talk about it sometime. You've kept it bottled up too long."

He shrugged and Irene rubbed her hand over her face. After a quiet moment she smiled at him.

"Hey, how about them Phillies?"

He looked at her, trying to make sense of the remark, his eyebrows raised in puzzlement.

She tapped him lightly on the upper arm with her fist. "Them Phillies, Bill.

You know. The baseball team. Isn't that the kind of thing guys say to each other when they don't want to talk about personal things? Hey, how about them Phillies? Eagles should have a good season. Hey, howzit hangin,' buddy? You know, guy talk."

Laughing, he reached around her, pulling her close.

"I think it was a mistake for you to come, but I'm glad you're here."

THE VIST FROM Vaughn the day before had been both difficult and pleasant. The old feelings between the two brothers had made them immediately easy with one another, yet little they had to say had bearing on the present. Buckman would not reveal himself. Vaughn tried getting him to open up. He asked questions, rephrased them, and tried again when Buckman gave evasive answers, and repeated them again. It was clear to Vaughan that his brother was in trouble. There was no other reason for his sudden return.

"I know you're in trouble, Billy Buck," Vaughn had said. "I'm ready to help you. All you've got to do it let me know what's going on and what to do."

Buckman had hugged his brother. "No trouble, Vaughn. Just a long overdue visit."

"Well Pa sure is giving you a warm welcome, going off and getting drunk again. Any sign of him yet?"

Buckman shook his head.

"He's a mean bastard. Always was." Vaughn had said.

Buckman nodded silently and that was the end of their discussion of Calvin.

After a few more beers Vaughn left, making Buckman promise to come to him if there was any trouble, Vaughan reached out and clasped Buckman's shoulder. "You're my brother, Billy Buck, the best of us. I'll do anything to help you when you need me."

Later that day, a visit from Wilfred and Charlotte had been difficult, unpleasant. They sat in the kitchen with Buckman, Irene and Velma, Wilfred staring at Irene in the shadowy room, looking for traces of pregnancy. When

Buckman went to get a glass of water, Wilfred followed him to the sink, talking just loudly enough for the women at the table to hear.

"You're going have your hands full, Billy Buck, what with both these broads knocked up."

Buckman was still thinking of a response when Irene stood up and came over to the sink. She stood on her toes to look Wilfred straight in the eyes.

"Moose, I'm sure you don't mind me calling you Moose. You're probably proud of the name, although why a man would want to be nicknamed after such an ugly and stupid animal is beyond me. Moose, I'm not a broad and I'm not pregnant. I am a good friend of Bill's, and I came up here to spend some time with him, maybe get to know some of his family, which hasn't proved to be an easy or especially pleasant chore. Now, Moose, if you're so damned interested in pregnancy, I suggest you do something to help your daughter here."

"She's Calvin's problem, not mine," Wilfred said. "And Billy Buck's too, seeing as how he's come home to live with the old man. Right Billy Buck?"

Then he went to the refrigerator and took a beer. Grabbing Charlotte's arm, he turned to Buckman as he spoke. "It's time to get the fuck out of here. Billy Buck's got himself a girlfriend as uppity as he is."

AT THE SAME time Koenig was parked at the end of Castile's driveway teasing himself with murderous fantasies, Buckman stood at the edge of the field, holding Irene close and thinking of the visits from his two brothers, one drunk but well meaning, the other mean and ill intended. He was in deep shit if he needed their help.

They were still walking along the edge of the field, headed toward the house, when a car pulled into the driveway and stopped by the back porch. The man driving got out and walked toward the door. He saw Buckman and Irene, waved, and turned, coming toward them.

"Who's that?" Irene asked.

"No idea, but it's too late to run and hide."

They met at the lower edge of the cornfield. The man was tall and thin, his clean shaven face ending in a sharp, ax shaped chin. Thick black hair stuck out from under a low flat topped hat with a wide brim. He wore a black suit and a red, regimental striped tie.

He held out his hand to Buckman. Smiling at Irene, he spoke with an accent more like that of eastern New England, Maine, and New Hampshire, than that common to many of the people in western New England.

"Good afternoon. By God, you must be Calvin's son Bill. Your brother Wilfred told me about you. My name's Dye, Reverend J. Erskine Dye, pastor of the Canaan Forks Missionary Alliance." He used the formal but rarely spoken name for the Old World.

"Bill Buckman. This is my friend, Irene Shoemaker. In all the time I was growing up here, I can barely recall hearing folks calling this godforsaken place Canaan Forks, except maybe in the newspaper, something like that."

"God doesn't forsake anyplace," Erskine Dye said, still smiling at Irene, shaking his head as he did. "Down at the church we don't much care for calling this area the Old World. It's got evil connotations we'd just as soon forget about. We call it Canaan Forks, and we call the church the Canaan Forks Missionary Alliance."

As he spoke, Erskine Dye kept looking at Irene. His eyes were pale blue, the whites clear as an untouched piece of paper, as empty of feeling as any she had ever seen, except, perhaps, for the man who had come to her house looking for Buckman.

He turned to Buckman abruptly, the smile disappearing. Buckman was sure it was one he used on women only. "Where's Calvin? I didn't see him in church today. Not him, or Velma. Why is that?"

Buckman shrugged. "I haven't seen my father since the day after I got here."

"Drunk again." Dye shrugged as he said it. "I suspected as much. What about Velma? Why didn't she come?"

"I suppose she's overwhelmed by having company."

Dye narrowed his eyes. "I hear from her father and mother that she's got herself in a family way."

Buckman stared at him without answering.

Erskine Dye shook his head, pushing his face into a parody of sorrow. "By God, there's just so much sin in this evil old world that God has charged us with cleansing. The girl's got herself pregnant by her own grandfather. No wonder the poor old man's gone off on another one of his drunks. He's been lonely since your mother died, his life empty of comfort and joy, and this young girl comes along and takes advantage of him. Well, I've come to pray for her and to see if I can give him some ease."

He patted Buckman on the shoulder and walked on ahead. Mounting the porch, he opened the back door.

"Velma," he cried, his deep voice resonating in the kitchen. "It's Reverend Dye, Velma. I've come to talk with you."

"You can't turn him loose on that child," Irene said. "For chrissakes, Bill, do something."

Buckman sped up, reaching the porch before the screen door had swung fully shut. Erskine Dye stood in the kitchen, his hat still on. Velma was nowhere around.

Buckman cleared his throat. "This isn't the best time for you to see Velma, Reverend Dye."

Dye swerved around, his eyes wide with anger. "Not the best time? It certainly isn't the best time. The best time would have been before she got herself in a family way. But this is the time the Lord has chosen for me to see her. This is the time when I'm here, and I'm going to talk to that girl. Pray with her. I'll thank you to leave to me any judgments on what's the best thing to do and the best time to do it."

By the time he finished, Erskine Dye's voice was barking as he snapped words at Buckman.

"And I'll thank you for leaving us alone, Reverend." Buckman nearly spat the preacher's title. He put his hand on Dye's shoulder and tried turning him toward the door. He might as well have tried moving a boulder from the sliding falls.

Ignoring him, Dye called Velma's name again.

"Stop it right now. I want that child left alone." Irene was standing by the table, her face red with anger.

Erskine Dye smiled his smile. "Now, Miss Shoemaker, surely you don't want Velma to be left without religious counsel today. After all, it is Sunday, the Lord's Day. By God, it wouldn't be appropriate for the child to continue in uncounseled sin."

"It's Ms. Shoemaker, Mr. Dye, and yes, I want her to go without your counsel today." Irene placed herself between Dye and the door from the kitchen to the rest of the house.

His smile widening, Erskine Dye's voice almost sounded as if he were chuckling. He shook his head. "No, no, no, no, Miss Shoemaker. You can't mean what you're saying. Velma needs me. If something should happen to her and she was unredeemed, Satan would claim her as his own, and as sure as God sent me to redeem her, Satan will make her his own if he can. Now, I suggest you get out of my way."

His smile suddenly disappeared. He placed his hands on Irene's shoulders and moved her aside.

"Velma, it's Reverend Dye. I'm coming upstairs to find you. You need to pray with me, child. You need to ask God's forgiveness for what you've done to your grandfather and to yourself."

Buckman grabbed his arm, swinging the Reverend J. Erskine Dye around.

"Get out of here, Reverend. Now."

Dye shook him off and moved again toward the door to the parlor. This time Buckman grabbed him with both hands, pulling him back into the kitchen, forcing him toward the back door and out onto the porch.

His eyes wide, their pale blue a piercing cold, Erskine Dye pulled away from Buckman. Straightening his coat, he leaned toward him, nearly whispering his warning.

"Don't ever touch me again, Buckman. I may be a man of the cloth, but by God, I'm a mean son-of-a-bitch when you cross me. For your father's sake, I'm leaving, but this household is part of my mission and I'm not abandoning those who live here and need me. Calvin is a member of my congregation and

Velma is too. Her sin and his weakness have called me here today and they will keep calling me back until I have fulfilled the Lord's will. If you keep on trying to stop me, you won't be the first sorry bastard to get in my way, and you won't be the first to regret it. Jesus may be the way, the light, and the resurrection, but Erskine Dye is the vehicle by which you get to Jesus. And you know what happens to someone who stands in the way of a running vehicle. Especially a locomotive and by God, let me tell you, Buckman, I'm a locomotive for Christ. I run on His tracks and my whistle sings His song. You be careful of crossing in front of me. Understand?"

He backed down the steps and moved through the shadows of the trees to his car. Irene had come out on the porch and was standing next to Buckman, watching Dye as he prepared to leave. Just before he got in the car, he smiled again at Irene.

"Shoemaker? You wouldn't be of the Hebrew persuasion, would you? Some of the good Christian members of my congregation would be offended if they knew someone of the Hebrew kind was staying in poor old Calvin's home. Jesus himself would be offended, don't you think?"

He shut the car door, started the engine, and backed around by the garage. He was halfway out the drive when Velma joined them on the porch.

"The Reverend scares me something bad awful," she said.

Irene nodded.

"He just threatened us," Buckman said. "It probably wouldn't hold up against him in court., but I don't doubt what he meant."

"Me neither," Irene said. "That man is almost as much a danger as whoever's doing the killing back at Worthington-Philadelphia."

Buckman forced a laugh. "He's smart, and he talks a lot, and he talks in full paragraphs, but he's a bullshitter like all preachers, and priests, all so-called holy men, and bullshitters can be scary. Rasputin, Franklin Graham, the Puritan ministers who burned women they believed were witches, all preachers, all smart, all bullshitters, all dangerous, all scary."

Velma said, "He's scary, but he ain't dangerous. He scares me that I'm going to go to hell. He's a reverend. Reverends look after your soul and make sure you don't get into the Devil's hands. It's the Devil who's dangerous, not the reverends."

Irene smiled at her. "Sometimes it's hard to tell the difference."

Velma frowned, her face scrunched in confusion. "Sure you can. The Devil's got horns and a tail, with feet like a goat and there's hair all over him and he's the bad one who eats little babies alive and tortures people forever if they done something wicked to their parents. Reverend says he throws them into burning lakes of shit that he's got down in Hell waiting for bad people. The Reverend's just a man, but he's holy, and he knows what's right from what's wrong and I'm scared of him because he can look into my heart and see I killed Grampy Calvin. And if he knows, he'll let the Devil get me and keep me forever because doing something wicked to your grandparents is just as bad as doing something wicked to your parents and killing Grampy Calvin was a wicked thing to do, even if it was an accident."

Buckman looked at her as sternly as he could. "The only way Erskine Dye is going to know about Grampy Calvin is if you tell him."

"Then you'd better not let him pray with me, Uncle Billy Buck. He prays so hard that he gets other people praying even harder and they tell him everything bad they done so he'll beg Jesus to forgive them. He says Jesus can't forgive you unless he knows what it is bad that you done, and Jesus can't know unless you tell Reverend Dye so he can let Jesus know all about it and talk Jesus into forgiving you. If he gets me praying with him, I'll have to tell him all about Grampy Calvin, you know?"

Buckman looked at Irene, then back to Velma. "We'll just have to be sure the good Reverend doesn't get alone with you long enough to start praying."

Velma nodded, looking at him with relief.

THE COT WAS godawful. Irene lay in it for twenty minutes before deciding there was no chance of sleep if she stayed there. She got up, wrapped a blanket around her and walked across the hall into Buckman's room.

"I don't think much of your guest quarters."

He was lying in a double bed, reading a copy of *The New England Journal of*

Medicine. It was one of several magazines and journals he'd stuffed in his suitcase before leaving Upper Black Eddy.

Putting it down on his chest, he smiled at her. "I didn't want to be too forward and suggest you sleep with me."

"So, you put me in the world's worst bed and waited for me to suggest it?"

"Are you suggesting it?"

"You could be the perfect host and sleep there yourself, giving this bed to me. I'd say it looks pretty comfortable, judging from the way you're lying there reading."

"It's all right. Mother always called this the guest room. We never had any guests though, unless you count Calvin's buddies sleeping off a heavy drunk before going home." He looked at the wall for a moment, then continued. "Mostly it got used when Calvin cornered one of my sisters. Mother called it a guest room out of self-defense."

"She must have been a sad woman."

"She was. I used to wonder why she stayed with him. Why she married him in the first place. It wasn't until years later I realized she didn't have any choice. Back then, it was the Old World Way. You got married to whoever was close and convenient at the time and you stayed with them because you didn't know anything else. It's just the way everybody did it and there wasn't any questioning of the way things were. My guess is that it's pretty much the same way. The history of the old world is a story of people who don't know any better and they do worse."

Sitting on the bed, she took his hand. "So, are you going to be the perfect host?"

"I would be, if I knew what being the perfect host meant."

She dropped his hand, stood up, and letting the blanket fall to the floor, slipped into bed beside him. "You waited too long. I'll have to force the issue. I'm sleeping here."

"Where am I going to sleep?"

"That's up to you, doc."

He rolled over, facing her. With his right hand he stroked her face, holding her right hand in his left one.

"If it's up to me, I think I'll stay right here."

"Okay by me." She smiled and pulled close, pressing her lips to his. "Only let's go slow, very slow. It's been such a long time."

"For me too," he said, touching her lips with his tongue.

CHAPTER FOURTEEN

Philadelphia, Pennsylvania \ Monday, May 6

DRINKING HIS MORNING coffee, Koenig read through the poems he'd written the night before. They were first drafts, several of them rough, some of them almost perfect. Almost. A few were weak, candidates for the trash can, but it had been a good night's work, a substantial start on a new book the editors at Yale University Press had been asking him to send them.

Several years earlier, his agent had suggested he approach one of the quality commercial houses with his work. Koenig refused. The commercial houses, he believed, even the best of them, still published for a general audience. Koenig wrote for what he considered an academically respectable audience, people who read the specialized journals and haunted the corridors of university English departments, professors who taught in Master of Fine Arts programs and their students.

Nobody but Koenig, and perhaps a rare one or two of his victims, would understand the primary level of meaning in his work. Most people wouldn't understand the secondary level. To do so required a sophisticated audience, educated people who would appreciate his use of mythic ritual, his brilliant interplay of imagery reflecting the elite cultures of both the Asian and European traditions in literature. A general audience could never understand or appreciate what he did and even attempting to reach them would be a waste of time and effort. Publication by anything other than a university press would denigrate his work.

He placed the poems in three piles. Those which were nearly ready for submission, once he made a few revisions; those which needed extensive revision, and those which were to be thrown away.

The first pile was the largest. The major revision pile contained half a dozen, some needing only a line or two of work, some needing total rethinking. There were only three in the discard pile. He burned the rejects, starting with the dangerous piece, "The Castle Dungeon." It wasn't a bad poem, but the title and imagery pointed too closely to the facts of Donald Castile's death. Koenig liked balancing on the narrow edge, but he wasn't a fool.

Until a few years ago, he had never thrown any of his work away, thinking future graduate students would find everything he'd written indispensable to doing their doctoral dissertations on the work of Christopher Koenig. When he realized how important it was to control one's image, to ensure he would be seen only in the most favorable light, he went through everything he had ever written, keeping only the work by which he wanted others to judge him.

At nine a.m. he stopped, put the remaining poetry away and began planning the search for Buckman. He'd start with his office. If he didn't find anything there, he'd go back to the Shoemaker woman's place and put more pressure on her. This time she wouldn't catch him off guard with her intellectual pretensions.

First, he took a shower. Standing in the hot water, his arms raised in the air, he decided once Buckman was dead, and the Shoemaker woman as well--she had seen him too closely when he came around asking about Buckman, and besides, she had engaged his interest, a fatal mistake--once they were both dead, he would try retirement again. Oh, he'd kill, certainly, but only for the sheer pleasure of the hunt and its bloody finale, perhaps even finally allowing himself the indulgence of tasting blood.

That was for the future. For the first few months, perhaps even the first year, he would concentrate on his poetry. He had enough material to last a lifetime, and if things did run thin, there would always be inspiration from the recreational kills. He smiled at the thought of killing for the joy of it, free of commercial taint.

He didn't allow himself to think of the last time he had tried retiring, how desperate he had felt prowling the streets for random victims. He didn't allow himself to think of the paperback vampire image of himself he'd carried in the back of his mind as he stepped into shadowed alleyways, following lonely people through the nights as they led him to their deaths. There was no point in allowing such thoughts to contaminate this new decision.

They were irrelevant.

This time he would do things correctly. While the poetry would dominate, the kills would also be works of art. They would be done with style and grace, in the proper frame of mind for a respected poet seeking new and fresh images and ideas.

He certainly needed a fresh start.

The whole Worthington-America thing had thrown him off balance. He'd probably even botched the Blanchard kill. The more he thought about it, the surer he was that he'd left bruises around head and face when the fool struggled, trying to surface for air. The police will know it wasn't an accident. He should have killed the entire family. He still could. Go back later and finish them. It would serve Blanchard right to be the cause of their deaths.

Silently he cursed himself. It wasn't like him to be so careless. He should be at the peak of his powers. In both professions. Still, there was nothing about the kill which could point to him. That he was sure of. He wasn't that far gone.

Getting out of the shower, he dried himself and crossed to the shaving mirror. Its surface was thick with steam, obscuring his image. He wiped the glass with the towel, but the heavy steam in the room clouded it immediately. The shave would have to wait until it cleared. He wasn't about to risk nicking himself.

BUCKMAN'S OFFICE WAS as much a dead end as the house had been. Koenig studied the diplomas on the wall. If he could get access to records at Princeton or Jefferson, he might find something in Buckman's background that would give him a clue as to where he'd gone to ground. It wouldn't be a difficult thing to do, given his knowledge of the workings of university records systems and how to get around the second rate bureaucrats who ran them.

Still, it would be a long shot, hardly worth the visibility trying to get his hands on the records would require. There was too much of a chance that someone on a university campus would recognize him and wonder why a poet of his stature would be prowling through the files of a doctor who would shortly be declared missing, and who, if things worked right for Koenig, would soon be dead.

Looking through the office was more frustrating than the search of Buckman's house had been. There was nothing he could use. He'd have to go after the Shoemaker woman again. That was fine with him. She had to be killed anyway. He might as well do it now, work off stress from the frustration of trying to find Buckman had been causing him.

THERE WAS NO answer to his knock on her door. Sunday's and Monday's newspapers sat on the porch and mail was still in the box. Checking to see if anyone was watching, Koenig put on a pair of rubber gloves, then slipped a lock pick in the door and opened it. Gathering up the newspapers and mail, he went inside.

The place was empty. Had been for several days. There was no odor of cooking on the stale air and a hallway light had been left on, presumably to convince housebreakers there was someone home.

After going through the mail, he dropped it on the hall table next to the answering machine. There was nothing from Buckman, nothing about him. There were bills, an invitation to a wedding in California, a letter from her sister, several professional journals, half a dozen catalogs from upscale companies offering Vermont marble pie rollers, electronic gadgetry, and authentic reproductions of museum pieces. He smiled. What was an authentic reproduction anyway? Jesus, the language was in trouble. Aside from a handful of poets like himself, no one was dedicated to its purity and integrity.

He went through the house, looking in drawers, scattering letters and notes piled on dresser tops, tables, and desks, checking the pockets of the clothes in her closets, even taking old newspapers and magazines out of the paper bags she had stored them in for recycling, thinking perhaps he'd find something stashed in with them.

Nothing.

Nothing to indicate she even knew Buckman.

And now she was gone, leaving no indication of her whereabouts.

His rage blossomed. At Buckman. At Irene. At himself. Mostly at himself. At his ineffectiveness. It seemed to be growing.

Before realizing what he was doing, he took a knife from the kitchen and returned to Irene's bedroom. There was a large closet filled with clothes he had already looked through. Her dresses, blouses, skirts, and slacks draped crookedly from their hangers or lay scattered on the closet floor. It wasn't enough. One by one, he carefully slashed them, throwing the remains in the middle of the bedroom rug. When there were no clothes left, he dug the knife into the mattress on her bed, pulling cotton batting and springs out, strewing them among the shreds of her clothing. Then he went through all the closets in the house, as well as both guest bedrooms, repeating the process.

Disappointed, he went downstairs. It would have been such a pleasure to kill her, force everything she knew about Buckman from her, then kill her. He stood in the hallway, thinking of ways he could have killed her, making the death appear to have been an accident. Suddenly he caught himself, realized what he had done in the house.

It frightened him. The loss of control was intolerable. Control had always been the main sourced of his pride in himself, his work. His margin of safety. His whole way of being. Control of language and action. He had to re-exert it. Without control he was nothing. Just another crazed killer. Just another tone-deaf fiddler with words. He sat on the stairs, trying to calm himself when his eyes fell on hall table with its answering machine. Leaning over, he clicked the incoming message play button.

"This is Bill. I'm calling from Canaan, returning your call."

He listened to the conversation, heard the Shoemaker woman telling Buckman about Koenig's visit, his questions, heard her call him a most frightening man, heard her tell him she would see him soon, heard soft affection in their voices before they hung up.

Perfect. He felt like singing. Canaan. Somewhere in New England, from what she said. Buckman was in Canaan. He'd find the place, and when he did he'd find the Shoemaker woman too. He'd bet on it.

Horrible man? The most frightening man? He smiled.

Taking care of these two was going to be sheer pleasure.

CHAPTER FIFTEEN

Canaan, Massachusetts \ Monday May 6

EARLY MORNING SUNLIGHT streamed dully through windows that looked as though it had never been cleaned, making mottled patterns on the wall. Waking, Buckman turned to see Irene sleeping on her side, her back to him, breathing softly and smoothly. Reaching over, he touched her hair, remembering how slowly they had begun last night, and how quickly they had given in to their passion. Only then were they free to be slow again, to explore, talk, and love again.

She looked lovely, lying next to him. It was strange though, seeing her here in the Old World. In this place he had done everything to forget. Put behind him. He was not the same person who had left the place so many years before. The William G. Buckman, M.D. of Philadelphia and Upper Black Eddy was not the same person as Billy Buck of Canaan Forks. He had extricated himself from that history.

Sure.

He laughed without humor.

Buckman was Buckman, and he was here in the Old World, where he'd been raised, if you could call what his parents did raising him. Where he had grown up. And suddenly the past was now. His present was here. His profession was in his mind and in his hands, his love was in his bed, a bed in Calvin Buckman's house.

Shaking his head, he rubbed his eyes. His entire adult life had been spent saving lives, or at least prolonging them. He prided himself on that. Friendships came and went. His marriage had come and gone. The skills and knowledge he carried as a physician went on. They were part of him. They were at the core of his being. Now, here in the Old World, running from death he had already confronted his father's death, hiding it by burying the body in a cornfield, sucked in by the dark complexities of life here, his history once again part of a straight line, instead of the separate blocks he preferred.

He slipped out of bed, dressed, and went downstairs, planning to make a pot of coffee and take a mug up to Irene. Velma was in the kitchen, sitting at the table, staring out the window. She looked up as he came in.

"I like your girlfriend, Uncle Billy Buck. Is she going to have a baby too, like daddy says?"

"I don't think so, Velma."

"She could have a baby and her and me could raise our babies together, you know. They could be friends, couldn't they? Like me and my sisters?"

"Would you like that?" Buckman started making a pot of coffee.

She shrugged. "I don't know. I don't guess I'd know what to do with a baby, you know?"

"I know, Velma."

"You really think I should get one of them abortions?"

He nodded. Resting a hand on her shoulder, he gave it a reassuring pinch.

"Even if Reverend Dye says it's a sin?"

"It's not a sin to make a smart choice about your own life, Velma."

"Daddy and Grampy Cal always told me that I was a dummie. Dummies can't make smart choices because they're dumb."

"Well, I say you can make a smart choice. Think about what your life would be like if you had a baby to take care of."

"It would love me, wouldn't it, Uncle Billy Buck? Don't babies have to love you if you're their parent?"

"Do you love your father? Your mother? Did you love Grampy Cal?"

She frowned. "Sure, I loved them. They're my parents and Grampy Cal's my grandfather. Or he was my grandfather. You have to love them."

"Does it feel good to love them?"

She frowned again, wrinkling her nose and shrugging. "I don't know how it feels. I never thought about it, you know?"

"You think about it, Velma. Think about it and talk to Irene after you see the doctor this morning, all right?"

She nodded. "Okay, Uncle Billy Buck. And then you'll tell me what to do, right?"

"I can't tell you. I can give you my best advice, but I'm not going to tell you what's right for you to do."

IRENE SAT IN bed drinking from the coffee mug Buckman had brought her. Sitting on the edge of the mattress, he told her about the conversation with Velma.

Shaking his head, he sighed. "I don't know what to do about her."

"You said she wanted you to tell her what to do, right? So, you need to convince that child to have the abortion, that there's no way she can take care of a baby alone, and that she certainly wouldn't want to take it into her parent's home. Remind her of the terrible things her father and her grandfather did to her, and how her mother stood back and let it happen. Make her understand how that would start the whole sick cycle of sexual abuse all over again. You tell her she ought to do it, Bill."

"I'm not sure she's smart enough, or strong enough to understand, and legally, it's her choice. She needs to make her own mind up."

"You're acting like a doctor dealing with a patient. Think like her uncle. There's no one else to help her. It's up to you."

BUCKMAN DROPPED IRENE and Velma off at an ob-gyn office in Canaan Falls, picked up a copy of the *Boston Globe* and went to Vic's Café. Drinking coffee, he munched on an English muffin with a slice of ham and paged through the paper. Squirreled away in the back pages he came across an item on Blanchard's death, one of those short, syndicated pieces about violence in other regions of the country, as though detailing a man murdered in his suburban Philadelphia swimming pool somehow absolved Boston of the horrors associated with its own violent crime.

Sixteen column lines in length, the article gave Blanchard's name, described the death, and said he had worked for a large Philadelphia hospital. The death would have looked like an accident, it said, except for bruises on the victim's head, where the killer had held him under water. It concluded, *the murderer is assumed to have been a prowler caught in the act who killed Blanchard to protect himself, trying to make it look like a suicide. A police investigation into the death is continuing.*

Buckman read it three times. Prowler, sure. Whoever had killed Blanchard was probably the same person who came to his place in the middle of the night. The same person who had come looking for him and frightened Irene. It was too much of a coincidence to be anything else.

He thought about calling the Philadelphia police and telling them what he knew. Sure, he told himself. That would be a clever move. They'd ask for verifying details, including his whereabouts and the next thing there would a leak of information and there would a picture of him in the paper there, an accompanying article telling the world where he was.

Now that he was sure of what was going on, sure how Castile had been having patients murdered, there was no reason to think he'd be safe with the Philadelphia cops. Some of the city's top politicians sat on Worthington-America's board of directors, or on at least one of the many boards which interlocked with Worthington-America. Insurance. Steel. Petroleum. Banks. High tech firms. If he talked to the cops, and the cops talked to the police commissioner, and the police commissioner talked to the Mayor, the Councilmen, his friends on the boards of the banks, insurance companies, if that happened, Buckman was dead. Irene was dead. Just like Blanchard.

No thanks. He'd keep his mouth shut and his profile low. He had enough to deal with in the Old World. Calvin dead. Velma pregnant. And now Irene was here, and they had spent the night making love. It was all more than he bargained for when he decided to come back here to hide, exchanging the danger of the real world for the complications and risks of the Old World.

Folding the paper, he paid his bill and drove down to the Big Y supermarket where he picked up a three pound bags of coffee, two regular, one de-caf, six steaks, several packages of boneless chicken breasts, frozen haddock, assorted fresh vegetables, broccoli, asparagus, lettuce, half a dozen hard, square tomatoes and four jars of various Cajun spices, along with ingredients to make sauces for the vegetables. He'd had the last can of Dinty Moore beef stew he ever planned on eating.

Leaving the groceries on the seat of the pickup, parked in the store lot, he wandered down Franklin Street, looking in store windows, studying the faces of passersby to see if any might be childhood schoolmates. If they were, he didn't recognize them.

Probably didn't want to.

He had left Canaan with no regrets. Without the slightest interest in going back and renewing old acquaintances. It was only idle curiosity which led him to peer into the faces on the sidewalks. Even if he recognized some, he doubted he'd say anything to them. What would they have to talk about, their lives spent here in Canaan, his on the outside, practicing medicine, but just as dull and routine?

At least until Castile started his cost containment program.

What would he have to say to them? Want to say to them? His boyhood had been spent in the Old World, barely a part of Canaan, except by accident of political subdivision when the boundaries of the towns and cities of Massachusetts were formalized by the Commonwealth, sometimes resulting in splitting villages, whole communities, between two municipal governments. Children of the Old World kept to themselves, hiding the dark secrets of their lives from the rest of Canaan. As a boy, Buckman had spoken of his youthful dreams only to Vaughn. Never to Wilfred, Dave and his other brothers and sisters.

What if he saw Fred Henry, Jake Barnes, Gaven Stevens, Jody Varner, any of the old jocks and school heroes he'd known as a kid? If he recognized them, they him, what would they say? What would he tell them?

Hey, I'm a doctor in Philadelphia, but I'm on the lam from a hit man who's been killing my patients.

No shit, Bill. I'm running my old man's shoe store here in the Falls.

And I've got a muffler shop down in Graham.

On the lam, hunh? Where did a sheepie you pick up that term, Buckman?

Miami Vice? Only thing you sheep fuckers in the Old World are ever on the lam from is the game warden.

Buckman started from his thoughts. From what deep recess in his subconscious had the word sheepie come from? He hadn't thought of sheepies since leaving twenty-five years ago. It was a name kids from the Falls used to call boys from the Old World, a reference to a widespread belief among proper Canaanites that every male raised in the Old World had to have sex with a sheep before he could be considered a man.

He'd forgotten all about the name and the alleged practice. Now it came flooding back. Buckman knew only of two boys who had done it with sheep, and they did it after hearing the story, in perverse retaliation at the schoolyard taunts.

You say we fuck sheep. I'll show you what fucking sheep is, asshole.

One of them had been Bobby Thompson, who was killed in a tractor accident the following summer. The other had been Wilfred Buckman who did it in Calvin's barn, with Vaughn and Dave as witnesses. After it was done, Vaughn told Wilfred about an article he'd seen in *Coronet Magazine.*

"It said if you fuck an animal your pecker will dry up and fall right off."

Wilfred had laughed at him, but the brothers had caught him several times a day over the following weeks, checking to be sure everything was all right.

No. Buckman did not want to meet anybody from his school days. He wanted to pass unnoticed in Canaan Falls, get back to Calvin's place and make plans.

The ob-gyn people would evaluate Velma for an abortion; tell them where to have it done if they didn't do abortions. Then he and Irene could talk to her about the procedure. He knew she was right about it being his responsibility to convince her to go through with it.

That done, they could concentrate on their own plans. Should they stay in the Old World indefinitely? Not what he wanted, but it was safe, a remote place, and the killer couldn't have any way of tracing them here. The countryside was beautiful with its spring greens and white water streams. And Calvin planted in the cornfield. Wilfred and Charlotte slipping around, trying to find out his every secret. Vaughn and Dave drinking themselves to death in their trailers down by Wesley Johnson's Store.

He could return to Philadelphia and confront the issue straight on. If Blanchard had been murdered by whoever Castile had hired, Castile might be ready, frightened enough, to turn State's evidence and testify. Being in jail would beat being dead, and if the killer murdered Blanchard to keep the lid on things, it made sense he'd go after Castile too. Going back would be risky. The killer would be looking for him, probably for Irene too.

Canaan wasn't the answer. Philadelphia wasn't the answer. Maybe he should go to Harrisburg. Or Washington. Report what he suspected, what he knew but couldn't outright prove, to State or Federal authorities.

He shook his head. His thoughts were jumbled. Fragmented. He wasn't thinking clearly, and it frustrated him. Angered him. As a doctor he'd been trained to analyze, to clearly think things through to a diagnosis. He'd come to think of himself as an intellect, an authority. And the people around him had treated him with the deference due a figure of authority. Now he was out of his depth. The problem facing him wasn't medical and he didn't know what to do. It required a kind of action for which he wasn't prepared. A kind of thinking he hadn't been trained to do.

Maybe he and Irene should run away to Mexico, or the Caribbean. He'd vacationed once on St. Ursula, a small independent British island in the West Indies. They could go there, stopping in Philadelphia only long enough for her to clean out her bank accounts and for him to put the house in Upper Black Eddy on the market with a Realtor who'd sell it, take care of all the paperwork and the settlement, then discreetly send the money to an account in the islands.

He didn't know what to do. He looked at his watch. Right now, he had to pick up Irene and Velma and get back to Calvin's place. Maybe they could figure it out together. Buckman and Irene, that is. Velma wasn't much help at anything.

They were waiting for him in front of the office.

"You know what I want?" Irene spoke as she held the door open for Velma.

Buckman shook his head.

"A milk shake. A super thick chocolate milk shake with vanilla ice cream, so heavy a spoon will stand up in it."

"Sounds good to me," he said.

"Velma wants one too. I've been thinking about it ever since we got to town, and we've already discussed it and it's settled. Two milk shakes. Three if you want one."

He grinned. "Milk shakes sound better than the things I've been thinking about this morning."

He drove back downtown, pulling into a parking spot in front of Vic's Cafe. Inside, they ordered their shakes and while they waited, Irene filled Buckman in on their discussion with the doctor.

"He doesn't do abortions in the office," Irene told him. "But he will do it Wednesday afternoon at the hospital in Graham. He said she still has plenty of time to get it done."

Buckman nodded. "I thought so, but I wanted her checked carefully first."

Velma lowered her eyes to the table. "I'm afraid, Uncle Billy Buck. It's a sin to have an abortion."

He asked her, "Can you afford to raise this baby?"

She shook her head.

"Would you want to go back and live with your parents, if they'd let you, to raise it in their house?"

She shook her head again.

"What would you do it you had the baby?"

"I don't know, but it would be somebody to love me. Nobody's ever loved me much. Daddy and Grampy Cal used to say they loved me when they wanted to do it with me, but all they ever did was hurt me, you know?"

Irene spoke. Her tone of voice was soft, the words direct. "You are going to get the abortion, Velma. You need to. You have no money and nobody to help you once your uncle and I leave here. You can't take care of a baby on your own. You will have the abortion."

Velma's face paled. They were silent for a minute while the waitress brought the milk shakes. When she left, Velma took a long sip, then looked at Irene. "You and Uncle Billy Buck are going to leave here?"

Irene nodded. "Someday, probably soon. We don't live here, Velma. We don't want to live here. We have our own lives to think about."

"I thought you was going to take care of me. I got nobody to do that now Grampy Cal..." She stopped, looking around the cafe. "Now that Grampy Cal's gone, you know?"

"Listen to Irene," Buckman said. "She's right about this."

"You want me to do it too, Uncle Billy Buck?"

He nodded.

"You say it's all right to do?"

He reached across the table for her hand. "I think it's a smart thing to do."

She gave him a small smile. "You're a doctor. You wouldn't tell me to do a dumb thing, or something wrong."

"We both want what's best for you."

She sipped at her milk shake without talking. When it was finished, she loudly sucked air at the bottom of the glass, then finally looked up at them.

"Then I'll do it. If it's a smart thing to do, I want to do it. I don't think I done very many smart things in my life, you know?" Using the back of her hand, she wiped the remains of the milkshake from her lips. "I want to do something smart. I don't want to be a dumbie no more."

When they returned to the truck, a policeman stood writing a parking ticket, his back to them.

Buckman walked up to him. "What's wrong, officer?"

Erskine Dye turned, the ticket pad in his left hand. He smiled broadly at them.

"Meter's expired, Mr. Buckman." He tipped his hat to Irene and Velma.

Velma gasped loudly. "I didn't know you was a policeman, Reverend Dye."

"The church doesn't have much money, Velma, so I make my salary here and what little bit the church raises I put right back into books for the Sunday school, grape juice for the Lord's Supper services and such things."

He bent close to her, peering at the bandage on her chin. "What happened to you, child?"

Her throat went dry. Instead of answering, she choked and looked at Buckman.

"She tripped on the porch steps and fell. Hit her chin on a rock in the yard."

Looking from Buckman to Velma, he shook his head. Then, handing the ticket to Buckman, he spoke softly, politely. A light smile on the corners of his mouth pulled the flesh of his chin tighter than usual. Buckman thought he could almost chop wood with it.

"It's only two dollars if you go pay it at the police station right now. Wait too long and they'll add on a five dollar penalty. If I was you, I'd do it right this minute. This is your father's truck. He won't look kindly on getting a five dollar ticket. Besides, if you forgot it altogether it could cause him a barrel of problems with the Registry of Motor Vehicles. I suppose he's home recovering from a drinking binge."

"He still hasn't come back." Buckman took the ticket Dye was holding out for him.

"I don't like this, Mr. Buckman. Not a bit. A man like Calvin doesn't just disappear. He might crawl a little too far into the bottle from time to time, but he always crawls out and gets back to farming that land of his. Sometimes I think it makes him a better churchgoer, knowing his weakness the way he does and looking to make amends for it through the church's work. I'd be worried if I was you."

"I don't much like it myself, Reverend, and I am a little worried. Rest assured, I'll let you know as soon as he comes home."

Dye nodded. "And you Velma, be more careful, child. You could do yourself real damage falling like that."

Buckman gave Dye a polite smile and walked next door to the police station. When he came back, Dye was gone. Irene and Velma were sitting in the truck, the girl's face white, her whole body trembling.

"I can't do it, Uncle Billy Buck. The Reverend Dye, he knows all about Grampy Calvin and the abortion you want me to have and everything, and he'll send to Hell if I do it."

Buckman looked at Irene who rolled her eyes, shaking her head.

"What do you mean, he knows. Did you tell him, Velma?"

Eyes wide, tearing, she shook her head. "No Uncle Billy Buck, honest. I never said nothing, but Reverend Dye, he knows things."

"If you didn't say anything, how can he know?"

"He's a reverend and a policeman too, so he knows things. Somehow, he knows I sinned with Grampy Cal and that I'd sinned by saying I'd have an abortion. He probably knows I killed Grampy Cal and he's just waiting to arrest me."

She started to cry, her trembling giving way to a deep racking shaking. "He's going to drag me to Hell. I don't want to go, Uncle Billy Buck. Don't let me go to Hell."

Her sobbing drowned out the words. Irene reached toward her and put her arms around the girl, her to her shoulder.

Buckman tousled her hair briefly and turned the truck off Franklin Street, heading back toward the Old World. He didn't bother telling Velma that she'd been born and raised in Hell.

CHAPTER SIXTEEN

Philadelphia, Pennsylvania / Monday May 5 - Tuesday May 6

BACK AT HIS apartment, Koenig got out his road atlas, turned to the back pages and began going through the list of towns and cities for all the New England states in the index at the rear or the book. He found four Canaans and one New Canaan, all in New England. Connecticut had both a Canaan and the New Canaan. The rest were in New Hampshire, Massachusetts, and Vermont.

He dialed Vermont information, asking for any listings for Buckmans in Canaan. None.

Canaan, New Hampshire had a Zachary Buckman and an M. Buckman. When Koenig called, Zachary said he had a cousin, William, who ran a catering business in Manchester. M. told him she had no Buckman relatives, just a bunch of no good in- laws, and said she was going back to her maiden name of Papineau as soon as her divorce from Zachary was final.

In Canaan, Massachusetts, he found a Wilfred Buckman listed. He dialed the number, asking the man who answered if he could speak to Dr. William Buckman.

"Doctor? The snot fuck's a doctor? That's news to me, mister, and it's probably nothing but horseshit."

"Is he around?"

"What do you want him for?"

"We have business."

"He left here as soon as he got out of high school. Thought he was too fucking good for the rest of us."

"Where did he go?"

"Don't know. Don't care."

"You haven't heard from him, haven't seen him?"

"Why should I? Why should he get in touch with me after twenty-five, thirty years? Only reason would be if he'd got his ass in trouble, you know? Like you, maybe. Are you looking to make trouble for him?"

"No trouble, Mr. Buckman. As I said, we have business."

Wilfred hesitated briefly, just long enough to whet Koenig's already honed suspicions. "Don't matter much if you are trouble for him. I ain't seen him or heard from him since the day he left Canaan with his goddamn nose in the air. You got business with him, find him. You've probably got a better idea where he is than me. You do find him, tell him that none of us back home give a rat's ass if he dead or alive."

Hanging up, Koenig was sure Buckman was in this Canaan. Wilfred had been too cagey. From the tone of voice and the things he said, it was clear he didn't like his brother, but he wasn't about to betray him either.

Just to cover all bases, he called Connecticut information. There was a William Buckman, Sr. in Canaan, no Buckmans in New Canaan.

William Buckman in Canaan, Connecticut sounded like an old man, his voice frail and wobbly.

Koenig asked, "Do you have a son, William?"

"I certainly do." The old man's voice strengthened with pride. "He's a fine man, my son."

"Is he around, Mr. Buckman?"

"He's up in Hartford, sir. A member of the State Senate there. I keep trying to get him to run for governor, but he tells me the time's not right for him. One of these days, though, it will be. I just hope I live to see it."

"I hope so too, Mr. Buckman. Thank you."

Koenig hung up, surer than before that his man was hiding out in Canaan, Massachusetts. Smiling, he stretched out on his bed. A good night's sleep and he'd be ready to drive to Massachusetts in the morning.

IT WAS NEARLY dark. Erskine Dye pulled his car into the garage alongside the Canaan Forks Missionary Alliance rectory. It had been a slow day. He'd rousted a bunch of teenagers who had been hanging out around the back of a pickup truck parked in front of Eileff's store on Franklin Street, given thirty overtime parking tickets, missed collaring a shoplifter at the CVS drugstore, and arrested a paraplegic for driving her electric cart on the sidewalk, threatening to run down people unless they gave her the right of way.

Inside the house he went to his room, quickly trading his police uniform for a black suit, white shirt, and shoe-string tie. Ten minutes later he was back in the car, setting out to make calls on sick members of his congregation. He also wanted to stop by the Buckman place. There was something peculiar, something wrong going on with them and he wanted, needed, to find out what it was.

If the son was to be believed, Calvin Buckman still hadn't come home, but he wasn't sure about the son. There was a false note about him. He wasn't like the other Buckmans, Wilfred up on the Windybush, Vaughn down in his trailer home, the others scattered around. He knew them all, had visited with them at one time or another, either in their own homes or when they came to see Calvin. They all belonged to Canaan Forks, to their evil Old World. The ways they lived and drank were familiar sins to Erskine Dye. He knew them and he knew how to use them to his own ends.

But not Bill Buckman. He was an unknown.

Dye had never even heard of him before he turned up in Canaan Forks. Now he was here, acting like he owned Calvin's place and he had some woman with him, a Jew, if he guessed right, with neither of them wearing a wedding ring. She might be an infidel by birth, but this Buckman seemed to be one by choice. He didn't treat the Reverend Erskine Dye with the proper respect and deference.

And something odd was going on with Velma. She wasn't acting like herself, those dull eyes darting around like some animal about to be caught and shot. It bothered him. He had to know. What he'd have to do was get her alone. Start her talking without the uncle and his girlfriend around. He could count on Velma being dumb enough to tell him everything. Even if she'd been told to keep her mouth shut.

He looked at his image in the mirror. Straightening the tie and setting the hat at the proper angle, he ran his hands over the sharp edge of his chin. Something was sure as blazes going on with the Buckmans and he was going to find out what. He prided himself on his ability to discover peoples' secrets. He had the reverend's smile and the reverend's way of talking soft, making people feel they could trust him and making them feel their eternal souls were bound for the hot coals of the fires of Hell if they didn't tell him what he wanted to know. After all, he was Jesus' locomotive, wasn't he?

He thought of the time when Leon Shippee died several years before. Dye had noticed how frightened his widow, Noreen, had been acting before and during the funeral. As though riddled with guilt. He'd called on her every day for the next week, talking to her, praying with her, doing everything in his power to convince her to open up to him, to unburden her soul.

Finally, she broke down. Weeping, slapping her shoulders and upper arms with her palms, she told him she'd been unfaithful to Leon once, years before, while he'd been off working somewhere in the south. She'd lived with her memories of sinful ways through the years, wanting to confess to him, have him forgive her, but she'd been afraid. In the last days of his life, as he had lain in his bed sweating and moaning with pain, she'd come close to telling him on three different occasions.

"But you never did?" Dye had made the question sound like a reproach.

She had shaken her head, tears streaming down her face.

"Why not? Why not tell a dying man of your sin and receive his absolution? You'd have sent him to heaven with the good deed of forgiveness as his last act on earth, and you'd have saved your own soul from Satan's foul burning lakes of human excrement."

She had sobbed, throwing her arms around Dye's shoulders. "What should I do, Reverend Dye? How can I make up for it now? I don't want Satan to take me."

Dye had pushed her away. Holding her wrists tightly, watching her wince against the pain of his grip, he shook his head.

"It won't be easy, Noreen. A sin like that against your husband, never confessed, never receiving his forgiveness, it's a terrible thing. He could have absolved you easily, but it's harder for me to do it. I'm not the one sinned against. It was Leon who suffered."

"But Leon didn't suffer, Reverend. He never knew."

Her voice had sounded desperate. Dye thought quickly and moved in.

"He suffered, Noreen. He suffered by not knowing. By not understanding what was going on all those times through your married life when you were holding something back from him. He suffered the injuries of ignorance. You held back the truth and in so doing, you held back yourself, keeping a secret place in your soul, a place where your own husband couldn't reach you, even during the most private moments in your marriage bed."

She had sobbed, breaking off his speech.

"What can I do, Reverend? How can I make it up to him?"

Erskine Dye slowly shook his head, the expression on his unsmiling face relentless, void of compassion or pity. "You can never make it up to him. Leon is dead, Noreen, beyond your confessions, beyond forgiving your sins. He's too busy basking in the eternal joys of Heaven, where you never will be. While Leon's singing God's praises and enjoying the blessed and everlasting company of His son, our Lord Jesus Christ, you will be paying for what you did here on earth, for your betrayal of him."

She had brightened, smiling at him.

"Then it doesn't matter, does it? Leon isn't suffering anymore. I can stop worrying about never having told him and maybe God will feel bad for me and forgive that I cheated on Leon."

"Leon might not be suffering, but somebody much more important knows what you did. You have to worry about him now."

Noreen had looked at Dye with confusion and fear.

"Who is it, Reverend Dye? Who else besides you and me knows about what I did back then?

He knew he had her and pounced. It made him smile with pleasure, even now, staring at himself in the mirror as he remembered the look on her face.

"God. God knows, Noreen." His voice was harsh, rasping the words through clenched teeth. "God knows. And oh, Noreen, how he hates what you did. Oh, how he hates you for doing it, how he hates you for never confessing it, not even to him. It's God's forgiveness you need to seek now, not Leon's. God hates you for what you did and Jesus weeps over it. You've got to beg forgiveness, Noreen." Forming his face into a fearsome grimace, he stared into her eyes, snarling as he recited the words of Jonathon Edwards he had memorized while touching himself under blankets.

"The God that holds you over the pit of hell, much as one holds a spider or some loathsome insect over the fire, abhors you, and is dreadfully provoked.

"How do I do that?" Her voice shook, her body trembled.

He had loosened his hold on her wrists, pushing his face down into hers, wetting his lips as he smiled.

"You do it through me. I'm your pathway to God's forgiveness."

Three weeks later, Noreen Shippee signed her farm over to the Canaan Forks Missionary Alliance, retaining the rights to live in the house until her death, at which time it would become the church's rectory. Six months later, she died. Erskine Dye moved in the day after Noreen's funeral.

Now all he had to do was turn his charm on Velma. He'd make the Buckman farm his first stop of the evening.

BUCKMAN ANSWERED THE door. Erskine Dye walked past him and stood looking around the room. He glared at Irene, who sat at the kitchen table holding a glass of wine. She barely nodded at him before taking a sip from the glass. Velma was at the sink, washing dishes.

Crossing the room, Dye nodded back, smiling his broad reverend's smile at Irene. He went over to Velma, placing his hand on her shoulder.

"How are you this evening, Velma?"

"I'm fine Reverend Dye." Her voice shook and she dropped a plate into the sink. It clattered against the porcelain and broke.

"I'm sorry, Velma. I hope I didn't make you drop that plate. Are you all right?"

"I'm doing good, Reverend. I'm real good."

"You don't look well, child."

She turned her face away, concentrating on picking up fragments of the plate. Buckman came over and took Dye's arm, leading him toward the table.

"Really, Mr. Dye, you must sit down and have a cup of coffee with us. We've already finished dinner, or I'd offer you some food too."

Spreading his arms in an expression of his inability to provide the food, Buckman pulled out a chair and gestured for Dye to sit at the table across from Irene.

"Perhaps I can take your hat, Mr. Dye. Surely you don't intend to wear it in our house."

Hiding his embarrassment, Dye handed him the hat and cleared his throat.

"I've come to invite you to our services next Sunday, also to our midweek prayer meetings, all three of you, and I'd like to see Calvin there too. He should be back by then, don't you think?"

"I certainly hope so, Mr. Dye."

"It's Reverend," Dye said. "Reverend Dye."

"I'm not religious," Buckman said. Hanging Dye's hat by the door, he poured a cup of coffee, placed it in front of Dye, pulled a chair out and sat between the preacher and Irene. "As I told you this afternoon, I'm more than a little worried about my father."

Dye nodded, looking silently into the dark surface of the coffee. Buckman was clever. He'd out-maneuvered him, leading him away from Velma and pulling the business with the hat and refusing to call him Reverend. Maybe he ought to go away, forget about the Buckmans, forget about whatever was going on here. Maybe this Buckman was too much for him.

As soon as the thought rose, he tamped it down. He'd been in Canaan Forks long enough to be sure no one here was too much for him. No one living here and no one who'd left here. They were a constant stock, these people. They were his people, his congregation, his flock, his sheep to shear.

He looked up at Buckman, catching his eyes and holding them. He looked like Calvin, younger, stronger, taller, even brighter, but he had a Buckman face. The nose was the same, and the lips. They could be on Calvin, Wilfred, Dave, Vaughn, any of the others. They just happened to be on this strange Buckman, with his outside ways, even the western Massachusetts hill town accent lost, buried under some other way of speaking.

He wished he knew more about accents. Then maybe he could tell where this Buckman had been, and that would be a clue to what he'd been doing and what he was doing here. As it was, he could tell what was missing, the hill town vowels and characteristic pauses, but he could not put his finger on what was there.

He cleared his throat. "You will come to our services, then? Prayer meetings are on Tuesday and Thursday nights, seven o'clock."

"I doubt if we'll be able to make it, Mr. Dye," Buckman said.

"How about you, Velma? You'll come, right?" Dye twisted around in his chair, smiling at Velma who was still standing at the sink, her back to him.

"I don't know," she said, her voice barely audible above the sound of running water.

"You've been away from services for a while now, child. You need to renew your praying, renew your faith. I'll stop by and pick you up if your uncle and his friend aren't going to come. It's for your own good."

"I don't know, Reverend." She shook her head, still standing with her back to him.

Dye took a sip of coffee and stood up, walking over to her. Shaking her head, Irene grabbed Buckman's wrist as he started to get up after him. He sat back down. She was right. Getting up and stopping Dye would only increase his suspicions. They were aroused enough as it was.

"Well, you think about it, Velma. God and I want you to come and pray with us. I'll stop by here at six-thirty tomorrow night. If you've decided to come to church with me, I'll drive you down. Understand?"

She nodded, still not looking at him.

Patting her on the shoulder, he walked to the door, taking his hat from the hook on his way out, the screen door slamming behind him. He stood on the porch, looking back into the shadowed kitchen, the yellow bug light on the ceiling glowing dimly on his face.

"It surely would be a pleasure if you all would join us, but Velma needs to come, for the good of her soul." He looked beyond Buckman and Irene, waving at Velma who had turned around and was staring at him through the door. "You're a member of the church, Velma. God expects you there. I expect you there. Don't disappoint us. The fate of your soul could lie in the balance. You understand?"

He turned and was gone. A moment later they heard his car start up and drive off toward the road.

"What am I going to do, Uncle Billy Buck? I can tell by the way he looks at me that he knows about the baby, he knows about everything. Grampy Cal. The abortion. I can tell by the way he looks at me that he knows about it all. I'm going to go to Hell. I know I am. He'll send me straight to Hell and I'll spend eternity in boiling lakes of cow shit, just like Grampy Cal always said." Her face was whiter than it had been before and she was shaking, crying. Irene quickly moved toward her, taking her in her arms.

"Don't you worry about him, Velma. How could he know about your grandfather? Just don't worry."

"He knows. Jesus must've seen me kill Grampy Cal with the skillet, and then he seen me and Uncle Billy Buck bury him out in the field. He seen it all, you and me at the doctor's office, and all, and Jesus told God and God told Reverend Dye to send me to Hell."

"Forget about Dye," Buckman said. "He's just another man and he's trying to get information out of you, trying to use you for some reason. He doesn't know a thing. He can't. You make him sound as though he's God himself."

Velma swallowed hard, tears soaking her cheeks.

"He knows everything, Uncle Billy Buck. I can tell he does. He knows it all and he's going to make God send me to Hell, just like he said."

"He doesn't know a damn thing, Velma."

She wailed, her eyes wild, her face wet with tears. "Don't say that Uncle Billy Buck. Don't say damned. That's what the Reverend is going to do to me, damn me. Send me to the shitholes of Hell."

Buckman fought to keep rising anger and frustration out of his voice. "Velma, he doesn't know anything. And even if he did know about the baby it wouldn't mean he knew about the abortion, let alone know anything about Grampy Cal. He thinks something is wrong here because of the way we've all been acting. He's trying to find out what it is by scaring you into telling him."

Still half-wailing, Velma screeched, "He scares me awful bad, Uncle Billy Buck."

"For Christ's sake, get a hold on yourself." Buckman's exasperation burst through his voice. Startled by it, Velma shrank from him, then ran from the kitchen to her bedroom, sobbing loudly as she went.

KOENIG WAS ON the road by seven Tuesday morning, his stereo blasting out Wendt's arrangement of Mozart's "The Marriage of Figaro," played by the Amadeus Ensemble. It was a beautiful cool spring morning as he crossed the Delaware on the I-95 bridge, whistling along with the music. *The New York Times* forecast of unseasonably cold weather, with the possibility of snow in the hills of western New England, seemed unbelievable.

He was feeling good. On a high. Blanchard and Castile were dead. In another day or two, Buckman would be out of the way, the Shoemaker woman too. It would be easiest if she were in Canaan with him, saving him the problem of tracking her down separately.

Then he would be able to put this goddamn Worthington-America business behind him. The high vanished as he realized again how stupid he had been to have gotten involved. It was pure lack of judgment. Thinking it through, he was convinced he never would have listened to such a crazy idea five years before. He would have told Castile he was on the wrong track the first time, the very the minute he approached him.

His lack of judgment worried him. Perhaps it was a sign of aging, although he wasn't that old. He certainly didn't need money. And the excitement of the kill was missing. They were the wrong kinds of kills. The satisfaction wasn't there, even if some of the victims were among the impure scum he preyed upon. Killing sick, dying people in a hospital wasn't his style, no matter how much élan he tried bringing to the job, and no matter how much he got paid for doing them. There was little pleasure in the work. His successes with Blanchard and Castile had helped. There were traces of the old joy as he recalled their deaths.

Reaching over, he fumbled through the glove compartment until he found a pack of cigarettes he'd stored there long ago, for the time he knew would come when he'd have to have a smoke. It had been over a year since the last time, and before that, several years since he'd had one. He'd quit when he was thirty-three. Since then, he'd had seven cigarettes, each one deeply satisfying. Lighting it, he took a deep drag and opened the car window a crack. It tasted wonderful, felt wonderful, even old as it was, stale from sitting in the glove compartment for a year and a half.

Later, hands tight on the steering wheel, he approached the top of the Tappan Zee Bridge. Glancing briefly to the right, he could see the buildings of Manhattan rising in the clear spring air. The water below was grey and choppy. He hugged the middle lane, as he always did on bridges, carefully watching for trucks in his rearview mirror. Once over the bridge, he headed for the Cross Westchester Parkway, turned off on the Hutchinson River Parkway which would feed him onto the Merritt and Wilbur Cross Parkways.

Miles farther on, passing the New Canaan, Connecticut exit, he smiled at his cleverness. Buckman was almost his. This was one kill he knew will give him the old pleasure. He'd set it up to give him the greatest possible amount of joy.

Shortly after ten the sky turned a leaden grey and rain hit his windshield. By the time he crossed the line into Massachusetts the raindrops were heavy, and he could see small sodden lumps of slush running down the glass. It was snowing heavily as he reached Graham and the snow was piling up on the ground. In Canaan, it was already several inches deep. Singing to himself, Koenig drove down the main street of Canaan, Massachusetts. He was about to deliver a finale to the Worthington-America plan.

CHAPTER SEVENTEEN

Canaan, Massachusetts \ Tuesday, May 7

STANDING ON HIS porch, Erskine Dye watched snow fall from a deep gray sky, trees and wires bending from the heavy white cover. Freak late spring snows can wreak havoc in New England, felling trees and utility poles, scattering live wires over the ground. After living in the western Massachusetts hills for nearly twenty years, he still hadn't adjusted to their grim cold. Even at the height of summer, late July and early August, there were often nights heavy with the promise of winter, filling him with longing for his native Georgia pine country. Yet, despite the climate he thought of as abominable, he had only once before seen such an unseasonal snowstorm.

Years before, shortly after he had first arrived in Canaan, during a frigidly cold May picnic he was holding for his fledgling congregation, it had started to snow and he had laughed outwardly when Luther Stone, one of the first men in Canaan Forks to join the church, came out with an expression he would hear many times over the years. The Sunday school children had been standing huddled around the barbecue, holding their shivering hands over the fire, ignoring the sodas and ice cream Dye had brought to the picnic. Luther had come up and clapped him on the shoulder.

"We got six seasons here in New England, Pastor. Spring, Summer, Fall, Going into Winter, Winter, and Coming out of Winter. You might as well get used to all six of them if you're going to build a church here."

He didn't laugh anymore when someone said it. Instead, he inwardly cursed the climate and the frozen ways of its people. Still, this was the place of his calling. The cold winds touching him with the forechill of death were part of God's plan for him, just as it had been part of God's plan for him to leave the warm Georgia pines and come here.

THE OLD WORLD

He had been in the second semester of his freshman year at Emory University when the call came. The first semester had been difficult, his grades low, confused by Atlanta's Godless ways, he missed Stoney Creek and the embrace of the Free Will Baptist Church where his father preached. The intellectual cacophony unsettled him, ideas of all kinds swimming in the air, threatening to drown out the hymns and preaching of Stoney Creek, driving them from the forefront of his mind.

He'd written his parents, telling them he was thinking of giving up his scholarship and coming home where he belonged. He wanted to serve God, he told them, not study Godless things in a Godless university in a Godless city.

His father wrote back, saying he would be foolish to come back. Those who served God did it best in Godless places. Stoney Creek already had a servant of God in Ephraim Dye. It didn't need another one in Erskine. If he believed God intended for him to be His servant, he should start looking for the place God intended for his calling.

The next day in his American History class, the professor was talking about Jonathan Edward's sermon, "Sinners in the Hands of an Angry God." The title gave him a thrill, and after reading the sermon, he went to an encyclopedia and read about Edward's life. He was especially fascinated by the years in Northampton, Massachusetts, and Edward's final break with the church there. A few days later he found Northampton in a road atlas. Studying the names of nearby towns, Canaan struck a chord. With such a name, he knew it had to be the place to which God was calling him. A week later he was in Canaan Forks, the section of town people called the Old World, seeking people for his congregation.

Life in Canaan had been hard for Dye. Far from his family, suffering the inhospitality of the climate, surrounded by deeply sinful people, he struggled to keep his faith simple and pure. Over the long years there he'd grown to understand the necessity of manipulating these fallen creatures for the sakes of their souls. At first, he had regretted the moral complexity the task involved, but gradually his regrets faded into pleasure at his cleverness in clearly understanding God's will and leading people into following it, often against their own wills.

That pleasure sustained him in a hostile world. Standing on his porch, watching the wet May snow piling up on brittle limbs, covering the ground with frozen whiteness, he thought of himself as living in a singular and self-imposed Babylonian exile, serving God in his own, private covenant, he alone chosen for this mission. The idea pleased and sustained him. Thinking of it, he shivered lightly with pleasure.

A moment later he heard a sharp cracking sound and a maple limb the size of a small tree crashed to the ground a few feet from the house. Just missing the garage roof, it blocked the drive. He shook his fist at it, roaring his anger into the falling snow. Now he'd have to saw the damned thing up before he could get the car out.

Going inside the house, he sat at his desk and started making a list of things to do once he got the driveway open. The last item was to call on Velma Buckman, reminding her again of the prayer meeting at seven o'clock.

"YOU GOT ANOTHER goddamn phone call at my place last night." Wilfred tooted his horn and leaned out the car window, shouting toward the house.

Buckman came out and stood on the porch, rubbing his arms against the cold, and squinting his eyes as he looked at his brother, the car half hidden by the thick snow falling through the air between them.

"Who was it?"

"How should I know? Guy asks for you, don't say fucking nothing about who he is or what he wants, except that he wants to talk to you. Said you and him had business."

"Did he say what kind of business?"

Wilfred shrugged. "I didn't ask him. All I told him was the same thing I told your girlfriend in there when she called, that I didn't know where you were, and I don't give a shit. I'm goddamn tired of phone calls coming to my place for you. I hope this was the last one. If you're going to stay around here you ought to talk Calvin into putting a phone in, you know?"

Nodding to shut him up, Buckman shivered again, increasing the speed with which he was rubbing his upper arms, his breath heavy in the air.

"Thanks, Moose."

Wilfred started to roll his window up, stopped and looked back at Buckman, his lips pulled back from his teeth in a taunting grin.

"This guy sounds like trouble, Billy Buck. More trouble than your girlfriend, for sure."

"I thought he didn't tell you anything."

"He didn't have to say nothing, the guy had the coldest, meanest voice I ever heard. Colder and nastier than pig shit in February. He's trouble Billy Buck, and I don't want a goddamned thing to do with him or his fucking trouble. He comes to see you, keep him here, and keep his trouble here, you understand?"

He lit a cigarette, throwing the match out the car window onto the ground. It hissed in the snow.

"Whoever he is, whatever he wants, it's got nothing to do with you, Moose."

"Better goddamn not have anything to do with me. You keep your trouble to yourself, eh?"

"Don't worry."

"I ain't worried, Billy Buck. You're the one that ought to be worried, the way that guy's voice sounds. I mean, like it was coming out of a fucking grave, you know? I ain't worried a bit. I'm just telling you about trouble and how I don't want nothing to do with it."

Buckman looked at him, struggling to keep an even, relaxed expression. "There won't be any trouble for you, Moose. There'd be no reason for it."

"So you keep saying, but it don't mean a goddamn thing unless there's no trouble." Wilfred put the car in gear and slowly started inching away from the house. "Any word from Calvin yet?"

"Nothing."

"Fucking asshole." Wilfred drove off, rolling up the window as he went.

Buckman went back inside. Light from the ceiling fixture barely cut the cloudy darkness which seemed to ooze in from the storm.

"I've got to go out for a bit," he told Irene.

"I heard what your brother said. That man's found you. The one who came to my place."

He nodded. "I think so. I'm going down to Vaughn's trailer. I think I'm going to need him after all."

"THERE'S BUCKMANS OVER in the Old World." The hardware clerk scratched his head as Koenig paid him for a spool of ninety pound test fishing line.

"Don't know much about them. People from that part of Canaan keep pretty much to themselves. Sometimes their boys make good at high school football, or some other sport and they stand out for a while, pictures in the newspaper, things like that. Then they'll drop out of school and just disappear back into the Old World. Seems to me there was a Buckman played football, twenty, thirty years ago, but that's about all I can remember."

Thanking him, Koenig took the bag with the line, sticking it in his hunting jacket pocket. He wore a shoulder length black wig and a false beard, both expensive and, he believed, next to impossible to detect as fake. Anybody trying to describe the man who went around asking questions about the Buckmans would tell about a scraggly redneck with a Maine hunting license. He'd taken the jacket and license from the summer home of a lawyer he'd killed several years before. The plastic frame covering the license had a carefully placed daub of mud over the date.

Outside the store, he stood on the sidewalk, snow falling heavily around him. Cars skidded on the street, a small group of onlookers staring at a cop arguing with the driver of a pickup which had plowed into the back of a Datsun. An elderly woman sat behind the steering wheel in the car, rotating her neck as a small stream of blood ran from her left forehead.

The hardware clerk was the seventh person he'd asked about the Buckmans. He'd decided there was no point in calling Wilfred again. It was obvious he'd been lying the first time he called. The best move was to find out as much as he could from townspeople. So far, all he'd learned was there were Buckmans in the Old World, which was an isolated section of Canaan, the part of town looked down upon with great disgust by the good burghers of Canaan Falls. He felt a low growl of frustration rumbling in his throat. Killing Buckman wasn't going to be a problem, not really, but he resented having to spend any more than five minutes looking for him.

He wandered into a pizza parlor/sandwich shop, ordered a hot meatball sandwich, a Coke, and asked the counterman about the Buckmans.

He shook his head. "Never heard of any Buckmans around here, but I've only been in town a couple of years."

"Somebody told me they lived in the Old World."

"They might as well live in Siberia for all of me, mister. I know what part of town they call the Old World, but I've never been there. No reason. I don't go hunting and I don't like to fuck twelve year old children and sheep."

He passed the sandwich over the counter and turned to draw the Coke. "There's something might help," he said, handing Koenig the soda.

Koenig took a sip, leaning his elbows on the counter. "I'm all ears."

"With the police station next door, I get most of the cops in here for lunch, nearly all of them in at one time or another during the week. I've heard them joking about one cop who's a minister over in the Old World, they say. Maybe he could help you."

"What's his name?"

"Erskine Dye. Sort of a strange character. Doesn't hang out with the other cops when they come in, just sits alone, over there in the corner by the plate glass window. One or another of the cops will kid him, something like asking if he's married any brothers and sisters lately, or any fathers and daughters. He just glares up at them and goes back to reading. You might check with him. He knows the Old World. Maybe he could find your Buckmans for you."

VAUGHN WAS DRUNK. Country music filled his small, dark trailer as he lay sprawled on the couch, singing along with the radio. Dirty clothes, hunting magazines and back issues of *Penthouse* and *Easy Riders*, along with several hard core magazines and video tapes, were piled on tables and chairs, and scattered about the floor. Large jar lids overflowed with cigarette butts, powdered ash ground into the rugs and upholstery. The place smelled of stale tobacco smoke and burnt filters, dirty laundry, rancid dishes, and open bags of garbage.

Grinning and waving, Vaughn tried standing as Buckman came through the door. He stumbled against the coffee table, lurched forward, and landed on the floor, missing hitting his head on the side of the woodstove by less than an inch. He turned over and waved at Buckman.

"Hey, it's Billy Buck, little brother Billy Buck. How're you doing, Billy?"

Buckman shook his head, smiling out of exasperation as he reached down to help his brother up. "At least I'm standing and sober."

"What's going on, Billy Buck?" Vaughn grabbed the hand and pulled himself upright, crashing against Buckman and breathing heavily into his face.

"I need help, Vaughn."

Vaughn smiled, nodding. "I'm your man, Billy Buck. I said I'd help you and I will. Hell, what's a big brother for if he can't help his little brother out? Right?"

"Maybe you ought to wait until I tell you what I want you to do."

Vaughn shook his head. "It don't matter. We're brothers and I'll help you. Just tell me what's wrong."

"I can't tell you, exactly. You've got to help me without knowing the details of what's wrong."

Vaughn laughed, waving his arms toward Buckman, barely maintaining his balance. "I'll tell you what's wrong, Billy Buck. What's wrong is that I'm drunk on my ass. I ain't going to be no good to nobody like this. You better get me sober if you want me to help you with anything."

Buckman made a pot of coffee. Medically, he knew coffee wouldn't sober a person up, but it was something to do while he tried getting through to his brother.

Vaughn grinned at him and pulled on his parka.

"I'm going outside to puke, Billy Buck. Ain't nothing for getting sober like a good finger stuck down the throat and some cold air. A good puke, a good shower and I'll be ready to do anything you got that needs doing."

Twenty minutes later he was out of the shower, drinking his third cup of coffee.

"Why is this guy after you, Billy?" Buckman was amazed by how sober his brother seemed. His hands were shaking, and his eyes had a small, pained look, but he seemed steady and his voice was firm.

"I know things about him."

"Like what?"

"That's what I can't tell you, Vaughn."

He shrugged. I don't give a rat's ass if you tell me or not, I'll still help you, but I'd sure shit like to know what's going on with you. Just for the knowing, not for anything else. I just like knowing things."

Buckman shook his head. He wasn't about to go into the details. He didn't want to tell Vaughn about himself. If people in the Old World learned about his life since leaving, it would be like losing it, bringing it into continuity with his old life, dissipating its separateness. He'd give Vaughn the drama without the substance.

"He's killed people and I know about it."

"And he's out to shut you up?"

"He's got no choice."

"Well fuck him, Billy Buck. We'll just kill him first, right? We'll blow him the fuck away."

"That's what I was hoping you'd say."

"Shit, that's the only thing I could say. So, where is this guy?"

"I don't know. All I know is that he's headed this way. I don't know when, but he's coming. We've got to be ready for him."

"You know what he looks like, so we can ambush the son-of-a-bitch before he gets to you, right?"

"I've never seen him close up and wouldn't recognize him. Irene's seen him, but from her description, he was probably in some kind of disguise."

"Who's Irene?"

"A friend." He paused. "A good friend. The best. Maybe more than a friend."

Vaughn nodded. "We'll find him, Billy Buck. Even if it means letting him find us first. Then we'll blast him. Hell, if you can't kill some fucker for your little brother, who can you kill them for?"

"Did you ever kill anybody?"

Vaughn put his palms together, then sprung them apart, only his fingertips touching. He looked at Buckman, closed his eyes, then opened them, smiling.

"Outside of Iraq?" He shook his head. "I don't think I even killed anybody over there. I always shot off into the bushes where there wasn't nobody to kill. If I did kill anybody it was a mistake, some poor bastard hiding in the thicket so he wouldn't get shot or shoot nobody. But that don't mean I can't do it if it's an important thing to do. Hell, the goddamn Army trained me a hundred and ten ways to kill a man. And it's important to know things like that if this guy is trying to kill you." He sat on the couch and stretched. "Now, you got a plan?"

"I want to set up an ambush, a place near the house where you can hide, and I can act as bait."

Vaughn nodded. "He comes looking for you and I blow him away. Sight the fucker up and kapow, he's gone for good, right Billy Buck?"

He aimed at the wall with an imaginary rifle and made the sounds of shooting they'd always used as kids, playing cowboys and Indians in the woods and along the banks of Buckman's Brook.

"I guess that's what I'm hoping for, Vaughn."

"You guess? You'd sure as better be damned sure. Once I sight in on the son-of-a-bitch and pull the trigger there ain't any not being sure. He's dead, by God."

Buckman didn't answer, letting Vaughn's comment stand for itself. He'd never be sure, just as he'd never allow himself reflective time to have doubts.

It would happen and he would bury it. He would not deal with the moral issues it could raise for him if he indulged himself in the luxury of thinking about it.

Vaughn seemed not to notice. Getting up from the couch, he pulled on his jacket.

"No point in waiting, Billy Buck. Let's do it."

THE SNOW WAS falling heavily as Erskine Dye lugged the last piece of the maple limb off to the side of the driveway. He cursed his luck, cursed the weather, cursed the heavens and he cursed the hands of God for sending the heavy snow which had caused the limb to drop. It was a kind of cursing he'd done a lot of lately. Not that he believed it did any good. He'd come to doubt the efficacy of both curses and prayers over the last few years.

He still believed in the church. It was his career. The job on the police force in town gave him his medical insurance and retirement pay, and the money it paid was an essential part of his income. But it was the church which served him the best. It housed him. It supplied him with adoring worshippers who carried out his suggestions and hung on his words. It paid him a small salary and its members wrote him into their wills. The church was fine. The problem didn't lie with the church.

It was faith and scripture, the underpinnings of the church, he'd come to doubt and disbelieve, although he managed to keep the depth of his disbelief from emerging fully into his consciousness. The doubt was bad enough. It crept over him in the middle of the night, as he woke from dreams which left him trembling and afraid, dreams nearly forgotten in the instant of awakening, leaving only terrible images and nameless fears rippling through him.

Like the one about finding himself in Hell, trapped in eternal pain, walking back and forth on the permanently snow-covered roads of the Old World, preaching in his church, shopping in Wesley Johnson's store, and visiting all the families of his congregation each week. The only thing setting it apart from his daily life was the knowledge he was in Hell. Forever in the Old

World. Forever in winter, lost to the warm Georgia pines and soft hills of his childhood.

His boots were cold, wet, and squishy. Leaving them on the step between the garage and his kitchen door, he brushed off his jacket and went inside the house. The bright florescent lights in the ceiling fixture glared on the white background of the wallpaper the last owner had put up. He'd never liked the ugly pattern, little red teakettles with white clock faces in them, surrounded by thin vines of ivy and ugly gold flecks, but he'd stopped seeing it after the third month of living there.

Hanging the jacket on a hook behind the door, he crossed to the counter and poured a cup of coffee. Fanning the steam toward his face, he listened to a weather report on WGHA in Graham. The snowstorm was expected to last through the night and into the following afternoon, growing heavier by midnight and beginning to taper off in the mid-morning. Already the main roads were treacherous and the back roads impassable. Interstate 91 and the Mass Pike were open, their speed limits reduced to forty miles an hour. The weather and road condition reports were followed by a list of closings and a warning to everyone in the listening area not to drive unless necessary.

"Late Spring storms such as this are particularly dangerous," the announcer said. "Most people have removed their snow tires and are not prepared for the slippery condition of the roads. If you have somewhere to go, forget it and relax at home."

Erskine Dye cursed again. If the roads were going to be bad, maybe he should cancel tonight's prayer meeting. He shook his head in fury, thinking of how a cancellation would throw his whole week off balance. Prayer meetings were his favorite church function. He didn't have to preach a sermon, working himself up in a lather of righteousness. It was an evening he could spend pleasantly discussing the divine inspiration of scripture and the work of the church, an evening of church business and finances, conversations filled gossip about members of the congregation, juicy tidbits scattered about with a few prayers and hymns. It was his time to ingratiate himself with members of the congregation, especially older ones looking into the abyss, desperate for ways to save themselves the pits of hell, willing to do anything, give him anything for assurances that they would get to enjoy the endless pleasures of heaven.

The women and men who came on Tuesdays and Thursdays dressed more casually for prayer meeting than they did for Sunday worship services. Dye liked to see the young girls in their tight fitting jeans. He'd been increasingly thinking about them as he went to sleep at night, picturing them dancing about him, clapping their hands, singing his praises, fighting over his favor, and begging for his touch. When this began to happen, he knew it was time to preach his love sermon again.

From time to time over the years, he'd been with one or another of the girls in the congregation. It never lasted long, and he was sure he never did them any harm. He thought of it as bringing them to Jesus through him. Love God and do as you please, because if you love the Lord it would be impossible for to displease him. Erskine's love sermon was built on his interpretation of that idea. Each time he gave it, he could see the excitement in several of the young girls' eyes. Eventually one of them would come up, flirting, wondering if she could do anything for him at the church, or at home. He'd praise her, praise the Lord, and be pulling those tight fitting jeans down over her sweet little butt within a week.

Then, a few weeks later, his eyes filled with tears, he would tell her they must stop sinning, beg God's forgiveness for their forbidden love. They'd get down on their knees and he'd raise a prayer, confessing to God how he loved this young girl, but knew God intended for him to remain single and pure. "Oh Lord," he would say in a voice broken with repentance, tears streaming down his cheeks. "I have strayed, we both have strayed, and all we want to do is to best serve your holy interests. Thank you, Jesus, for sending such sweetness to me. Through this young woman's pure and holy love I have found the way to rededicate myself to your calling. You have sent her to me as a divine instrument, playing the tune for both our salvations. I promise you Jesus that neither of us will sin again.

The girls were always flattered, embarrassed, confused by Dye's prayers, thankful their brief affair was over, glad of God's understanding and sworn never to talk about it. Ever. It was an easy promise to keep. Their fathers and uncles had forced many similar promises from most of them. Dye, unattached to any particular woman, was free to continue roving his congregation, the image of propriety.

Now his needs were building once more. Soon, he would give the love sermon. Next week, or the week after at the latest. He didn't want to cancel tonight's prayer meeting. Besides ruining his week, it was too much trouble. He'd have to call WGHA and have the cancellation put on their list. Then he'd have to call members of the congregation who had telephones. Still, there'd be those wouldn't get the word and he'd have to deal with their angry grumblings about plowing their drives with tractors and coming to the church at risk of life and limb, only to find no prayer meeting.

He knew who they'd be, elderly men and women with no phones and no taste for listening to the radio. He'd have to placate them, offer them coffee and tea, a few prayers and send them back to their farms. He'd end up holding a mini-prayer meeting anyway, and without the young girls. They wouldn't show up. They'd have heard the radio or gotten a phone call from someone who did, and they'd be home watching television, or they'd be rolling in the sack somewhere with one of those young boys with only lust in their hearts, their souls empty of God's grace.

Damn. It wasn't fair. A spring storm would not make him cancel. If anybody got stuck in the snow, injured, or killed, coming to the meeting that would just have to be the price they paid for their faith and dedication. Their gateway to heaven. He smiled, nodding to himself. He liked the sound of the phrase, their gateway to Heaven. He'd preach a sermon on it if anybody was maimed or killed trying to get to the church. He stretched and smiled. The matter was settled. There would be no cancellation of the prayer meeting.

Pouring another cup of coffee, he went into the living room and sat on the sagging couch. Old newspapers and magazines were scattered about, and six boxes of religious pamphlets stood piled against the wall next to a bookshelf filled with small statuettes of smiling animals. Except for the clutter and his meager personal possessions, everything in the house was just as it had been the day Noreen Shippee died and left it to him.

The phone rang. Putting the coffee down, he crossed to the hallway and picked it up.

"Reverend J. Erskine Dye."

"My name's Roger Teeter, Reverend Dye. I need some help and I've been told you might be able to give it to me."

The voice on the other end was strange. Blank. Deep and blank. Empty of feeling. He'd never heard anything like it. Whoever it was didn't sound as though he wanted any spiritual guidance.

"What can I do?" He answered smoothly, composing a professionally concerned tone.

"I'm looking for an old friend of mine who I believe is living somewhere near you."

"I know almost everyone here. Tell me who it is, I'll tell you where to find him."

"Buckman. Doctor William Buckman."

Dye's mind raced. Buckman a doctor? He thought how unlike the rest of the Buckmans he was. That, and his own sense about something unusual going on at the Buckman place, it figured. He smiled into the receiver as he began to stall, sure that here was something he might be able to use to his advantage.

"There are Several households of Buckmans in this area. William doesn't ring a bell. Certainly not a doctor. The closest doctors to Canaan Forks are over in the Falls. You need a doctor, look in the telephone directory."

"I'm not looking for a doctor, Reverend. I'm looking for William Buckman, Bill. He just happens to be a doctor."

"I don't know him."

"But you know Buckmans."

"Some of them are members of my church."

There was a pause on the other end. "Finding Doctor Buckman is very important to me."

Dye nodded, still smiling to himself. "There's a prayer meeting here at the church Thursday night." He scratched his upper lip. "There's also one tonight, and if some Buckmans are there they'd be able to tell you something. Too bad about this storm, though. I doubt if you'd make it here given the condition of the roads. Where are you now?"

"I'm in Canaan Falls."

Dye laughed. "Forget it Mr. Teeter. I was going to say if you were calling from the phone in Wesley Johnson's store you might be able to come tonight, but there's no way you're going to get into Canaan Forks until the storm's over and the roads are cleared. Plan on coming Thursday night. I'll make sure there are some Buckmans here. You can talk to them, see if any of them knows this Dr. William Buckman. Who knows, you might even find our worship service valuable."

"Thursday night is too long a time to wait. I'll come tonight."

Dye laughed softly into the receiver. Whatever Teeter wanted, it was clear that he was in a hurry. He'd push him a little farther; sound out his haste.

"You're not going to get here in this weather. No one's going to be driving into and around Canaan Forks this afternoon and this evening. I'm just hoping a few of the people who live closest to the church will be able to walk to the prayer meeting. You'll have to bide your time and wait for the storm to let up."

"I'll be there tonight."

There was a click and a dial tone.

Dye went back to the couch and sank in, drinking his coffee. The conversation had confused him. Calvin's son a doctor? That would be an odd turn of events; especially with scum like Wilfred, Vaughn, and Dave, to say nothing of the other brothers and sisters. He couldn't imagine Calvin producing anything other than drunks and brutes. Besides, if there'd been a doctor in the family wouldn't he have heard about it? Everybody in the Forks would know.

Still, it was odd, the way this Bill Buckman had suddenly appeared in Canaan Forks. Dye had never even known there was another Buckman son.

And then there was the Shoemaker woman who was with him. She sure as hellfire wasn't the type of woman the men around here liked, or the type who liked them. She'd go for a doctor, though. She was pushy and high toned in her ways, like city women are. And she'd been completely unimpressed by his standing in the church.

He was fascinated by the questions swirling in his thoughts. If Calvin's son was a doctor, what was he doing here, living in Calvin's house with the woman? And where was Calvin? And how could he use the answers once he found them out?

Beyond waiting for this Roger Teeter to show up, there was only one way to get information. Go to Calvin Buckman's house and ask questions. He put on his jacket, went to the garage and pulling on the wet boots, started walking. He wasn't about to risk driving in this weather.

CHAPTER EIGHTEEN

Canaan, Massachusetts \ Tuesday, May 7

KOENIG WAS FRUSTRATED. He had to get to Canaan Forks. Looking through the drugstore window at the heavy snow, clenching and unclenching his fists, he watched it pile up, white and heavy. He thought of Robert Frost's poems, tight, bitter little things, carefully crafted to mask a dark and violent heart. He felt close to Frost, a poet who knew how to say one thing to himself, another to a choice audience of readers, and make both statements satisfying, profitable.

There were no poets in the late Twentieth Century like the great ones of the first half. No Eliot. No Pound or Frost. No Yeats. On one hand the world of contemporary poetry was dominated by effete academics prancing around with their MFA degrees and on the other hand vulgar popularizers, all whiners, not a giant among them. He stood alone, carrying on the elite traditions of the past, adding his own unique elements to the mixture, sure, once the literary history of the second half of the Twentieth Century was written, the name of Christopher Koenig would be a major chapter.

A woman walking a small dog passed the window, leaning forward into the wind, her clothes white with the damp snow, the dog straining against the leash. Koenig watched her move and suddenly found himself thinking of the pleasure he would find in killing her, in putting his lips to her wounded neck and drinking deeply. He shuddered, afraid that someday he'd do it, give in to the impurity of the urge and drink, betraying himself, his calling.

Right now. It was possible. Easy. He could follow her home. Not even be noticed in the falling snow. He could watch her go in, wait outside for a few minutes, allowing the anticipation of the kill to build. Then let himself in. Be done with her and be gone, his desire spent and on his way to Canaan Forks to talk with the Reverend Dye before anyone found her.

It was a pleasant thought, and the shivers of pleasure unnerved him. He chased it from his mind. A distraction. There had been many distractions of late. Not just the idea of drinking from his kills. He'd played with such images for as long as he could remember, always before discarding and nearly forgetting them quickly. But within the last two years the idea of doing it had given way to taunting and frustrating fantasies, their power over his imagination increasing. He resisted them as decadent and impure, capable of attracting unwanted attention to his kills. The kind of thing that could bring him down. He knew what the forensic people could do with the saliva they'd find. And the press would love it. What a heyday they'd have with vampire killer headlines.

Even without saliva tests, giving into the sickness of the urge would add a dangerous dimension to killing. It would also mean losing his professional edge. He'd seen too many middle aged men do foolish things. Life wrecking things. Leave wives they had loved for years, women who had loved them back. Idiots, starry eyed horny for some young body they wouldn't even be able to talk to once they got their rocks off. Or respected accountants who'd embezzled from lifelong employers, running off to hide in easily detected resorts, living off the money, celebrating their wealth with foolish abandon.

Giving in to his thirst, to this desire for a random kill, would be equally adolescent, going back to the spontaneous murders of his youth. He'd be no better than the fifty year old husband looking for youthful sex, the embezzling accountant looking for the wealth of his young dreams. Too much of his life had gone into perfecting the art of the kill to blow it now and risk losing everything on the whims of impure desire. Shaking his head, he took a deep breath and watched the woman disappear into the storm.

It was time to get to work. Pulling his eyes from the spot he had seen her last, he looked at the street. It was filling up with four wheel drive cars and trucks, yellow snowplows attached them. He grinned and snapped his fingers, then returned to the phone booth. Fifteen minutes later, he was walking into the local car rental agency where a Jeep was waiting for him.

PEERING THROUGH THE dusty window on the Buckman's porch, Erskine Dye could see Velma crying, hear her thick muffled sobs filling the room. Irene Shoemaker was on the couch beside the girl, holding her hand and speaking softly. Buckman sat at the kitchen table watching Vaughn clean a .30-30, running soft white patches of cotton into the barrel with a ramrod. A black twenty-two caliber pistol sat on the table by his hand.

"It ain't right, Uncle Billy Buck. Reverend Dye'll find out I'm going to have the baby and he'll send me to Hell."

Through leaky windows and thin walls Dye could make out her words. Velma pregnant? The knowledge sent a shiver down his back. Lord, but he'd love to break down the door and rush in, yelling about how he really was going to send her straight to Hell, straight to the burning coal fires of damnation and Satan's eternal torture where her only companions would be homosexuals and Jews and Blacks and murderers and all other varieties of human vermin, where she would never see the friendly faces or hear the comfortable voices of family and friends from Canaan Forks.

And she'd get down on her knees and beg him not to do it. Please, she'd say, don't send me to Hell, Reverend Dye.

Then he'd say he'd spare her if she'd tell him what was going on in Calvin Buckman's house. Tell him about the baby she'd mentioned. Tell him about sin among the Buckmans and why her uncle and the Shoemaker woman were there. Tell him where Calvin was. Why he'd run off. Tell him what it was she'd done that was so evil she was afraid he'd send her to Hell. If she'd open all the secrets the Buckmans were hiding and confess all her own sins, he might just try to convince God to forgive her and prepare a place in Heaven for her. That was his kind of power. That's what being a preacher was about; the thrill of having people acknowledge their depravations and iniquities and holding possibility of the Lord's forgiveness over them.

Excited, he almost pushed his shoulder to the door, ready to crash it open. Then he thought of Buckman. Calvin's son would never let him say the first few words of Hellfire before telling him to shut up and get out. It would be best to wait. Do what he'd come here to do. Invite them all to the prayer meeting again and slip around the subject, trying to find out what this Roger Teeter wanted and what this business with Buckman being a doctor was all about.

He knocked.

Buckman grabbed the pistol, motioning for Irene to open the door. Nearly knocking his chair over, Vaughn moved toward the door, holding the half cleaned rifle like a club. Dye came into the room, brushing snow from his jacket, smiling at the four of them. Velma's jaw hung slackly as she shivered in the draft.

"It's him, Uncle Billy Buck, come to send me to the Devil. He's going to see all these guns and know something's bad wrong. Oh Jesus, maybe if I tell him what I done he won't let the Devil get me. Maybe he'll tell God to let me be." Tears streamed down her cheeks as she cringed against the stove.

"I don't want you here, Dye." Buckman lowered the pistol, resting it back on the table.

He glanced at Velma, trying with his eyes to tell her to hold on, but she was as close to the edge as he'd seen her. If Dye made the right move, said the right thing, she'd go over and tell him everything.

"I only stopped by to remind you of the prayer meeting at the church tonight."

"You've already reminded us."

Dye hesitated. His response had to be plausible. He could see Buckman's eyes narrow, his hands clench. "The snow worried me," he finally said. "I thought you might figure it was canceled because of the bad roads, but I'm not canceling. Everything's going on as planned. People who can get to the church should plan on coming. I just wanted you to know."

Buckman nodded. "Now we do."

Dye held his arms out toward the girl. "You should be at the meeting, Velma. God's been missing you. Jesus has been missing you." He smiled, softening his voice. "I've been missing you, child. And I can tell you've been missing all three of us, me, God, and Jesus. You need us, don't you? You need us real bad."

Wide eyed, trembling, Velma nodded, pulling at Irene's grip, trying to free herself.

Buckman took a step toward him. "Leave her alone, Dye."

It was too late. The girl broke suddenly away and ran toward Erskine Dye, throwing herself at his legs, wrapping her arms around them.

"Don't send me to Hell, Reverend Dye. Please. I didn't mean for it to happen."

Helping her up, Dye spoke softly to her, playing the opening carefully, watching Buckman and Vaughn.

"I'm sure you didn't, Velma. You're a good girl. You've always been a good girl, haven't you?"

She nodded, sniffling. "Always, Reverend. Almost always, anyway."

"But you did something bad this time, right?"

"But I didn't mean it, Reverend Dye. I didn't mean to do nothing bad. Please, you got to believe me."

He answered in his deepest, smoothest voice. "You knew making a baby with your grandfather was a bad thing to do, didn't you Velma?

Before she could answer, Buckman stepped in, pulling Velma's hands away from him and leading her over to Irene. "I'm sorry, Reverend, but Velma won't be able to come to your prayer meeting tonight."

"And why not, Doctor?" Dye stressed the last word.

Buckman turned, face stiff with anger and surprise, his stomach churning. He wanted to crash the pistol across Dye's smug smile. He had a quick violent fantasy; unlike any he'd had since his childhood. He could almost see blood pouring from the man's face. He chased the image away, carefully ignoring the preacher's use of the title, doctor.

"She can't come because we have family business."

"Business which Velma is obviously unhappy about." Dye smiled his voice loud.

Buckman shrugged.

Dye leaned toward him. "Why don't you let me take her to the services? It would save you the trouble."

Buckman shook his head.

"Surely you don't want to deny this poor child the comforts of the worship she's so obviously in need of. Look at how distressed she is."

"Reverend Dye's right, Uncle Billy Buck. I need to go to the church awful bad. If I go to the church Reverend Dye won't send me down to Hell. I don't want to go to Hell, Uncle Billy Buck." Tears streamed down the girl's cheeks as she strained against Irene's hold on her arms. Her breath came in sharp, noisy gulps and she was trembling.

"You're not going to Hell, Velma, count on it." Buckman looked at Vaughn, who had been listening with wide eyes.

"Take her up to her room. I don't want this creep upsetting her any more than he already has."

Velma looked from Buckman to Dye, her eyes moving wildly as Vaughn took her hand. She pulled away, again throwing herself at Dye, grabbing his arm, her gulping sobs the loudest sound in the room.

Dye stroked her hair. "It's all right, Velma. You confess to me and I'll see to it that Jesus does all right by you. You understand?"

She managed to nod her head. "I done bad things, Reverend Dye. Things they send people to Hell for doing. You got to save me."

Again, Buckman pulled her away, this time leading her to the living room, Vaughn following closely behind. She tried getting away, back to Dye, but Buckman's grip was firm. He turned her over to Vaughn and came back to the kitchen, standing in the middle of the room, several feet from Dye.

"I've already thrown you out of here once, Dye. Do you want me to do it again?"

The preacher stood still, staring into Buckman's eyes. "What's wrong, Doctor?"

"Mister, Reverend. Mr. Buckman. Where did you get this doctor business?"

Dye laughed. "From a friend of yours, Doctor Buckman. Roger Teeter? He called me, looking for you."

"I've never heard of him. And if I were a doctor, why would I be living here and not practicing medicine?"

"There could be many reasons." Dye was still smiling, staring into Buckman's eyes.

This was wonderful. He surely was onto something. No doubt. Buckman was backing away, even physically, inching closer to the stove and farther from Erskine Dye. All he had to do was push a little harder, handle him like he'd handle one of the punks he arrested any Friday or Saturday night in the Falls. Preachers and cops could always make people back down if they played their cards right. And Erskine Dye knew how to play his cards right. It was his stock in trade in both professions.

"Maybe you killed a patient, accidentally, of course. Or maybe you've been selling prescription drugs and the police are after you. Oxy maybe? Those are just guesses, you understand. I don't know why they'd be after you. Or why anybody else would, but this Teeter surely wants to find you. I wouldn't be surprised if he's eager enough to try driving through the snow to get to the prayer meeting tonight."

"I don't know anything about him."

"Then why are you cleaning all these guns, Doctor? And why were you so jumpy when I came to the door?"

Off guard, Buckman didn't know what to say. Dye's questions were coming too fast, and he hadn't prepared a story. He'd been winging it since he came back to the Old World.

Irene saved him. "They belong to Bill's father, Reverend Dye. We noticed they were covered with dirt and rust. Vaughn said we should clean them. And it's mister, as he said earlier, not doctor."

Dye rolled his eyes, pulling on his preaching voice. "There are lies in this place. Lies on all your lips. Lies in all your eyes. That poor child you won't let me help has heard them all and wants freedom from them. You saw how she threw herself at me. How you had to force her away and take her from the room. Lies blow through men's hearts on winds from Hell. Now I have some choices to make, Doctor, and you're going to help me make them."

He paused, staring at Buckman as Vaughn came back into the room. "The girl's in her bedroom, Billy Buck."

Buckman sighed. "Maybe you ought to stay with her, Vaughn."

He shook his head. "She'll be all right. Said she wanted to lie down for a while."

Buckman started to reply but Dye cut him off. "I'm not backing off, Doctor Buckman, Velma or no Velma at my prayer meeting. I told you I had some choices to make, and you'd best listen to me. This Mr. Roger Teeter is going to be at my place as soon as he can get through the storm. Perhaps sometime today if he has four wheel drive. I'm going to have to see him, listen to his questions and decide how to answer them. You could help me decide by telling me the truth."

Buckman sat at the table, folding his hands around the butt of the pistol. It was time to take charge. Taking a deep breath, he raised his eyes to meet the preachers.

"If I were a renegade doctor running from the police, wouldn't killing you be the smartest thing for me to do? With the medical skills a doctor has, it would be easy to make your death look natural, or like an accident."

Dye moved closer to the door, his eyes fastened on Buckman's.

Vaughn came back into the room, picking up the rifle he'd been cleaning earlier. "By God, wouldn't many people around here miss him, for sure. He's got people around here scared shitless of the Devil and forgetting all about the Lord. That don't make for much of a religion in my book. I say the best thing to do with him is dump him out on the road and run him over a few times with Calvin's pickup."

He grinned at Buckman, waving the rifle as he spoke. "Of course, we'd have to beat him over the head so's he couldn't run away before we ran him over."

Dye flinched briefly, then made another smile. "You could do everything you say, no doubt, Doctor, but you'd still have Roger Teeter coming after you. What is he? Police? The enraged parent or husband of someone you killed by mistake on an operating table? I talked to him on the telephone, Doctor, and his voice gave me chills. I can only imagine how it would sound to the person he was after. It's up to you what I tell him when he shows up at my place asking about you and looking for you."

Vaughn brandished the rifle. "See, Billy Buck, we ought to crush this son-of-a-bitch out on the road, run the pickup over his neck and leave him out there like any other roadkill. Won't bother anybody to have him gone, except for a few of the older people who like to think of their sinful neighbors screaming in lakes of burning cow shit, and the crows and dogs would be happy to have his holier than thou little body to chew on."

Buckman nodded. "It's an attractive idea, Vaughn."

"You bet your ass it's an attractive idea, Billy Buck, and we could do it easy. Just let me bash him one with this here rifle butt and we'll haul him out there and run the fuck over him until we're tired of doing it."

"The Lord is my shepherd. I do not fear you." Dye heard the emptiness of his voice as he made another smile. It didn't come as easily as the last, which had been difficult enough for him. He hadn't heard God's voice in a longtime. Hadn't felt safe in God's hands in a long time. Hadn't thought much about God at all, beyond how he could use him to force obedience from the members of his congregation.

"We could do it even more easily, Vaughn. If I was a doctor, like the Reverend here thinks, I could give him a simple shot of something that would make him drop dead of a heart attack. No marks. No violence. We'd leave him dead in a chair at his house."

"I suppose we could, Billy Buck, if you was a doctor. But since you say you ain't no doctor, I got an idea that'd be even more fun than running his neck over with the pickup. Let's stake him out behind the house, put dog food on his nuts and turn Calvin's hounds loose on him. That'd be some fun, don't you think?"

Buckman gave another nod, pretending to think about it. He hoped Vaughn was serious. He wasn't prepared to do anything quite so horrendous to Dye, but the kind of creative violence Vaughn was displaying might come in handy later, when Teeter showed up.

Teeter. It was the first time he had a name for the man who had come after him at his home in the Bucks County night, a name for the man who had murdered patients at Worthington- Philadelphia. Teeter. An innocuous name. Like a child's playground toy. Teeter-totter.

"Let him go, Vaughn," he said at last.

Dye visibly sank with relief.

"Shit, Billy Buck, you're spoiling all the fun."

"Maybe, but he's not important."

Dye took a deep breath, expanding his chest. "But Mr. Roger Teeter is, right Doctor Buckman?"

"I've never heard of Roger Teeter."

"He's heard of you."

Vaughn snorted. "Hell, he's doing it again. Let me get the dog food and the tent stakes, Billy Buck."

Irene walked over to Dye, putting her hand on his arm. Starting, he pulled away.

"I think you'd better go now," she said. "Bill's still in a pretty good mood, but you're working on him. Pretty soon he'll start listening to Vaughn's good ideas and you'll find yourself in more trouble than a thousand hours of praying could help you out of."

Dye answered softly, looking at her conspiratorially. "Why's he here? How come Calvin's son is a doctor and what's he doing here? Hiding out like he is? Why's he doing it?"

"Just go, Reverend Dye. It's best for all of us. Go and forget about us. Soon enough we'll be gone from Canaan Forks and your life can get back to normal. That's what you want, isn't it? Things back to normal? Your church and congregation in good shape? Your health?"

Erskine Dye nodded. Those were the things he wanted, weren't they? He thought of the young girls who came to his prayer meetings in tight jeans. It was surely time to get the love sermon out, polish it up a bit and preach it.

But he wanted more. He wanted to know what was going on with the Buckmans. Perhaps there was a scandal here. A good scandal could be a gold mine, something that would make normal sinfulness pale. He'd never been able to preach effectively against incest and drunkenness and the array of sin and abuse committed by the people of Canaan Forks. If he had been prideful enough to try, they would have laughed, accusing him of misunderstanding their way of life and the rights that come with it. But something was wrong here. Something was far more awry than Canaan Fork's version of normality. And he wanted in on it.

He forced another smile, giving Irene the trace of a bow. "You're right, ma'am. Those are the things I want."

He walked to the door, standing with his hand on the knob. "You tell that child to get herself down to the prayer meeting tonight, hear?"

"I don't think she'll be there," Irene told him.

He shrugged, giving it up with one last try. They would expect no less of him. "It's in her own best interest. I can tell she needs prayer."

He went out into the snow and started walking home to wait for Roger Teeter.

CHAPTER NINETEEN

Canaan, Massachusetts \ Tuesday, May 7

NEARLY SLIDING INTO a ditch, Koenig dropped his rented Jeep into four wheel drive and pulled out of the skid. Snow heavy branches from trees growing close to the roadside slashed against the Jeep's sides. Once back on the Windybush Road, he stopped and looked at the Black Horse Pike below. Wesley Johnson's store was down there, nestled somewhere among the scattered farm buildings and houses, smoke curling from their chimneys.

The minister's words over the telephone had told him enough. "If you were calling from the phone in Wesley Johnson's store you might be able to come tonight."

Koenig's task was simple, find the store to find Dye. Find Dye to find Buckman. Find Buckman and this damned business will quickly be over. He patted the canvass bag on the seat next to him, feeling the hard lumps of the silenced pistol and the sharpened knives inside.

Humming to the Mozart coming from the tape deck, he put the Jeep in gear and started slowly back down the Windybush. His hands ached from gripping the steering wheel. The road wound down through sharp turns, edged by steep drop-offs into rocky woodlands. The snow seemed to grow deeper with every fraction of a mile he drove, bouncing over buried ruts and potholes.

How did people manage to live in these backwoods, backwater bush towns, always driving on roads like this, far away from concerts and poetry readings, without the theater, without fine cinemas and decent restaurants? Life would be totally barren without the higher culture of city life. Overlook urban street scum. Ignore the mindless pettiness of the solid citizens. Even in the decadence of the present, there were always places in cities where the life of the mind was catered to, where it was appreciated, regarded as a mark of civilization.

And Koenig thought of himself as the most civilized person he knew. A poet. A scholar. A lover of fine music and art. He had spent a lifetime cultivating his tastes and, whenever possible, eliminating people who existed on levels below his.

Suddenly, driving past a small house alongside of the road, paint long ago chipped away, porch roof barely hanging onto the house, he understood what kept people here. Even with the thick layer of snow, he saw piles of trash, hulks of discarded cars and farm equipment in the yard, out-buildings fallen into little more than piles of gray lumber. People lived here because they didn't care about anything beyond eating, defecation, and fornication.

The whole valley was filled with prey. Later, once he was retired and bored, it might be an interesting place to cleanse. Much later, of course; once he had put all his business in order. Buckman had come from this sordid world. He almost laughed at the irony. His immediate concern, the person he had come here to kill, was one who had pulled himself out of this squalor and become a man of some accomplishment. Allowing himself a broad smile, Koenig sighed. It would be quite appropriate for him to return to Canaan Forks sometime, preferably during predictably warm weather, to do the cleansing. Preoccupied with thoughts of future kills, he skidded into a horseshoe bend, nearly sliding off the road again. Pulling out of the second skid, the Jeep stalled briefly, then bucked hard as the engine caught. Koenig was knocked against the door. Sharp pain shot up his left arm.

Pulling to the side of the road in a rage, Koenig hit the steering wheel with both fists, the impact intensifying the pain in his arm. The situation was abominable. Jeeps were for redneck idiots to run around in, wrecking forests, deserts, and any other open land they could drive through, tearing up the soil and ruining stream beds. Resting his head against the back of the seat, he briefly entertained a fantasy in which he was hiding in a blind, high in a tree, shooting at four-wheeling rednecks, watching their heads spatter like red hail against the interiors of their wildly swerving Jeeps. He allowed the images to drift through his mind until, realizing what he was doing, he straightened and banished them. Playing with thoughts of kills, random and unpaid, had just ended up with him nearly having an accident. He needed control. Now more than ever. And he was indulging fantasies. Where was his edge? His intellect? Was reason deserting him?

After several minutes, he started driving again, more slowly than before, tension and the pain from the arm churning his rage. The engine missed, ran smoothly for a few moments, then missed again. Koenig cursed, screaming at the windshield. It was all wrong. The Worthington job had been wrong from the beginning. He had been wrong to take it. Bad judgment. He'd never thought of himself as having bad judgment, but he'd bought into Castile's asinine plan, hadn't he? Damn foolishness. There hadn't even been the appropriate pleasure in it, unless he counted that he had found in disposing of Blanchard and Castile. They had been fine kills. Among the best. There was poetry in them.

Now he was here, driving around in the snow-covered backwoods of New England, trying to clean up the last of a bad job, the grand finale in cleaning up the results of his error in judgement, something that had he been more careful, if he had thought things through more carefully, he would never have to do. It was all wrong. The weather was wrong. The engine sounded wrong. He hit the steering wheel again. The pain returned with such sudden sharpness, he nearly passed out and his foot slipped off the accelerator pedal. The Jeep a stalled again.

His cry of rage filled the cab. If he didn't kill himself driving off the road, this frigging car would probably quit on him and he'd freeze and die in the snowstorm. And all because of Buckman. Goddamned Buckman. This was one kill he'd enjoy above almost all. Maybe it was the one after which he would drink. He could drink Buckman's blood, wait for it to process through his kidneys then piss it out, spraying it over the bastard's corpse. He smiled. There was poetry in the fantasy.

Then it caught up with him, the sick urge raising its images again, just minutes after he'd chased them off. What was happening to him? He was losing control of some vital aspect of himself, but what was it? He looked at his reflection in the rearview mirror, baring his teeth and snarling.

After several failed attempts, he got the Jeep started. Driving slowly through the swirling snow, he tried and failed to banish new images of a dying Buckman floating around the air before him, throat slashed, eyes wildly trying to comprehend what had happened to him. Absorbed in the thought as he entered a series of sharp turns shortly before the Windybush ended at the Black Horse Pike, he didn't notice the large oak felled by snow, lying across the road. When he did finally see it, there was no time to avoid the crash. The Jeep slowly bounced off the tree and slid downhill into the woods, coming to rest against a boulder, its front end destroyed, the hood up, blocking the windshield, steam pouring from the engine.

Uninjured, Koenig howled in rage, the sound rising through the snow like the wail of a wounded and hungry carnivorous predator.

THE GUNS, CLEANED, oiled, and loaded, Buckman lined them up on the kitchen table and sat in a chair staring at them, a cup of coffee untouched in front of him. Irene walked over from her position by the porch window and picked up the pistol.

"My father had one like this. We used to take it out to the dump and shoot rats."

"Quite the traditional American pastime." Buckman smiled without humor. It was the first thing he'd said since Erskine Dye left.

"I was the ace tin can shooter in the family. Dad and my brother would pop away with a twenty-two rifle, but I outshot them all with the pistol. Used to make them furious, especially since rifles are supposed to be much more accurate than pistols." She turned the weapon over in her hands, the shiny black surface catching the light and bouncing it around the room. "And even more especially, since I was a girl," she added.

Buckman's eyes traveled from her face down to the pistol in her hand. She was still turning it over. "It's loaded, you know."

She nodded. "The safety's on. I made sure. I know guns, Bill."

Vaughn picked up the .30-30. Pointing it at the window, he sighted along the barrel. "By god, this ain't no tin can we're talking about shooting today, right Billy Buck?"

Buckman nodded.

Vaughn gave him a black-toothed smile. "So, tell me Billy Buck, now the minister's gone, we can be square with each other. You a doctor like he says?"

Taking a sip of lukewarm coffee, Buckman slid his chair back. The legs squeaked against the floorboards. Rising, he walked to the window and stood directly behind his brother. "Would it make any difference if I was? Would it make any difference if I was a bank robber, hiding out here?"

Vaughn shook his head. "By god, I guess it wouldn't make no difference at all. Either way, you're my brother and either way I'd stand by you."

Buckman rested his hand on Vaughn's shoulder. "Thanks."

"No point in thanking me. It's the way things are, although, I'd like to think you're a bank robber instead of a goddamn doctor."

"Being a bank robber's a lot less complicated, you mean?"

Vaughn shook his head. "More honest, Billy Buck. A bank robber don't pretend to be nothing but what he is. He steals money, and that's it. Doctors, at least from my experience with them, don't want nothing to do with you unless you got money to give them for doing what they're supposed to do for you, which is make you healthy, like God intended for people to be. God never intended for people to have money, although he don't object to it none, so their ain't nothing wrong with stealing it, like bank robbers do. Hell, God didn't create money, people did. But I figure God meant for people to be healthy. He created them and he created health, so they're supposed to go together, you know? It ain't right for doctors to hold health over peoples' heads for money."

Buckman smiled at his brother. Vaughn was still the intellectual he'd been when they were kids, even if the ideas and information he intellectualized with were Old World primitive.

Taking the smile for agreement, Vaughn nodded. "So, I'm going to think of you as being a bank robber on the run, Billy Buck, and I'm proud of you.

It's a better than being a drunk like me and Dave, or Calvin, for that matter."

Irene interrupted. "Are you boys just going to stand here and chat about doctors and bank robbers, or are we going to do something about Teeter?"

"We're going to do something," Buckman said. "Vaughn's going to set up a sniper's nest in the barn, in the hayloft, where he can overlook the road and the yard. You and I are going to keep watch at the windows, me at the front, you at the back."

Irene asked, "What about Velma?"

"I'll bring her down here and we'll keep her in the living room."

"Let me get her, Bill. The poor kid needs a woman's understanding right now. Between what your father did to her and what Dye talks about doing, plus the uncertainty of everything around here, she's a wreck."

Irene left. She was back in thirty seconds.

"She's gone, Bill. Her bedroom window's open. It looks like she went out and jumped off the porch roof."

"The prayer meeting." Buckman's voice was a snarl. "She's gone to that goddamned prayer meeting."

Vaughn shrugged. "No big deal, Billy Buck. We just change our plans a little bit. Instead of waiting for Teeter here, we'll wait for him at the church."

STANDING IN THE road, shoes filled with snow, feet cold and wet, his gloveless hand numb from holding the canvass bag, Koenig shivered in the wind, watching the pickup move slowly down the hill toward him, the pain in his arm growing steadily worse.

The driver stopped as he came to where Koenig stood. The truck was a heavy four wheel drive model with huge tires, a rack of four large round running lights on the roof, and a gun rack with three rifles hanging in the rear window. Even with the windows shut, Koenig heard heavy metal blaring from the stereo. The driver, a boy in his late teens, leaned across the seat and rolled down the passenger's side window, shouting over the music.

"Is that your Jeep I seen back there, off the road and in the woods?"

Koenig nodded, answering softly. "I hit a tree lying across the road."

"I couldn't hear what you said."

Koenig made a face and pointed to his throat. "Turn down your music if that's what you call that noise. I can't talk any louder. Sore throat." He was damned if he was going to shout to be heard over the crap the boy was blasting into the pickup's cab. Cold or not, he wasn't going to be inconvenienced by anything less than Mozart. The discordant cacophonous roar of electric basses and guitars coming from the truck wasn't worthy of being called music.

The boy reached toward the dash and the sound stopped. Then he looked back at Koenig.

"I said I hit a tree that was lying in the road back there. The Jeep went down the hill and I'm walking."

"I seen the tree, then I seen your skid marks and looked down in the woods and seen your Jeep." Drinking from a beer can, the boy looked unsmilingly at Koenig. "I hooked up my winch and chain and moved the tree out of the way, so's I could get through, you know?"

Koenig looked back at him, without expression.

"Your Jeep's fucked up real bad, you know?"

"I know."

"I could've winched it up the hill, but there wasn't no good to come of it, you know? Ain't nobody can drive it like it is, all smashed up. It'd just be another hazard in the road, you know? Something for somebody else to hit and smash his car into."

"What good thinking." Koenig knew the boy could not comprehend the sarcasm in his voice.

The boy took another swallow of beer. "Look at all the shit you run into hitting that tree. Think of somebody hitting your Jeep. Could kill them, you know."

"I wouldn't want to be responsible for killing anybody." Koenig smiled at the boy.

"Want a beer?" He held another can out the truck window.

"No. Just a ride."

"Sure. Get in. Where are you going?"

Koenig opened the door, threw his canvass bag on the floor and taking the driver's offered hand, pulled himself up into the cab. Once seated, he picked up the bag and set it on his lap. Opening it quietly, he reached in, slipped his hands into a pair of rubber gloves, and picked up the gun, keeping it hidden in the bag.

"Your truck isn't easy to get into."

"It's them heavy duty springs and the big wheels. I got big wheels on it. I can take the fucker just about anywheres I want, you know? It's not like them trucks you see at the fair, you know, the ones that run all over each other and smash the shit out of things. Them mothers really got big wheels, but these here are plenty big enough for me, you know? I can take her out in the woods, drive any fucking place I want to with it, up and down streams. Ain't hardly nothing can stop this baby, you know?"

He put it in gear and started down the road. "My name's Carl Shippee. What's yours?"

"Roger Teeter."

The boy reached a hand over to Koenig. "Glad to meet you, Roger. So, where are you going?"

Koenig ignored the outstretched hand. "I'm looking for some people by the name of Buckman."

"We got a few Buckmans around here. Just a mile back up the Windybush Road where you walked from is Willard Buckman's place. You could've stopped right there if you'd've known."

"Maybe you could take me back there now." Koenig's fingers tightened around the gun as he spoke.

The boy shook his head. "I ain't got time. Besides, the driving sucks too bad to go back uphill, you know? Even with the tranny in low four wheel drive like I got it, driving up that hill would be a pain in the ass."

"Then you'd better let me out. I'll just walk back up there myself."

Stopping the truck in the middle of the roadway, the boy shook his head. "Okay, if you want. It's the first house you come to, on the left but it's shitty weather to be walking."

Koenig had his silenced pistol out, pointed at Carl Shippee. "I'm not going to walk. Too bad, Carl, you'd have lived a little longer if you'd been willing to put yourself out enough to have backtracked up there for me."

Before Carl could react, the pistol softly spat three times, the rounds pounding into his midsection. The boy jerked twice, then slumped silently against the door. Koenig pulled the body to the right side of the truck, climbed over it, and got behind the wheel. Within seconds he had turned around and was headed back up the Windybush toward Wilfred Buckman's house, slipping, sliding, but making steady progress up the hill. He could barely hear the Mozart he was whistling over the deep whine of the lower case four wheel drive. Maybe a visit to Wilfred Buckman would be more useful than talking to the minister.

VELMA REACHED Erskine Dye's house less than five minutes after Dye got back from the Buckman place. The hood of his car was steaming from melting snow and his footprints were still clear and sharp in the snow. She trembled and cried, standing outside the door, afraid to knock. Afraid of his voice, of his eyes, of the fate he might damn her to.

She'd never thought of religion as involving anyone other than Reverend Dye. In her mind, he was God, Jesus, and Satan all in one. There was no other figure. Just Reverend Erskine Dye, the man who could damn her to eternal pain in the boiling lakes of shit Grampy Calvin had told her about. Reverend Dye controlled her fate, and she had lied to him. Lied about Uncle Billy Buck being a doctor. Lied about Grampy Calvin being dead, telling him how Grampy had gone off to she didn't know where. Lied about Uncle Billy Buck getting her set up for the abortion tomorrow. She had lied and Reverend Dye knew all her lies. She could tell by the way he looked at her.

She raised her hand to knock. Lowered it. Raised it again, then stopped. If she knocked and he came to the door, what then? He would take her inside. What would he do to her there? Maybe there was a doorway leading straight from his cellar to Hell. Maybe he would drag her down there and drop her into the boiling lakes without even giving her a chance to pray for forgiveness. Yell at her in that deep voice of his, lightning coming from his eyes as he dragged her down the cellar stairs toward Hell.

Turning, she walked off the porch, moving away from Reverend Dye's house as fast as she could. She'd go to the church. There wouldn't be any steps leading down to Hell in the Church. The church was a good place. They prayed in church. And sang hymns. There was a kitchen in the cellar at the church, not steps leading down to Hell. There was a kitchen, with brightly painted walls and wallpaper around the stove and sink, bright wallpaper with pictures of flowers and vine leaves.

She'd always had fun in the kitchen. She and the other girls had made cookies and played games, sitting around the table gossiping and laughing. When she was younger, her Sunday School class would meet down there. Mrs. Chapman would pass out their workbooks and they'd color pictures of Jesus and His Disciples, play Bible quiz, and sing songs while Mrs. Chapman played the piano.

She walked on, feeling safer with each step she took away from Reverend Dye's house toward the church. The church was safety. Reverend Dye couldn't drag her off to Hell in the church. He'd have to listen to her. Hear how things got all confused and how Grampy Calvin made her do things with him and how she hadn't meant to kill him or to keep any of those secrets about Uncle Billy Buck from him.

She was halfway from the house to the road when she heard him call her name. A chill colder than the snow ran through her at the sound. She quickened her pace.

He called again.

She stopped and turned to look at him.

He stood on the porch, wearing his black suit, holding on to a post and leaning out, toward the yard, looking like he could grab her with his eyes and hold her there like he'd cast a spell. She stopped, her heart pounding.

"Where are you going, Velma?"

She stammered. "I didn't think you was home, Reverend Dye, so I was going over to the church to look for you."

He smiled at her, beckoning with his arm. "Well, I'm not at the church, child. I'm right here. You come on up here and tell me what's on your mind."

She stood still, as though the snow had become frozen snakes, grasping her feet and holding her motionless, threatening to fill her with cold poison if she took a step toward the house. Dye watched her for a moment, his smile unchanged.

"Velma, I said for you to come over here. Now what's the matter?"

"Nothing, Reverend Dye."

He nodded. "Then come, child. Let me help you."

When she didn't move, he came down from the porch and walked toward her. She tried running, but the snakes wouldn't let go of her feet.

"Why, child, you look scared to death," Dye said as he came up to her and took hold of her arm, his grip almost painful.

Saying nothing, still motionless, she looked into his eyes. She thought she saw cruel lightning flashing in the depths behind them.

"Let's go inside, Velma." He tugged at her, the grip tightening. She resisted for a moment and then her body turned to liquid, her strength gone, and she allowed him to pull her toward the house.

"Tell me what's wrong," Dye said once they were inside, standing close to the woodstove.

Shivering, she shook her head. "Nothing's wrong, Reverend."

He gave her as kindly a smile as he could force. "Then why did you come here? You must have wanted something."

She shook her head again. Maybe if she didn't say anything, he'd stop asking questions.

For a moment, she believed she might be right, as he shrugged and walked away, toward his kitchen. Then, at the doorway, he turned, his right hand hanging from the top molding, his smile no longer kindly.

"Something is very wrong at your house, Velma. I want you to tell me all about it. Everything. You understand?"

Her heart pounding harder, sure that he already knew about her and Grampy Cal making the baby and about the abortion too. Oh, Jesus, he did. She was sure he knew about the abortion Uncle Billy Buck had planned for her. And if he knew about the abortion, he must know about Grampy Cal and how she killed him. She was going to Hell, no doubt about it. She felt sick.

He saw her expression and dropping his hand from the molding, moved closer. "Your grandfather has been missing for three or four days, just about the time this mysterious uncle of yours seems to have turned up. And he's a doctor? What's going on with you, child? And what's going on at your place?"

He was talking about Grampy Cal still being missing. Maybe he didn't know everything. She didn't understand what was going on. Her throat was stiff, dry, and sore. Even trying to make words come out would choke her. She shook her head, gulping.

"Jesus wants you tell me, Velma. How can I help you if I don't know what's wrong?"

"There ain't nothing wrong Reverend Dye." It hurt to talk. She wanted him to stop asking questions.

He broadened his smile, leaning toward her, looking like she'd always imagined the wolf from Little Red Riding Hood looking. "I only want to help you, child."

"I don't need no help."

"Then why did you come here?"

"Reverend Dye, I.." She started to answer, but the words stuck dryly in her throat and her eyes moved wildly about the room, finally coming back to Dye, standing tall above her. His chin looked as though he was about to chop into her soul and cut the truth out of her.

"You're worried about the baby, aren't you?"

The kindliness in his voice soothed her, but her throat was too tight for an answer. She nodded lightly.

He nodded back. "But other things worry you too, don't they, child?"

She looked up at him, at the sharp chin and the smiling lips. Again, she nodded.

"Maybe we should pray about it," he said.

Velma looked down at the ash dust on the hearth in front of the woodstove.

"Praying on it would be a good idea, child. Prayer is always a good idea. Talking to God and Jesus unburdens your soul. It frees you. You want to be free of sin, don't you Velma? You want your soul prepared for Heaven, not doomed to Hell, don't you?"

She kept her eyes on the hearth, not wanting to answer, but unable to keep from nodding at his questions. Suddenly he grasped her arm, twisting it and forcing her to her knees on the middle of the living room floor.

"Then we're going to pray about it, Velma. We're going to talk to the Lord and you're going to tell him everything that's on your mind, everything that's bothering you. And if you don't tell him, if you hold anything back, me and the Lord are going to know about it and we're going to be right mad at you. You don't want me and the Lord mad at you, do you child?"

There was no smile on his lips and his chin was inches away, pointing at her face, dotted with small specks of spit. Just before she closed her eyes and began to talk, she noticed his cellar door standing slightly ajar.

"I don't want to go to Hell, Reverend Dye."

"Don't worry, child. Tell me everything and you won't ever have to worry about going to Hell. But if you don't tell me, well then, that old Devil is down there sharpening his claws and swishing his tail, just waiting for you."

CHAPTER TWENTY

CANAAN, MASSACHUSETTS \ Tuesday, May 7

KOENIG TURNED THE engine off and with a glance at the boy's body that had fallen against the passenger's door, he left the pickup, slammed the door, and waded through thigh deep snow to Wilfred and Charlotte's front porch, wondering again why people lived in such a vile climate. When he'd left Philadelphia, it had been full spring. Warm. Flowers in bloom. Leaves on the trees. Lilacs were blooming and soon the honeysuckle would blossom, filling the air with sweetness. Here it was dark and cold, a heavy snowstorm raging at the end of the first week in May. Choosing to stay in this climate didn't make any sense. He'd do what he'd come to do and get out of here. Maybe go to the Caribbean for a few weeks, lie on the beach and soak up some long overdue sun, writing poetry and reading, listening to Mozart.

Climbing the porch steps, his footfall muffled by the snow, he imagined the lives of these people, shadowed, limited, devoid of the pleasures of music and literature, they would be focused inward like this dark and narrow valley which contained and restricted them. The porch was bare, except for two frayed, pealing wicker rocking chairs and a rusty galvanized bucket half full of ashes.

He knocked at the door.

Someone pulled aside a curtain at the window, just far enough to see out without being seen. He heard the muffled sound of a woman's voice, then the rumble of footsteps before the door opened. The man who stood there would once have been a menacing adversary. Now he was blubbery and spent, wearing a bourbon red sweatshirt with brightly colored horses silk screened on the front. He peered resentfully at Koenig, as if no one unfamiliar should be knocking at his door.

"What do you want?"

"My name's Teeter, Mr. Buckman. Roger Teeter. I called you earlier, about a William Buckman. Remember?"

Wilfred nodded. "So?"

"I'm looking for this William Buckman. Doctor William Buckman. I think you can help me find him. I believe you lied to me over the phone."

Wilfred broke into a wide smile. "Doctor? The snot's a doctor? No way. Not Billy Buck. You got to have the wrong Bill Buckman."

"I don't think so." He kept his eyes tight on Wilfred's face as he pushed past him into the house. The sour smell of dirty clothes and dust, the stench of rotting food, assaulted him. For a moment he thought he'd vomit. He stood still, breathing shallowly, and looking at the dirty and littered living room.

"I didn't ask you the fuck into my house, mister."

Recovering his balance, Koenig smiled, shaking his head. "No, you didn't, but I came in, didn't I?"

Wilfred moved toward him, the shadow of a motion which once would have been quick and dangerous. Koenig moved easily aside, pulling the gun from under his jacket.

"You have a woman here."

"Just me." Wilfred seemed to be gathering himself for another move.

Koenig jabbed the gun into his stomach. "Call her."

"I said it was just me, fuckhead."

"I heard her voice when I was on the porch. Call her in here now."

"Maybe you heard the radio."

"You're too fat to be a hero, Mr. Buckman. I heard a live woman's voice in here. Call her or I start pumping bullets into your soft underbelly."

"Charlotte, get out here." Wilfred breathed deeply sucking his paunch away from the gun.

Charlotte came into the room, moving as quickly as her weight allowed, rushing toward Koenig, swinging a fire poker fiercely in the air before her, swooshing it as she came at him. Turning away from Wilfred, he shot her in the face. She lurched backward, crashing against a knotty pine cabinet filled with dishes. They jarred loose and fell to the floor as she did, shattering around her. The fire poker clinked against the broken china and lay on the floor next to her right leg.

He heard Wilfred gasp and swung back toward him, digging the barrel of the gun into his neck before he had a chance to do anything.

"Don't try, fat boy. I can take you out just as quickly as I did your wife."

"Fuck you."

Koenig laughed, pointing at Charlotte. She sat on the floor, surrounded by broken dishes, thick arms hanging limply, hands resting on the floor, her legs spread-eagled, the dimpled fat of her massive thighs showing through the tight pink acrylic slacks. Her remaining eye stared off toward the wall as blood poured from her ruined face, covering the white sweater and pooling in her lap.

"You're still alive, Mr. Buckman. How long you remain alive is in your hands."

"What do you want?" The gun pressing hard against his throat, Wilfred's words were a whispery croak.

"I want to kill you, Mr. Buckman. That's what I do best, kill people. Scum who litter the earth and use its resources without returning anything of lasting value. People who live without art, without reflection, like animals, leaving their refuse, both intellectual and physical behind. Litterers. Loiterers. I kill people like that. I want to kill you. Eventually I will."

He paused, smiling at Wilfred, increasing the pressure of the gun, grinding it deeper into his throat. "And I know what you want."

"What could I want from you, mister?" The words were barely audible.

"To live a little longer, Mr. Buckman. To live a little longer and to die with as little pain and suffering as possible. When you come right down to it isn't that what we all want? The way I see things, it's a universal human desire. Perhaps the prime universal human desire." He paused, looking upward as though thinking of something far away in time and space. "Or at least one of the prime universal human desires, don't you think, Mr. Buckman."

Wilfred didn't answer, his eyes watering as he stared into Koenig's face.

"Your wife died without pain. Poof. One minute she was charging me with that poker in her hand and the next she was gone, turned off a light bulb. I imagine she never felt a thing. Never knew a thing. One instant she was, the next she wasn't. Not a bad thing to have happen. I mean, look at all the people suffering long horrible deaths in hospitals, tubes coming out of every opening in their bodies, some of them new openings, all manner of machines hooked up to them. All those devices just there to prolong their lives keeping them going, drugged, and stupefied because they're in such awful pain."

"Is he really a doctor?"

"Is who really a doctor, Mr. Buckman?"

"Billy Buck. He a doctor?"

"So, you do know him."

Wilfred nodded once and winced from the pain of the gun barrel. "He's my brother, but I didn't know the snot was a fucking doctor or nothing like that. All I knew was that he thought he was too fucking good for us here in the Old World and ran off as soon as he finished high school. Ain't nobody heard nothing from him since then. Till he showed up here five or six days ago."

"Very good, Mr. Buckman. See how easy it is to tell me things? And you're alive. Isn't that wonderful? We have a deal; I want to know things and if you answer my questions, you'll stay alive. Where is he?"

"Why do you want to know?"

Koenig tightened the gun's pressure against Wilfred's neck. "It's enough that you understand that I want to know. My reasons shouldn't matter to you. Just tell me where he is."

Wilfred looked at Charlotte's body. He shuddered quickly, then sniffled, as though he were clearing his nose.

"I don't know where he is."

"Come now, Mr. Buckman. You were beginning to help me. I liked that. The more you help me, the easier it's going to be for you. Do you have any idea what it's like to die with a bullet in your abdomen? Gut shot, they call it in the Army. Terrible thing, a gut shot. A man left alone with a gut shot can last for days, each passing hour more painful than the last as infections build and blood pools inside the body. I'm sure you've heard about such things, right?"

Wilfred nodded again, eyes going back and forth between Koenig and Charlotte's body. His throat was dry, but with the gun tight against his throat, he was afraid to risk the discomfort of swallowing.

"Tell me what you want, mister."

Koenig eased the pressure of the gun, slightly. "Your brother, Mr. Buckman. I want to know where he is."

"He's not here."

He pushed the gun harder again. "I can see that, but you know where he is. Tell me."

Wilfred was quiet for a moment, then he sagged inward a bit and took a long breath. "He's down to Calvin's place."

Pulling the gun away Koenig motioned him toward the kitchen. "Draw me a map."

Wilfred pulled at the skin on his neck, reddened from the gun barrel. "You won't hurt me?"

"I will hurt you if you don't hurry. I want a map showing me how to get to this Calvin person's place."

"Our father. Calvin's our father," Wilfred said.

"It doesn't matter to me. Make the map. I want it to show me the house, any outbuildings, the contour of the land and the placement of the trees and bushes."

"What do you want all that for?"

"For no reason of any meaning or consequence to you."

"What will you do for me if I do it?"

"Like I said, kill you quickly, Mr. Buckman. Turn off your lights like I did for your wife."

"And you'll kill me slow if I don't?"

Koenig smiled and nodded. "Sit in the chair by the table, Mr. Buckman."

Wilfred did as he said.

"Now, take your belt off and strap your legs to the legs of the chair." Frowning, confused, Wilfred followed Koenig's orders.

When it was done, Koenig walked over to the sink, taking a serrated steak knife and a heavy carving knife from the drying rack. He spread Wilfred's left hand out on the table, leaning his full weight on the wrist.

"I'll show you what I mean, Mr. Buckman. You try pulling away from me, try getting your hand free, and I'll slit your throat. Do you understand? I'll slit it slowly."

Eyes wide, breathing rapidly, shallowly, Wilfred nodded.

Humming softly, Koenig raised the carving knife and brought it down hard, quickly cut off Wilfred's index finger.

Wilfred looked startled, then screamed. Grabbing the finger with his free hand, he tried to reattach it by holding it tightly against the bleeding stump.

"You see, Mr. Buckman, that was fast, minimal terror, minimal pain. Now, don't forget what I said about trying to get away from me. Try it and you die."

As he spoke, Koenig knocked the severed finger out of Wilfred's grasp, sweeping it to the floor. He took hold of Wilfred's left hand for a second time, once more leaning on the wrist, and began sawing at his second finger with the steak knife.

"This, Mr. Buckman, is slow."

Wilfred screamed again. He moaned. He begged. But he did not try to pull away. Doing so meant death, he knew. He tried not watching as the knife worked its way through the skin to the bone but, despite the horror and pain, he could not tear his eyes away from the sight. He wanted to faint, to pass out and escape, but he would not let himself give in. To do so could also mean death.

Then, suddenly, as though he had shifted slightly away from the moment, he found himself oddly detached, watching, thinking about what was happening to him, feeling the pain, the terror, but no longer part of it. It was an old trick he'd figured out back in high school, when he'd force himself to finish a football game with sprained ankles, twisted arms, once with a badly ripped cartilage in his knee. Another time, during his senior year, he'd gotten his hands on the ball when the runner fumbled at the annual Canaan/Graham Thanksgiving game, and he'd run sixty yards for a touchdown with a broken collarbone. He'd pushed the pain to the background and concentrated on the game, feeling nothing but the ground passing beneath his feet and hearing nothing but the cheering of his schoolmates in the stands.

Only this was not a game. No matter what he did, this man was going to kill him. No matter what he did, what he said, he'd be dead. Listening to the rasping sound of the knife as it sawed through his bone, he decided to play it like Moose Buckman one last time. He could almost hear the cheering crowd as he ran toward the goal line, the pain a distant companion.

Moose, they called. Moose, Moose, Moose. Moose Moose he's our man if he can't do it no one can Moose Moose Moose Moose Moose Moose he's our man...

"Fuck you," he hissed through lips barely parted. "Fuck you. Fuck your mother. Fuck your sister. Fuck your whole goddamn fucking family."

Koenig stopped sawing through the bone and laughed.

"That's good, Mr. Buckman. The death poetry of primitive man. I like it. I may find a use for it."

"Fuck your map. You can do any goddamn fucking thing you want to me, but you ain't getting no map and you ain't getting another word about Billy Buck out of me."

"That is a pity, Mr. Buckman. Not a word, eh?"

Wilfred stared at him, his eyes filled with tears, his lips twisted in an offensive lineman's sneer.

"Not even a please don't kill me?"

Wilfred stared.

"Not even another fuck you?"

Wilfred's teary eyes did not waver.

Shrugging his shoulders, Koenig sighed. "This is tiresome, Mr. Buckman. Goodbye."

Taking the knife away from Wilfred's hand, he brought it slowly and deliberately across his throat. Wilfred blinked, jerked backward, but all the while hearing Moose, Moose, Moose, Moose, he's our man, he kept his silent stare until the world wavered and he was gone.

Washing at the sink, the warm water running over the rubber gloves Koenig daubed at the blood on his face and clothes with a dishrag, he realized that not once during this kill had he been tempted to drink. Maybe he'd be all right after all. Maybe he wasn't falling into madness, or worse, middle-aged folly.

He went out to the pickup. Pulling Carl Shippee's body from the cab, he dragged it through the snow into the house, leaving it on the floor next to Charlotte's. Then he used a fallen branch to sweep the snow, covering the bloody tracks he'd made. Before getting in and starting the engine, he used a scarf he found lying on the floor and cleaned the seat and the inside of the door where Carl had rested after the shooting.

Driving back down the Windybush, looking for Erskine Dye's rectory and church, he started whistling an air from Mozart. Charlotte and Wilfred Buckman had been a pleasant warmup for the Buckman he had come to kill, and the kid driving the pickup had been a bonus. Not getting the map was a disappointment, but perhaps that would work out too. The Reverend Dye could well be another bonus.

"SHE'S IN THERE, Billy Buck. Her and the reverend are kneeling beside the woodstove, and mumbling, praying, from the way it looks."

Vaughn was standing on three cement blocks they had found and stacked atop one another in the snow outside Erskine Dye's living room window. Buckman and Irene stood below, bracing him. They were bundled in heavy jackets, sweaters, scarves, and wool hats, stiff and warm despite the spring storm blowing around them.

"The bastard." Irene's whisper sounded like a shout to Buckman, and he raised his index finger to his lips.

"I want her out of there before she tells him everything about us."

"Only one way to do that," Irene said. "We'll just go in and get her. Take her home."

Vaughn grinned at her. "Direct action. You got quite a girl here, Billy Buck."

Irene's face tightened briefly, then she shook her head and smiled. "Vaughn, girls are a lot younger than I am, and one whole hell of a lot less experienced."

Vaughn raised both hands in a gesture of surrender. Ignoring them both, Buckman walked to Dye's front door and opened it.

"Velma," he yelled in. "It's your uncle Bill. Irene, Vaughn, and I have come to take you home."

There was no answer. He went inside, Irene and Vaughn close behind. They were in a long center hallway. At the rear was the kitchen. Four rooms, two on either side, were off the hall.

"Velma," he said again.

Erskine Dye came from the farthest room on the left and stood in the hallway, arms folded over his chest.

"I know it all, Doctor Buckman. Your father, the abortion you've been trying to force this poor child to have, all part of the evil you've brought to Canaan Forks with you. The stench of corruption is all around you."

Velma appeared in the doorway behind him, her face stained with tears, an angry red mark on her left cheek. Rushing to her, Irene leaned over, gently touching the girl's face. Velma winced and pulled back.

"I didn't mean to get you in no trouble, Uncle Billy Buck, but the Reverend told me the Devil was waiting for me and said if I didn't tell him everything sinful that I knew about, he said the Devil was going to tear into me, and Jesus wouldn't love me, and I'd be tortured in Hell forever."

"Some man of God you are, you son-of-a-bitch." Irene spoke as she whirled on Dye, her eyes narrowed, her fists clenched.

Dye moved, as though to hit her.

"Don't," Vaughn said, pointing a pistol at him.

Dye's arms dropped to his sides as he backed away from Irene, toward the far wall of the hallway. He stood there silently, slumped, cowed, eyes going from one to the other of the three people before him. Velma was motionless.

"He's got a door that goes into straight into Hell down in his cellar, Uncle

Billy Buck. That's why I told him everything we done, about how I killed Grampy Cal by mistake and how we buried him in the cornfield, so nobody'd know, and all and about the abortion you got me set up for tomorrow and how you're a doctor and all. He said if I didn't tell him everything that was going on that he'd call all kinds of slobbery demons out of Hell and have them come up from the cellar to get me. He said they'd eat my body and drag my soul down to the Devil."

Dye looked at her, then at Buckman. Pulling himself out of his slump, he cleared his throat and spoke.

"Dr. Buckman, I'm an officer of the law and you're under arrest for conspiring to conceal an unlawful death. Whatever you say can and will be used against you. You have the right to an attorney, the right to remain silent." He paused for a moment, looking at Vaughn's gun. Then frowning, he shook his head. "I can't remember the specifics of the rest of it, Miranda, I mean, but that's the sense of it. You've been officially advised of your rights."

Buckman looked at him, almost smiling. "It's a little difficult to arrest a man who's having you held at gunpoint, isn't it Reverend?"

Dye shrugged. "I called police headquarters over in the Falls as soon as Velma told me about how she killed Calvin and how you buried him in the cornfield. They'll send men in here just as soon as they can get through the storm. In the meantime, I'm a police officer and you're under arrest. The longer you keep me prisoner, the harder it'll be for you."

"If Roger Teeter is what, who, I think he is, Reverend, then I'm the least of your problems." Buckman gave him a brief smile and quickly turned away.

"We got a real tough situation here, Reverend." Vaughn's Yankee hill town tones came from barely parted lips. As he spoke, he turned briefly and looked at Buckman. "A lot tougher than I ever realized."

CHAPTER TWENTY-ONE

Canaan, Massachusetts \ Tuesday May 7

SURROUNDED BY STOCKACE fencing, the Canaan Forks Missionary Alliance Church sat empty, snow quietly piling up around it, the drive and walkways empty of tire tracks and footprints. Snow clung to the low hanging branches, clumped on soft green shoots of maple blossoms. Thick, heavy flakes fell to the ground, silent and cold. Two squirrels ran around the top of the fence and jumped six feet up into the branches of an oak tree. The quivering branch sent clumps of snow thunking to the ground. Spring birds, confused by the weather, huddled close to the trunks, or hid in their nests, feathers ruffled against the snow and cold wind.

Inside the concrete block and frame building, dust motes hung in the gray light of the stormy afternoon. They settled on oaken pews, coated the ivory keys of the organ, landed on floors, windowsills, grayed the white cloth beneath the polished brass cross on the altar. The dust fell more slowly than the snow outside, but over the two days since Sunday's services it had formed a thin coat on every surface. Erskine Dye hired Perce Gareau as a caretaker to come every Wednesday and Saturday to vacuum and dust, as well as to open the church an hour before every service. Tuesdays, he thought of as his make do service, as far as the church being clean was concerned. It struck him as foolish to pay Perce to clean three times a week when two would do.

It was a small building, erected by Dye and a group of volunteers from the early days of his congregation. The sanctuary held seating for about a hundred people, a hundred and twenty-five if you counted the balcony. There was a sacristy, most of its space taken up by choir robes and boxes of pamphlets and just off the sacristy was the church office, filled by a large cherry desk Dye had found at an auction, two filing cabinets and more boxes of pamphlets and religious newspapers. Anyone trying to get from the desk to the farthest of the files would have to walk sideways. The basement had a kitchen and two Sunday school classrooms.

At six o'clock, an hour before the prayer service, Perce Gareau stopped his pickup in front of the church drive. Gunning his engine, he lowered the yellow plow and began scraping the asphalt clear. The heavy snow made the going difficult, and he had to be content with moving a few feet at a time, pushing a load off to the side and starting again. It took him half an hour to clear the drive and a small part of the parking area, stopping every few minutes for a sip from the whiskey flask he kept in his jacket pocket.

Convinced he'd cleared more than enough parking for the few people who'd be willing to come out on a night like this, he decided he was finished. Hell, he hadn't seen another person on the road since he left home to get here. It didn't make sense that many of Reverend Dye's flock would bother risking their asses on a night like this one was shaping up to be, not when they'd been to church just last Sunday and had another prayer meeting coming up on Thursday night. Hell, if it was up to Perce, he'd have canceled the whole shooting match.

He'd called Reverend Dye half an hour before coming out to plow and told him there wasn't much point in paying to have the drive plowed and the walk snowblowed. People crazy enough to dive on the snow-covered slippery roads on a night like this, just to come to a prayer service, were risking having prayers spoken over their damned coffins. Besides, by Thursday, this time of year, the snow would have melted. Cancel it, he suggested and save the bucks. But no, the Reverend said he was going ahead with the service. It was the Lord's will, he said.

Sure, Perce thought. And come the end of the month, Dye will be pissing and moaning about having to pay extra to have Perce clean away this spring snow.

Damned fool. Hell, Perce had nearly gone off the road two or three times himself getting here. But he'd made it and he'd done his best, and now he had to clear the goddamn snow off the walks, if he wanted to keep his contract with the church. Clear the snow, unlock the church, and turn on the lights. By God, he'd raise the heat up to sixty-five if it was cold inside. Tonight, it would be, no doubt.

THE PICKUP STARTED sliding sideways near the place Koenig had earlier gone off the road in the Jeep. Taking his foot from the gas pedal and turning into the skid, he glanced down the hill into the woods. The Jeep sat there, tilted awkwardly, nearly hidden by the snow which had fallen on it in the time since Koenig lost control, sending it careening down the bank.

He was startled when the pickup's wheels grabbed, the truck straightened, and he continued along the Windybush. A few minutes later, his heart pounding, he was on the Black Horse Pike headed west. He gripped the wheel, hoping that from here on things would go smoothly and that within the hour he would be done with the godforsaken hills of western Massachusetts, that Buckman and the woman would be dead, along with anyone else unlucky enough to get in his way. The only link between Koenig and Worthington-America would be gone.

He was struck again by his foolishness for getting involved with Blanchard and Castile. It seemed ever more like a watershed in his affairs, and he was far too fixated on it. Increasingly it seemed like it was time to put the business end of his life to rest and concentrate on poetry and, of course, the pleasure of an occasional recreational kill. Focus on those things which bring him pleasure and do them for their own sake, not as part of some crass commercial undertaking.

He remembered how Castile's face had looked the other night in Buckman's Upper Black Eddy house, saw again the eyes set at the instant death became inevitable. The memory merged with rhythms and images as a poem began working at him, words shaping themselves into lines. He spoke them aloud, felt their beat in the repetitive thumping of the snow tires and the thrum of the pickup's engine. For a moment he was completely lost in the world of the poem, and in that moment the truck skidded again, sliding off the road into a ditch, the front end folding against a tree, jarring him as it came to a stop.

Putting his head back against the seat, he roared his fury at the roof of the cab. Now he'd have to walk. He hit the steering wheel with both fists. Buckman's death would have to be a damned good one to make up for what he'd been going through. Making sure he had two pistols tucked under his belt, he got out, jumped into the deep snow at the side of the road. It poured into his shoes as he forced his way through the thick cover on the road, snow matting in his hair and blowing under his collar. His ears were aching, his hands numb, the rubber gloves no help at all. Swinging his arms to keep warm, he tripped over a rut hidden by the snow, sprawling face first in the snowy and muddy road.

When he stood again, his rage was as cold as his body. Nothing could compensate for this. Buckman's earlier escape had been bad enough. Now he was humiliated in his own eyes, walking along this snow covered road after losing the Jeep and the pickup, his clothes wet, muddy, his face scratched and bleeding lightly from the fall, his side aching where the barrel of the silencer had jammed into the flesh when he landed in the road.

Snow and wind made him shiver. Rage blowing through him made him shiver. Imagining Buckman's dying eyes made him shiver. He started moving down the road again, lurching more than walking, his feet aching from the cold. Pushing his hands deep into his pockets, he kept the fingers moving, clenching and unclenching them to chase away the numbness. He was going to need them warm and responsive.

Fifteen minutes later he saw the Canaan Forks Missionary Alliance Church sitting at the edge of a field, dark and half hidden in clouds of mist and thickly falling snow. At last, something had gone right. He'd found the church straight away, if he didn't count the two accidents and the distractions of the kid who'd been driving the pickup and the Buckman couple. At least he wouldn't have to try finding the minister's home. He'd go into the church, get warm, and wait for Dye to show up.

PERCE GAREAU HAD the lights on, the heat turned up and sat in the basement kitchen, sucking at his flask, and playing solitaire with a ragged pack of miniature cards he kept in his pocket, the solitaire a frequent distraction from the boredom lurking at the edges of his life. He'd stay down here until the service was over, then check the place out to make sure it was empty and lock it up until it was time to do the Thursday afternoon cleaning.

From upstairs he heard the door from the outside to the sanctuary open. Probably the Reverend or someone early for the service. Either way, it didn't involve him. He was the plowman and the caretaker. The Reverend Dye's preaching and sermonizing none of his business. All he needed was to be left alone to do his work and to get paid for it. He ignored the sound of footsteps crossing the floor above him. He didn't notice when they started down the basement stairs, turning only when the door from the stairs to the basement squeaked open.

A strange voice asked, "Reverend Dye?"

Perce didn't recognize the man standing in the open doorway. Even if it had been his own brother, he couldn't have been sure, given the shadow he stood in.

"No. He's not here yet. I'm the caretaker."

Perce didn't hear the shot. He saw a quick movement in the shadows, but the bullet creased his skull before the sound reached him. Not checking to see whether Perce was dead or alive, Koenig turned off the lights and went back upstairs to the sanctuary, leaving him lying unconscious and bleeding in the darkness of the basement.

"IT LOOKS LIKE your friend Teeter isn't coming, Doctor." Erskine Dye was smiling. "I'd wager he's still in town waiting out the storm. You should just turn yourself over to me and wait for the police. It'll go a lot easier on you if you do."

"He'll come. Here or the church."

Dye looked at his watch. "It's after six-thirty already. If he is coming, maybe he's already at the church."

Buckman nodded. "Then that's where we're going."

THE CHURCH WAS quiet. Light from three small ceiling fixtures shone from the large brass altar cross, the reflection shimmering on the door leading from the outside. Beside the pulpit, a mouse twitched its whiskers, then skittered across the floor and disappeared beneath the organ.

A blast of wind rattled the building. Koenig knelt in the balcony, shivering. His arm ached, his fingers till numb from the cold; he rubbed them together, the gun under his belt tight against his stomach, the other held lightly in his hands lying on the railing in front of him, glinting brightly in the light from the fixture hanging just above.

"WHOSE TRUCK?" Standing in the snow in front of the church, Buckman pointed at the pickup sitting next to the building.

Irene, Velma, Vaughn, and Erskine Dye were huddled beside him, their heads and shoulders white with snow. They had walked from Dye's house to the church

"Looks like Perce Gareau's," Vaughn said.

Dye nodded. "He's the church caretaker, plows the drive, opens the place before worship time, keeps the place clean and does whatever else I need done around here."

Walking over to the truck, Buckman looked in the cab. It was littered with beer cans, bags, wrappings, and Styrofoam cups from fast food restaurants. Several torn and dirty hunting and fishing magazines were on the seat, along with pairs of gloves and baseball hats with various promotional patches above their brims. A pair of large fuzzy dice hung from the rearview mirror.

Vaughn looked over the parking lot, went around to the back of the church and came back shaking his head. "I don't see no signs of nobody else here."

Dye shrugged. "Of course not. We're early. People won't start coming for the prayer meeting for another ten, fifteen minutes, and like I said, your Teeter won't be coming from the Falls tonight."

Buckman looked at him, then back at the church. "He'll come. If there's a way to get here from Canaan Falls, this man will do it. He's not about to give me a chance to get away."

Dye smiled at him. "He's from the police, right Doctor? Whatever it is you've done, he's run you to the ground. You should let me arrest you now, take you to the Falls as soon as the roads are clear and put you in custody. You do understand that you're officially under arrest anyway, don't you? I think I've made my position perfectly clear."

"If he was a policeman looking for me, Reverend, why wouldn't I just run? Get as far away from Canaan as I could? Why would I be coming here to look for him? You just don't know how to figure things out, do you?"

Rattling his lips, Dye shook his head and moved away, walking toward the church door. Buckman watched him, his form dark against the building, a small black hole in the white field of the world.

Warm in his heavy jacket, he shivered.

Unreal.

It was all unreal.

Unreal, the snow in May, bending the trees, snapping them like dry sticks, heavy laden branches lying on the ground, leaves showing through the snow.

Unreal, the events which had brought him here, those of his distant past, those of his recent past, those of the present.

Unreal, his being here, standing before a church in the Old World, where there had never been a church before, the strands of his life converging in a grotesque parody of symmetry.

It was all unreal.

Unreal.

KOENIG HEARD VOICES outside the church. Kneeling at the rail, looking out over the emptiness of the sanctuary, he saw the front door reflected in the brass cross. As he watched, it opened, a dark figure standing outlined against the light.

He picked up the gun, holding it in both hands, waiting for whoever was coming to move into the room and stand against the altar where he could make quick kills if the people coming in were his targets.

Erskine DYE SAW the church was empty and turned to Buckman. "I don't even see Perce. He's probably down in the basement with his flask and a deck of cards."

He walked into the building.

Buckman followed, standing in the doorway for a moment as Dye walked down the aisle toward the altar. Vaughn, Irene, and Velma came up behind him, crowding him through the door into the building.

"Looks like we beat him here, Billy Buck," Vaughn said.

Buckman stood beneath the balcony, straining to see into dim corners of the sanctuary. Wind blew through the open doorway, making the ceiling fixtures sway. The shadows moved with them, rising and falling in the corners like living beings.

He walked farther into the room, still under the balcony. Erskine Dye was standing in front of the altar, looking out over the benches, his eyes on Buckman.

"No one here, doctor. You're wasting your time and intruding on my church. People will be coming for the services any minute. Either leave so you won't interfere with our prayers or agree to be my prisoner and wait for me in my office in the back."

Vaughn's voice echoed through the building. "Shut the fuck up, Reverend."

"You shouldn't talk to Reverend Dye like that," Velma whispered. "He's a minister and this is his church. Talk like that to him and he'll send you all to Hell just like he's sending me."

Irene put her hands around the girl's shoulders, giving her a light hug. "Reverend Dye isn't going to send anybody to Hell. Not you, not any of us."

Velma glanced at her, then looked back at Dye, standing with his back to the altar, the brass cross bright and shiny behind him.

CROUCHING IN THE shadows of the balcony, Koenig sighted on Dye's forehead. The room was small enough for pistol range. Things would be fine.

Buckman was here. As soon as Dye said the word doctor, he knew. Now all he had to do was wait for him to come into view. He'd shoot Buckman first, then the woman and anyone else who might get in the way of his escape.

Then it would be over.

Worthington-America would be part of his past.

A stupid mistake corrected and the future assured.

BUCKMAN WAS ABOUT to walk to where Dye stood when Vaughn shoved past him, holding his rifle at shoulder height.

"Guns are hardly appropriate inside the church," Dye said, moving away from the altar toward the center aisle where Vaughn stood, peering around the room.

Vaughn was about to answer when he saw light glinting off a metallic surface in the balcony. Dropping to his knees, he fired into the darkness and rolled between two benches.

"Stop, for God's sake, stop," Erskine Dye yelled, rushing toward him, his hands outstretched.

Koenig fired, catching Dye in the chest. The minister spun around, crashed against the benches opposite where Vaughn was lying, and fell to the floor, blood spreading over his shirt.

"Put your hand over the wound, Reverend," Vaughn said.

Dazed, Erskine did.

"Press tight. It'll stop the bleeding."

Dye pressed, crying. "Doctor Buckman, help me. Please, help me. You're a doctor. You can help. Please, I don't want to die, doctor, please."

Vaughn shouted back. "Stay where you are, Billy Buck. He's in the balcony. You keep out of sight. It's you he's looking for. Reverend Dye's going to be just fine if he does what I told him to do. Hell, I seen enough guys shot in hunting accidents and over in Iraq to know what to do. He ain't hurt bad just so long as he don't let it bleed heavy."

In the balcony, Koenig moved on his belly, crossing to the steps leading down to the sanctuary floor, hoping to catch a glimpse of Buckman through the stairwell. The carpeting was rough, dust tickling his nose, threatening to make him sneeze.

Buckman looked at his brother. "Do you think you hit him, Vaughn?"

"If I did, it wasn't good enough. There wasn't no crash. And if there wasn't no crash, then he didn't fall down or drop nothing, which means he's still up there, still got a gun and still waiting to shoot you."

Koenig slithered without noise, a tight smile on his face. He was lying at the top of the stairs, his head and shoulders into the stairwell, elbows resting on the second stair down. He saw the woman and a young girl. He could get them both but shooting them would drive Buckman further under cover. Even now he was still standing out of his range of vision. Koenig's nose itched. He lay perfectly still, forcing the sneeze away. When it passed, he would get closer.

Vaughn was watching the front of the balcony, Buckman watching him, as Koenig began easing his way down the stair, stopping when his elbows were resting on the fourth step from the top. Buckman stood ten feet away, his back to the staircase. Slowly, Koenig lowered himself one more step. To get a good shot, he rested his elbows on the stair. It squeaked.

The girl started, and turning, saw him.

"Watch out, Uncle Billy Buck." She yelled and pushed Buckman, just as Koenig squeezed off a shot. As she did, she banged against Irene who tripped, knocking her head against the armrest of a bench.

Velma and Buckman fell. Buckman landed in the middle of the aisle, his left shoulder broken from the slug, his gun sliding across the floor, coming to rest by Velma's head where she had fallen between two benches.

Vaughn fired at the stairwell, missing Koenig who spun and fired in return. The shot went wild, knocking the brass cross to the floor. Koenig shot again, this time hitting the floor beside Vaughn's head, sending splinters into his cheeks and left eye.

Vaughn cried out and crawled farther back between the benches. Koenig took careful aim in Vaughn's direction. He had them now. The minister was down, the woman and girl were down and Buckman was down, none of them dead, but all out of commission. The one hiding between the benches was the only problem. Get rid of him and he could finish the others off quickly. He'd bring this business to an end and get on with his life.

He sat on the stair, holding his gun in both hands, scanning the room, the sneeze rising again. The minister was groaning on the floor, blubbering, Koenig thought. Disgusting. There was no sign of movement from under the benches.

Still, it was almost over. They would all be dead in a few minutes, and he'd be free. It was a good feeling. Forcing himself to relax, he looked at the scene below. An hour from now he would be gone, headed away from Canaan, Massachusetts. He'd leave the pickup in town, get in his car, and hit the Interstate. By tomorrow night he'd be sitting in his box at the Met, or listening to Mozart on his stereo, or perhaps eating in one of those small restaurants in New York he loved so.

The world was his tomorrow. Anything he chose to do he would do. The world of art and culture were out there. Waiting for him to come. To appreciate tradition and talent. All he had to do was kill these five idiots. Buckman. The woman. The other three. They were his. He loved the feeling, the anticipation. It was almost more pleasure than the kill would be.

Although the kill would be exquisite. He'd get rid of the four quickly, saving Buckman for last. His death would be the sweetest, the others were simple necessities.

Velma lay on the floor watching the man on the staircase. He'd probably come in from the door in the basement of Reverend Dye's house, the one the Reverend had down there that led into Hell. He looked like a devil. He was acting like one, shooting people in the church. Shooting the Reverend. Shooting Uncle Billy Buck. Although she didn't think any of them were dead, she knew the man was going to kill them as soon as he got the chance.

She watched him watching for her Uncle Vaughn, staring at the place where he was hiding under the bench. He was smiling, this bad man. It wasn't a nice smile. It was the kind of smile Grampy Cal would get when he told her stories about the Devil biting people's heads off and sucking out their brains. He was bad, this man on the stairs who was trying to kill her Uncle.

Using the shelter of the benches where she lay, she carefully reached for the gun on the floor beside her. She raised it to her face, aiming the slot and bead at the man's face, just like she'd been taught to do with the rats at the dump. When she had it lined up, she squeezed the trigger, hearing Grampy Cal and her father.

Slow, now girl.

Squeeze it so it don't jerk.

Hold your breath and squeeze slow.

Koenig saw her too late. Saw the black barrel of the gun. Saw the girl's face knotted in concentration as she squeezed the trigger. Saw the end of everything. In a cold instant he saw it was all gone, the poem which had been thrumming through his mind in the truck, the plans, the world he had created for himself, Christopher Koenig, the center of all knowledge and being.

The sound of the gun loud in her ears, she saw the man fly back, his gun dropping to the floor below. He listed sideways and sank down the stairs. When he stopped, he lay on the floor, arms stretched out like wings, a small dark hole oozing blood on the right side of his forehead.

Vaughn came out from under the benches. He checked Buckman, Irene, and Erskine Dye. They were all right. Dye's wound was serious enough, but he'd stopped the bleeding by following Vaughn's instructions and would survive. Irene had regained consciousness and Buckman was getting to his feet. Holding his wounded shoulder, he walked over and stood looking down at Koenig, whose gun lay on the floor a few feet from his outstretched arm.

Buckman picked it up and stuck it in his rear pocket. As he did, Dye moaned in pain. He walked over to see if he could do anything for him beyond what Vaughn had already done.

Velma stood nearby, the gun still in her hand. Vaughn reached over and took it from her.

"You've done real good, Velma," he said.

She looked up at him, then at Buckman who had come back, once he saw that Vaughn had done as much for Dye as he could have, given the situation.

"Did I, Uncle Vaughn? Do good?"

He nodded. "Real good, Velma. Real good."

"You think I did good, Uncle Billy Buck?"

Buckman sighed, then smiling at her, he winked at his brother. "You heard your Uncle Vaughn, Velma. You done real good."

Irene slipped her hand into his.

"That's the first time I've heard you sound like somebody from Canaan, Massachusetts."

He squeezed her fingers. "I almost feel like someone from Canaan, Massachusetts."

"Almost."

"That's about it."

"Is that good?"

He laughed. "It means I won't come back here to live, but I'm not afraid of it anymore. I think I understand how much of it I carry with me, and how much of it I've outgrown. There's no use running from it anymore."

"That's good," she said.

He nodded.

She held his hand tightly, silent for a minute. When she spoke, her voice was nearly a whisper.

"I envy Velma."

Buckman looked at her, eyebrows raised. "How? What's to envy about her?"

"She got him."

He rubbed his eyes with his good hand. "Teeter?"

"Or whoever he was. I wanted him, Bill. I fantasied killing him. For Melinda. And Velma got to do it. That's what I envy."

Buckman smiled at her, shaking his head. "I don't know how I feel. I'm glad he's dead. Besides Melinda, he killed a lot of other people, patients I cared for and cared about, and he tried to kill me. Still, odd as it may sound, but I've never thought about taking a life. My whole life has been predicated on saving it, or at least prolonging it."

"Would you have killed him if you had the chance?"

He didn't answer.

Freeing his hand, he walked to the church door and stood looking out at the snow. It was falling more heavily than when they came in. Already the recently plowed parking lot was covered with more than an inch. The police certainly weren't going to get there before the storm ended. No one was going to come to the church that night, and none of them were going anywhere.

Across the room, Koenig inhaled sharply, pleased to find he was alive. He'd seen death coming, felt it enter him, and yet, he was still alive. His head throbbed, his right eye was blinded from blood flowing from his temple, but he was breathing. He lay still. Controlling the pain, keeping his breath as shallow as possible, he watched the room through the slit of his left eye. Everything was blurred. He could see a human form in the doorway and a group of people standing farther down the aisle. Someone was lying on the floor near them.

Nobody was paying him any attention. He'd get out of this. If he wasn't dead, he wouldn't die. Not this time. He had too much left to do. Poetry to give the world. Purifications to accomplish for it. These gifts would be selfless, free of the taint of self-gratification his earlier work had grown from.

He had been further purified. The moment he'd felt death enter him he'd been changed. Everything had left him. Vanity. Greed. He had died and he had been reborn as he lay here in the church aisle. Creating poetry and creating death would cease to be done for pleasure. His work would be solely for the world's improvement, markers of the age and beacons to the future. Just as Eliot's work had defined his time, and Ginsberg's work had defined his, so Koenig's would define this time and point to the future. Starting here, tonight, in this church.

The irony of it pleased him.

Carefully, slowly, so no one would see him move, he reached for the second gun he had under his belt.

Buckman watched the snow, smooth and white, covering the Old World.

The churchyard and road beyond, the parking lot, all disappeared under it, indistinguishable from one another. In the lights from the building, he could see trees and shrubbery bending, threatening to crack under their heavy cover. He was trying to avoid thinking, trying to lose himself in the snow just as the boundaries between yards and roads were lost. The effort made his head ache. He saw Calvin's body covered by the plaid blanket lying in its cornfield grave, the first few clods of dirt and rock scattered over it.

He wanted to go back to Philadelphia. Get back to his work. Find another hospital and lose himself in its routine, in its sanitized rooms and careful procedures. It was all possible, and he would do it, but it would never be the same. The Old World had returned. Or he had returned to the Old World. Either way, his past had penetrated his present and he knew he would never be free of it. Irene had been here and she knew where he came from, what he came from, just as there were people here who knew about his life. When the police investigations were finished, there would be more. He would be news, his present and past worlds known to one another.

He shrugged. It didn't matter. He was who he was, and he would get on with his life. Healing. Saving savable lives. Building something with Irene.

Koenig held the gun under his chest. When the time was right, he would slip it out and start the kills. He had to get them all to continue his mission. Slowly, he moved a finger toward his good eye, wiping it clear.

It was Buckman in the doorway. Good. He was the prime target in every way. He was also the closest target. Turning his head slightly aside, he looked at the others. They were occupied with themselves. He looked back at Buckman who stood unmoving in the doorway, outlined perfectly against the churchyard lights on the snow.

He pulled the gun from under him, aiming it at Buckman. His hands were shaking. He took a deep quiet breath and held it. No good. They still shook. There wasn't much time. He'd have to do something fast. Buckman would move, or the others would see him, and he'd lose his chance. Shaking hands or not, he had to shoot. His finger touched the trigger.

The more Buckman thought of Irene, the better he felt. He liked her. He loved her. He knew he could be in love with her, stay in love with her for a long time. Nothing else much mattered. Not the Old World. He would deal with that. Not the horror of the events surrounding Worthington-America. He would deal with them too. He could deal with pretty much anything now. Behind him he heard the soft voices of the others discussing what had happened. Under them were the pained moans of Erskine Dye. For a quick moment Buckman found them satisfying. It served the bastard right.

As long as he wasn't dead. Nobody deserved to be dead. Except maybe Roger Teeter, if that was his name, lying on the floor behind him. He was dead and it was good. Damned good. Dye was only hurting and that was fine with Buckman. He sighed and turned to rejoin the others.

The first thing he saw was Koenig, resting on his elbows, blood pouring down his face, a wide smile on his lips, his gun pointed shakily at Buckman's chest.

He turned cold, feeling his death. Before he had a chance to move, Koenig fired. The shot was off, missing him by several feet. Before Koenig could shoot again, Buckman pulled the gun he had put in his back pocket and shot back. The bullet crashed into Koenig's face, just above the bridge of his nose.

He died without a sound.

CHAPTER TWENTY-TWO

Canaan, Massachusetts

VAUGHN BANDAGED BUCKMAN'S shoulder and Buckman cleaned Vaughn's eye, taking the splinters from his cheek before tending to Dye and Perce Gareau. He fixed a makeshift infirmary for them in the church basement, where they had found Perce. Using cushions from the pew benches for beds and several layers of altar cloths for blankets they made Perce and Dye as comfortable as they could.

Dye slipped in and out of consciousness, each time warning Buckman that anything he said could and would be used against him. Perce came to, demanded his flask, drained it, and slept through the night.

It snowed until late the following morning, blocking the roads completely. It was the middle of the afternoon by the time the police arrived. Buckman told them everything he knew about the dead man in the sanctuary and his suspicions concerning the deaths at Worthington-Philadelphia, as well as about Velma accidently killing Calvin. They listened, astounded. The Canaan police rarely had anything more exotic than a minor drug bust involving speeders out on highway.

IT SEEMED TO Buckman that it took forever for them to check his story, during which time Velma had her abortion and Calvin was reburied in the Canaan Forks cemetery, next to Wilfred and Charlotte. Charges of concealment of a wrongful death, stemming from the cornfield burial, were filed against Buckman and Velma, but were quietly dropped as the District Attorney's office came to understand the events surrounding it. There was talk of bringing Velma up on manslaughter charges, but again the District Attorney quashed it, convinced she would never be found guilty, given

Calvin's history of abuse. Erskine Dye spoke of pressing charges of assault on a police officer against Buckman, but never went through with it once the Chief of Police in Canaan told him he ought to give Buckman a reward for saving his life.

Castile's body was discovered in Buckman's cellar when the Pennsylvania State Police went there to see what they could find to verify his story. The authorities were suspicious but cleared him after a long and difficult coroner's hearing.

As the police discovered Koenig's identity and information about him surfaced in the media, there was a run on his books. People were buying poetry who had never read it. Yale University Press ordered a large second printing, tying in distribution with the major chain booksellers who were featuring it in cardboard display racks in the front of their stores with large color pictures of Koenig and the caption, "Works of the Killer Poet."

Everyone speculated upon what made such a brilliant and respected writer get involved in what the press was calling The Worthington Thing. No one knew, or was likely to know, the full story on Koenig. It died with him. While he left at least fifteen full manuscripts of unpublished poetry--for which mainstream publishers outbid the university presses and slowly released books over the next several years--Koenig left no journals dealing with his double life, no notes on his work which touched upon it. Attempts to discover the truth of Christopher Koenig would supply dissertation topics for countless doctoral candidates in literature and psychology.

Buckman arranged for Velma's sister Edna to be appointed the girl's guardian. Edna and her husband moved into Wilfred and Charlotte's house, taking Velma with them. It looked to Buckman as though life with them would be only a little better for her than it had been with her parents, but there was little he could do about it, or any of the Old World ways. Unless he chose to stay there, practice medicine and offer an alternative to tradition and the Reverend Erskine Dye.

He never seriously considered it.

VAUGHN WAS DRUNK the day Buckman and Irene left the Old World. He stood in the yard at Calvin's place, weaving back and forth, promising to come to Philadelphia and visit."First chance I get, Billy Buck, I'll be there."

"I hope so, Vaughn," he said. "I could get you some treatment, for the booze and everything else."

Vaughn laughed. "Just what I need, Billy Buck, treatment. Think I'll give myself another one right now."

He took a long swallow of wine, waving the bottle at them.

Buckman watched him through the rearview mirror as he pulled the Porsche onto the Black Horse Pike, following Irene's car. The snow had long since melted, the world green and lush again. At the top of the Windybush they pulled over and got out, looking down at the valley.

"It's beautiful country," Irene said.

"Would you like to go back, stay a little longer?"

"Not on your life."

"Want to visit it sometime again?"

She shrugged. "I don't know. You?"

"Not for a long time. But I'll come back at some point. No reason not to."

He looked down at the Old World, its tin roofs and smoky chimneys, its winding gravel roads, its plowed fields and forests creating contrasts of sun and shadow. He'd run from its troubling ways, from the pain it caused him as a boy and young man. He hadn't understood it then. He didn't understand it now.

He'd gone to a world he believed understandable. Medicine. Science. The hygienic world of the hospital where questions of life and death seemed manageable. Now it all seemed the same, the Old World, the new one he'd run to years before, both with their darkness, both corruptible, fallen.

Looking over at Irene, he smiled.

"Where are we going?" He asked.

"I thought we were driving back to Philadelphia."

"After that."

"Where do you want to go?"

"Someplace warm. And bright. Someplace where I don't have to think for a while."

"That's what I want. Not to think. How do we do it?"

He shook his head. "I don't know, and I don't want to think about it."

She laughed and kissed him on the cheek. "Just as long as we can hang out together not thinking for a while, before getting back to our lives and work."

"And more hanging out?"

She nodded. "I hope so."

He looked over at her, the promise in her smile almost prevailing over his dread of a future in which the earth was trying to rid itself of pestilent humans before they could destroy ecosystems that had evolved over uncounted centuries, through uncounted species, some successful, some, like humans, disastrous failures. Perhaps, he thought, Kurt Vonnegut had been right in his novel, *Galapagos*, picturing earth's salvation through the devolution of humans into seal-like creatures unencumbered by the brain power of *homo sapiens*, or George Carlin, with his wide-eyed proclamations of how humanity was circling the drain.

A breeze blew up from the valley, carrying leaves and maple seeds, their small green helicopters whirring through the air. He nearly smiled; without humans screwing up the environment, vegetation would flourish. A hawk coasted on wind's currents, gliding, circling below them as it searched for prey. The last thing Buckman smelled before getting in his car was the odor of wood smoke.

He carried it with him for a long time.

Works by Wilson Roberts

Fiction

The Cold Dark Heart of the World
Incident on Tuckerman Court
The Serpent and the Hummingbird
Borrowed Trouble
Poets' Seat
All That Endures
Shadows and Acts
A Place in Paradise
February Heat
Caribbean Ice
October Fury
Murder in Coral Bay
It Happened on St. John
Storms / Tales of Irmariageddon
Double Woods
There Will be Time
The Old World

Poetry

Before the Storm and Other Poems

www.ingramcontent.com/pod-product-compliance
Lightning Source LLC
Chambersburg PA
CBHW030619310726
48979CB00003B/798
9781515457848